Praise for *Valeria's L*

"What emerges is the soul of one small place you'll never want to leave." —*Atlanta Journal-Constitution*

"Since the days of Hawthorne, Melville and Poe, American authors have had a penchant for sweeping allegory . . . This tradition is carried on today by authors such as Cormac McCarthy . . . Toni Morrison . . . and National Book Critics Circle Award finalist M. Glenn Taylor . . . And now by novelist Marc Fitten . . . [*Valeria's Last Stand*] is an allegory which at first glance is a tale of love and lust but from a distance is clearly a symbolic rendering of the benefits and drawbacks of switching from a socialist to a market economy." —*Los Angeles Times*

"First-time novelist Fitten . . . riffs on classic village comedy with satirical glee. Evoking Gogol, Kundera, and García Márquez, with a touch of Fellini for good measure, Fitten concocts a shrewdly farcical tale of the endless battle between change and tradition." —*Booklist*

"In Fitten's madcap hamlet, it's never too late to find tender love (or reckless hate) . . . It's the low-intensity nature of the characters' conflicts and triumphs that gives Fitten's book its fairy-tale charm . . . But even with his light touch . . . his protagonists' final quests resonate." —*Time Out New York*

"[A] sharp-eyed debut novel . . . Emulates the fablelike tone of Calvino and Márquez, adding a heaping helping of Kundera-like sex and satire." —*Kirkus Reviews*

"Marc Fitten's excellent new novel has much to recommend it—wisdom, warmth, humor—but it is his creation of the title character herself that is his and the novel's most remarkable achievement. Valeria is every bit as sensual and irrepressible as Chaucer's Wife of Bath."   —Ron Rash, author of *Serena*

"Fitten writes with the grace and quiet wisdom of a village elder. This is a stunning debut."   —*Atlanta* magazine

"Warmly amusing . . . Enjoyable and poignant."   —*Library Journal*

"Fitten populates his fairy tale of a novel with bitter-coated sugarplums of characters . . . [who] manage to cheat, love, hate, drink, and make pottery for one another with a level of passion we're more accustomed to associating with the very engines of expanding or decaying empires. A beautiful debut."

—Rivka Galchen, author of *Atmospheric Disturbances*

Valeria's
Last Stand

A Novel

Marc Fitten

BLOOMSBURY
NEW YORK · BERLIN · LONDON

For Zita

Published by Bloomsbury USA, New York

All papers used by Bloomsbury USA are natural, recyclable products made from wood grown in well-managed forests. The manufacturing processes conform to the environmental regulations of the country of origin.

LIBRARY OF CONGRESS CATALOGING-IN-PUBLICATION DATA
Fitten, Marc.
Valeria's last stand / Marc Fitten.—1st U.S. ed.
p. cm.
ISBN-13: 978-1-59691-620-3 (hardcover)
ISBN-10: 1-59691-620-6 (hardcover)
1. Middle-aged women—Fiction. 2. Love in middle age—Fiction. 3. Man-woman relationships—Fiction. 4. Villages—Fiction. 5. Hungary—Fiction. I. Title.

PS3606. I8655V35 2009
813' .6—dc22
2008035290

First published by Bloomsbury USA in 2009
This paperback edition published in 2010

Paperback ISBN: 978-1-60819-209-0

1 3 5 7 9 10 8 6 4 2

Typeset by Hewer Text UK Ltd, Edinburgh
Printed in the United States of America by Worldcolor Fairfield

"The great matters of nations cannot make us forget the modest matters of the heart."

—Milan Kundera

Book One

One

Valeria never whistled. Nor did she approve of people who did. In sixty-eight years, what Valeria had learned to be a truth about character was that people who whistled were crass. Whistlers were untrustworthy and irresponsible. They were shiftless. They were common. Butchers whistled. Peasants also. When they were supposed to be tending to their fields or completing any number of tasks peasants are meant to complete, Valeria was certain she could find them instead with their chins wet from a half liter of beer, sitting in the village's tavern, whistling at the slutty proprietress, and telling off-color jokes.

As for the butcher, he was the worst kind of whistler. He whistled right into his customers' faces. Blew his fetid breath right into the nostrils of anyone who visited him. Certainly, a visit to the whistling butcher on Monday was a trip to the health clinic by midweek.

Valeria thought about it while scrubbing the grout of her portico floor early in the morning. She was certain that the queen of England did not whistle. The Hungarian president did not whistle either. She followed a line back through Soviet history: Trotsky may have whistled; Lenin, certainly not; Stalin only whistled in madness. Subsequent leaders of the Soviet regime never whistled, not even Gorbachev. Yeltsin? Valeria's stomach turned when she thought about Russia's head of state. Yes, Yeltsin probably whistles, she decided.

And prior to the Communists, or reformed Communists, or whatever they called themselves these days, the aristocracy they had replaced had never whistled either. The Hapsburgs certainly never had. Valeria scoffed just imagining it. A whistling Hapsburg!

She brushed away a stray leaf with the back of her hand. She remembered hearing the village's mayor whistle and she swore.

True, it had only happened once, and in his defense, he did not know he was being spied upon. Still, Valeria *was* watching him. She did not like him. She did not approve of his flashy German car and flashier young bride. She considered the mayor to be nothing more than a cleverly trained chimpanzee, though more gauche and obtuse than any chimpanzee could possibly be.

Valeria sighed. The mayor was who he was, like everyone else of his generation. The young were all too gauche these days. Since the Soviets had exited Hungary—unceremoniously, she might add—the country had sidled up to the West like a cheap moll. In fact, self-respect seemed to have deteriorated. Adolescent men appeared from nowhere. They drove expensive cars and kept company with expensive, long-legged women, women who were useless in all capacities save sex, who lacked any apparatus that might make them useful to society's betterment. They certainly were not revolutionaries, these women. What with their narrow hips and small breasts, these simple-minded, androgynous-looking sexpots could not even breed tomorrow's revolutionaries. Valeria thought of the mayor's bride giving birth and laughed. Ornaments! That's all the new woman was good for these days—decoration. *Why, just imagine it,* Valeria thought, *allowing oneself to be treated with the same disdain children have for holiday ornaments when they are rushing to get to their sweets and presents. Just imagine it— allowing oneself to be set aside casually, or thrown to the ground violently, or shattered against a wall, or, at best, if they were very, very lucky, to be stuffed in a box until the next holiday season.* Valeria shook her head. *Imagine it!* A generation of women reared to turn off everything within them except the capacity for easy compliance to wet sex.

Valeria scrubbed more vigorously. Her face flushed.

Meanwhile, she thought, meanwhile, the mayor and his cronies slapped one another on their backs. They filled their bank accounts . . . blew smoke at the citizenry . . . had the nerve—the audacity, really—to call the whole stinking flea circus a democracy. Why, the Communists were philosopher kings when compared with the backslapping capitalists in charge of Hungary's *new and improved* free-market system.

Valeria spat at a speck of white bird shit and scratched it with a short fingernail.

She wiped her brow. Nothing was sacrosanct anymore. Ultimately, that was her problem with this new system. It bred contempt. The masses need the inviolable. Even Stalin knew that. The proper care and feeding of the masses requires and demands opiates! But the capitalists ran roughshod over everything. They left nothing untouched or undefiled. Even the insignificant succumbed to market pressure. Things as inconsequential as her favorite Brazilian soap operas were being interrupted with screaming ads for French douches and toilet paper! Why? Who allowed that? What was the point of it? How did screaming commercials—decibels louder than the program itself, so loud she couldn't escape them even when she went to the wash closet (yes, she even heard them in there)— how did screaming commercials (four times during her last program) make a democracy? It made no sense . . .

And then to top things off, the mayor was a whistler!

Thank goodness, she thought to herself. Thank goodness they lived in a small village, deep in the prairie, in the middle of nowhere —and oh how Valeria was thankful for this point. She could rest assured that even the mayor's whistling, loud as it was, would fall on deaf ears. If the mayor—only the cleverest of peasants—wanted to whistle, it did not matter; no one of importance would hear him and think less of the village. In fact, if, from afar, the queen of England or the Hungarian president happened to hear the mayor's whistling as they were writing one another letters, they might look up for a moment and wonder, but then they would shrug and write the faint whistling off as wind stirring a distant crop of sugar beets; the mayor's tinny whistle would be as insignificant to their ears as leaves falling on forgotten hunting grounds—as insignificant a sound to their cochleas as the candelabra flickering in their studies.

Except lately, the mayor himself had started bringing foreigners in. As though he had intuited that he needed an audience. Investors, he called them. Hardly any outsiders had ever come through their village before, and it had been that way as long as Valeria had been alive. In fact, Valeria remembered watching German tanks as a young girl along with her friends as the machines sped along the horizon making their way to Russia. Then, later, on the horizon again, she watched as British tanks arrived. The phalanxes hammered one another for days. And still later on, as a teenager, she watched the horizon for three days as a parade of Russian tanks made their way to Budapest. None of the tanks ever turned in their village's direction. They were always heading toward coordinates more valuable, toward more interesting or important places to occupy. While this should have been cause for great relief, to some it was almost an insult. Indeed, it damaged the psyche of the villagers so much, this sheer disinterest by the tanks—by anything really—that when the new expressway was built, the villagers insisted that the signs not mention their village at all.

"Reaching us isn't really worth anyone's petrol," some said.

"We only have one thermal spring anyway," said others. "Tourists would be better off at Balaton."

The Gypsies working on the road crew shrugged and offered the villagers the blue road-sign, which was quickly mounted in the village's tavern.

Things change, however, and the mayor had his hand in all of it. Foreigners were visiting all the time now, it seemed.

Valeria looked at her handiwork and nodded. The blue tiles were clean. They sparkled. The grout was bone white. She moved her bucket to the concrete steps. A child had offered to paint them for her, but she had refused. Clean was good enough for her. She pulled her brush from the sudsy water and attacked them. She couldn't help but think of the mayor, and she cursed again.

It was the people's fault, what this village was becoming. After all, they had voted the mayor in. The people of her village had put him where he was. Her neighbors! The most immoral, unreliable, uninformed, uninspired, and insane group of has-beens, alcoholics, pedophiles, perverts, unwed mothers, sissies, and Gypsies she had ever known. Her thoughts on this point were not exaggeration. She had lived in the village her entire life. She knew the village's citizens intimately for what they were—a shiftless group of malcontents, maladroits to the last scruffy-necked man, overweight woman, and unclean child. And all of them smiling and nodding as they pulled the lever that put in power a man she would not have trusted with her trash.

She washed up.

Valeria did not consider herself a killjoy. Not in the least. In fact, she kept a ring of keys at her side, like a jailer, and sometimes she liked to shake them. When she felt pleased or content, instead of whistling or smiling she just tugged at the string around her hips until the dangling keys—nearly one hundred of them—started to shake. She felt this act to be supremely appropriate to a woman her age. It was fun.

She left her cottage and headed for the market while it was still dark out. As she had for many years, she reached its entrance with her chin jutted forward and her eyes owlish just as the sun was peeking out. She clutched her basket ahead of her like a battering ram. She marched through the throng of shoppers and thought nothing of ramming her meaty elbows into the ribs of other women, or against the jaws of loud children, or against the backs of slow old men. If it meant she could save a few forints on the last of the tripe, or if it meant she might be able to purchase a fresh carp, so fresh that its tail still smacked against crushed ice, she would elbow her way through a crowd or ram them with her basket and then shout in her victims' astonished faces to boot.

She ignored the mongers hawking junk on the sidewalks out front. She had no regard for Chinese boom boxes, Polish electronics, German cassettes, or aluminum pans. She ignored the counterfeit sneakers piled high in assorted colors. She preferred to pass them as quickly as she could and head, instead, into the belly of the market, toward the stalls, where her neighbors displayed their fruits and vegetables.

Inside, she was like a raptor. She scanned the great hall, walked about, and investigated each and every cranny. The market was a place of commerce and Valeria acted accordingly. She allowed herself even fewer pleasantries while there. She haggled and harangued like a magnate and then bought little or nothing.

She jabbed her fingers into her neighbors' stockpiles, poking and handling their orange carrots, white carrots, turnips, rutabagas, tomatoes, parsley, pears, and asparagus. Most of these foodstuffs

Valeria grew herself. She had no reason to buy anything. She was merely inspecting, checking for quality.

Her neighbors shook their heads at her. It was the same scene every day. Some even shooed her away.

"Leave my food alone," they said. "Why are you touching that?"

Valeria ignored them and continued inspecting.

"It is always the people with the worst-looking vegetables who complain the most," she answered.

When Valeria found something she did not like or that she felt should not have been sold, she looked up at the vendor, focused on the sheepish face staring back, and shook her head.

"You're not selling this, are you?"

The vendor turned red. Whether out of anger or embarrassment one couldn't say.

Regardless, they all responded the same way.

"You're crazy. Get away from my vegetables."

"But you can't possibly mean to sell this?"

"Why not? Go away."

"I wouldn't feed this to my pigs," Valeria said. "You'll poison somebody with this."

A few shoppers would stop and listen. The vendor would shake her head and smile at them.

"Valeria, there is nothing wrong with my vegetables. I've grown them all in my garden. I eat them myself." The vendor smiled. Her eyes were full of rage.

Valeria then sniffed the vegetable in question and shook her head.

"How old is this?"

The vendor was speechless.

"Why does it smell like urine?"

The vendor shrugged.

"Are you letting your cat pee on these? You should be imprisoned," Valeria said and tugged at her keys.

She ruined sales. Villagers, though they didn't like Valeria, never questioned her knowledge. Every morning word traveled quickly through the market about who was selling rotten produce.

It was rare when Valeria found a fruit or vegetable grown better than one she could grow herself. In those instances, her eyes again focused on the vendor. Then she nodded her head in appreciation before asking, "Who are your parents?" The vendor answered and Valeria nodded, trying to remember. Then she congratulated the vendor, bought the vegetable, took it home, and examined it. When she could, she would save the seeds and crossbreed them with her own near-perfect vegetables.

Valeria was just as knowledgeable about the fish and meats. In fact, no one in the market was safe from her. Even the women who sold spices made sure to hide their older bags of seasonings when Valeria was walking by. Since the country had opened up to the West, even in Zivatar, new fruits and vegetables had been introduced. In what was once a room of potato browns and spinach greens, colors like orange and red stood out like Christmas lights. In the first heady days of capitalism, when exotic fruits were still a novelty, people who hardly ever went shopping made special visits to the market just to look at pineapples. Valeria wasn't interested in foreign fruits and vegetables, mostly because she could not grow them, but also because of their blatant sensuality. Tropical fruits were swollen with flesh and juice. They were sticky. They were uninhibited. The first time she held a banana, Valeria was offended.

"How can you sell such vile things at the market?" she asked.

"It's a banana, Valeria. You know that. Taste it."

Valeria peeked at it and shook her head.

"I will not. It's for monkeys."

"It's not. The mayor buys them all the time. It's good. Here, just have a bite."

Valeria tasted it. She had to admit that it was good. Still, tropical fruits disturbed her and, except for the occasional banana, she left them alone. Besides, they were ridiculously expensive. Only the young capitalists could afford them. Valeria noted that besides the mayor's love of bananas, the mayor's bride was always buying bags of oranges. Bags of them. Ostentatious is what it was. In the old days, families only shared an orange at Christmastime. One orange. It was a treat. Valeria was certain that for most families that was still the case. How long would it take a stick-like woman to eat a bag of oranges, Valeria wondered. And how could the mayor allow his wife to leave the house wearing more makeup than clothing? A woman with a slippery mouth, long legs, and no hips to speak of, carrying an expensive bag of Valencia oranges . . . what had the world become?

Even American vegetables were suspect. Valeria examined the vegetables from America closely. The label on one crate read: CALIFORNIA RED PEPPERS. She bought one, just to see what an American pepper tasted like. She wasn't impressed. The pepper looked nice enough, it was big and clean, without a mark on it, grown in a hothouse, no doubt; but when she took it home and cooked it in a stew she was disappointed with its blandness—no tang at all, nothing but nitrogen.

Sometimes, when Valeria had an abundance of anything in her garden, she would arrive even earlier in the morning, set up a stall of her own, arrange her vegetables by color, and sell them at a fair but high price. She always sold out. Though the villagers didn't like Valeria, when it came to the quality of her goods, they could not question her. Her fruits and vegetables were never too soft, never tasted like rot had just set in, and never, ever smelled like cat urine.

Valeria grew them on her two hectares of land. That was three hundred hectares less than what her grandfather had owned before the Communists took everything, but it was more than enough land to carry her through the winter and support her livestock.

Everything else was profit. Valeria felt she could afford to be caustic. She was often caustic.

But then one day, as she was checking brown spots on a young woman's cucumbers, something made her look up. Two aisles across from her, standing directly in front of her, facing her, she spied a man whose face she recognized but had never looked at. It was the village potter—a widower. He was eating a banana. He was holding it in a strong hand with long tapering fingers. With his other hand, he was snapping the heads off of mushrooms and handing them to the vendor, who dropped them into a brown paper sack and weighed them. Valeria nearly gasped when she saw how gallantly he carried himself. She wondered why she'd never noticed that before, why she'd never noticed him before.

"Darling," she said too loudly.

The woman selling cucumbers breathed a sigh of relief.

"Did you hear that, everybody? Did you hear what Valeria thinks of my cucumbers? The price has just gone up five forints."

Valeria scowled. "I said noth—"

"But you did," the woman interrupted. "I heard you. You were holding it. You were looking at it. You looked up. You said, 'Darling,' just like that. Like you were in love."

Valeria glared at the woman and cleared her throat. She dropped the cucumber and walked toward the potter, examining every inch of him. His hair was white and crept out from under his hat. It covered his ears. His moustache was also white . . . and clean. He looked like an old Prussian officer. He even carried his satchel with the strap crossing his chest. Valeria felt her face flush. She thought herself ridiculous—a blushing spinster. The potter looked up. His eyes caught hers. He nodded his head and smiled widely. He must have recognized her, she thought. She held her breath when he headed in her direction, but then he brushed right past her. Valeria stood still for a moment. Afraid he would disappear without her having said anything, she decided to follow him out of the market. In doing so she left early. It was the first time in twenty-five years. People noticed.

"Well, did you see that? She's gonna have to polish up a bit to get her claws into him," one woman said.

"You're right about that, but there isn't anything wrong with her that couldn't be fixed with the right wardrobe, curlers, and some cold cream," another woman said. This was true. Over the years, Valeria had made herself unattractive. Villagers were accustomed to seeing her grimace, seeing her sneer, and then hearing her curse before being pelted with a handful of chestnuts or whatever else she could get her hands on. It would have taken a stranger to town to appreciate any beauty Valeria might have had hidden behind her scowl or underneath her apron. It would have taken someone without the slightest knowledge of her history. History was really all that stood between Valeria and the people of Zivatar, after all. Over the years, Valeria had made herself an easy target of contempt by being so contemptible.

It was said, for example, that Valeria had cut down the church bells in a rage. This would have made an outcast out of anybody. Nobody knew this for certain, but most everyone agreed that it could not have been anyone else. The incident occurred in the late forties, just after the war had ended. In fact, they had only recently started ringing again.

It was said that the reason why she cut them down was because of her battle with her young lover—the butcher's son.

"She was a beautiful girl," the old men remarked with a wink when they told their grandsons. "With a reputation, if you know what I mean."

Most of the young men in the village, having never seen a young Valeria, didn't believe the stories. They couldn't believe that the old hag who had stung them with chestnuts and curses had been as attractive or lively as their grandfathers insisted.

"I don't believe that," one young man or another would say.

"She was a lovely young woman," their grandfathers insisted.

"Valeria? You must be getting senile in your old age."

"It's true. It's true. She was a lovely girl. She had rosy cheeks. She was healthy and long limbed. She had a firm bosom. She had the butcher's son arrested when the war just began. Who knows? He might have been conscripted eventually, but Valeria wouldn't even allow him the chance to die honorably in battle as cannon fodder against the British."

"That's right," another grandfather said. "And somehow, the Soviets got to him."

"The Soviets?"

"It was horrible. They sent him away to a gulag with Poles, Czechs, and Germans. That poor whistling butcher suffered terribly and he never returned."

"Imagine having to slurp down bowls of greasy soup and fight over crusts of bread," said some of the older men. "When you were raised on the choicest cuts of meat."

"Those were the same prisoners who repaired the railroads after the war."

"All because he wouldn't marry her."

"I heard it was because he had killed her grandfather in the old tavern."

"No, no, you are both wrong. Her grandfather found out about their affair and became furious. He went to the butcher and insisted that the two lovers get married. The butcher agreed, but his son refused. He was a handsome boy. He boasted all the time. I remember. Finally, Valeria's grandfather confronted him. He was so furious he was shaking. He pushed the butcher's son. The butcher's son pushed him back. The old man had a heart attack right in the middle of the pub."

The men stopped speaking and shook their heads. They listened to the wind far off in the fields and thought some more about the butcher's son.

"Hard labor," someone whispered.

"He liked to dance those goddamned Italian tarantellas, remember?" said another.

"When you think on it, it probably served him right."

The men imagined hard labor: laying railroad track across the country or digging holes and standing telephone posts upright, even during winter, even when the earth was cold, the wind was cold, the men were cold, and the sun was cold. All of that backbreaking work done by hand, with hammers, shovels, and pickaxes, and when those things broke, spoons, sticks, and fingertips. All the while Mother Russia standing over them with rifles at the ready: Comrades! You will learn the value of our revolution.

Valeria had placed her own young lover, a boy from their village, under the Russians' inhospitable care, sent him to a work camp far away, on the outside. And after the young man was sent away, after her grandfather had died and she was free to see whoever she wanted, there was not a man left in the village who would visit her, nor one that she would choose to see herself, her reputation notwithstanding. She cut the church bells down after that and sealed her fate as the village's outcast.

"What a waste of a woman," the old men muttered.

"Come on, Grandpa. You forget yourself."

Their grandfathers shook their heads. "You're not listening. I'm not talking about today. I'm talking about during the forties, before she became bitter, before she went crazy and cut those bells down. She was always in the fields watching her sheep . . . and those pigs. Do you remember those pigs? Before her grandfather died?"

Another old man would look up and nod.

"Do you remember how rich they tasted? How sweet? They had the sweetest-tasting pigs in the village. I don't know how they did

15

it. We had a roasting every October. We let the fat drip onto our bread. The whole village went out to her grandfather's field. Right up to the cottage steps. We fried the skin, seasoned it, and feasted right there. The same place where she lives today. Ah, the bread dripped with fat in those days. Don't you remember? The fat? And Valeria, in those days?"

"We did that every year until her grandfather died. He kept the village out of plenty of troubles in his time. Sold all those pigs to the British when they first appeared on the horizon. They rode those pigs out for two days. Remember? But after he was gone, if we wanted fat we had to find it ourselves. She would not share a thing."

The young men shrugged.

"She's a hag, and you're crazy."

"I'm not crazy. In fact, I should have asked her to marry me. The butcher's son really was a horrible man. Dancing goddamned tarantellas. A grown man. Who could trust a man like that? Maybe I should have asked her to marry me. She would have been livelier in the sack than your grandmother, that's for certain. Isn't that right? She would have been livelier than all our wives."

The other old men nodded. They smiled wickedly and licked their lips.

"She had hips!" someone shouted.

"And a bosom like a fat pigeon!" shouted another.

"Enough. Grandpa, really, how can you speak about Grandma this way?"

The old men would shrug. "I'm only telling the truth. Why do you think the women hate her so much? Why do you think they've let her remain an outcast all these years? Believe me, they're not so innocent. They prefer it this way. Valeria was a firework and they know it. Just take a look at her now. It's still there. A firework. She's safer when she's smothered. I tell you one thing. I tell you

16

this honestly, my boy. Had the day happened when I was out on a field and Valeria called me over to the poplar trees where she sat in the shade singing songs—yes, that's right, she used to sing songs in the shade of a poplar tree. They weren't Italian songs either. I swear, had that large-breasted woman ever beckoned to me that I should put down my pitchfork . . . leave my wife . . . abandon my children . . . cut off my legs . . . I tell you now, as certain as I am that your precious grandmama is a loudmouthed shrew, that you would not exist today. I would have left your sweet grandmama and your unborn father. I would have left them all to rot, if only for a day under the poplar trees with Valeria."

Grandsons at this point would shake their heads and either storm away or look around for help. But their grandfathers would not be still.

"And for years after," the old men concluded, "for years, that boy's family tried to appease her, to get her to help them get their boy released. Even during the height of the regime, when it seemed like they were counting every sliver of gristle, they gave her extra slices of pork. Extra slices! They even gave her knucklebones for her dog. Nothing. If you ever see her at the butcher's shop today, just watch her. She remains chilly with the entire family, right down to that fat toddler who's always playing in the freezer.

"If any of them smiled at her, she told them not to. When one of his relatives, while out hunting, came upon a parachute and a crate and opened it, only to discover U.S. dollars, sawdust, guns, and steaks—the first person they offered the meat to was Valeria. She refused, and then sent a letter informing the authorities in Budapest . . . that, my dear boy, that's the luck a man will have when Valeria falls in love. I just wish it could have been me."

Two

Countless bicycles were parked in an empty lot beside the market. Except for scrub and weeds, greenery had stopped growing there. The earth on the lot was rutted and misshapen. Under normal circumstances trying to navigate it sure-footedly was a challenge for anyone over fifty. Drunk, or as in Valeria's case, smitten, it was all she could do to keep from tripping and splashing into a puddle of water. The potter was the exception. He stepped gingerly over puddles and divots and made his way to his bicycle. He unlocked it and pulled it back. He sat on it and was about to pedal away when he looked up and saw Valeria standing directly in front of him. Their eyes met again. He stopped. She tried to smile.

"Yes, my dear? May I help you?" he said.

Valeria mumbled something.

"I'm sorry? I didn't hear you."

"A pitcher. I need a pitcher made," she said. "I was hoping you might make something special for me."

"Ah. Well, that's easy," he answered. "I've got some at the workshop right now. Why not come by this afternoon? You can take your pick."

Valeria nodded and stepped out of the way. Her right foot landed in a puddle. She would have cursed, but the potter was just passing her. He smiled, doffed his cap at her, and rode off. He even looked back and smiled a second time. Valeria could feel her heart racing. She dared not move her foot. Never mind that the water was seeping into her shoe and ruining her stocking. He hadn't noticed and she didn't want to call his attention to her clumsiness. She waited for him to leave and then ran to her own bicycle. She hurried straight home.

When she arrived back at her cottage, Valeria removed the stocking and washed her feet. She rinsed the stocking and hung it to dry. Then she unlocked the milk pail and stool and headed straight to her cow.

"Come along," she said to the animal as she sat down beside it and grabbed its teats. "I know I've already milked you, but I need a little more." The cow's head lolled about in discomfort, but with a hard twist of its tail and a smack on its rump, the beast settled down. Then, somehow, maybe sensing Valeria's insistence, the animal spurted and dribbled enough milk to keep a family of six for a day. Valeria rubbed a salve around the beast's udders and rubbed its ears when she was done.

"That's a good girl," she said. "This should certainly keep him for the rest of the week."

Valeria poured the milk into a canister and sealed it. She went back inside and bathed. She put on different clothes. It was clothing that she wasn't comfortable with, but they were made of softer fabrics and warmer colors, entirely different from the drab gray dress she had been wearing, was known for wearing.

Once she was ready, she hoisted the canister and fastened it to the back of her bicycle. She pedaled toward the potter's workshop. Villagers marveled when they saw her on the other side of the centrum. They stopped and pointed, surprised to see their harsh misfit so far away from her garden. Even more surprising, though, were the flowered skirt and kerchief she had changed into.

"Did you see that?"

"What is she wearing?"

"Was she smiling?"

"Where is she headed?" they wondered aloud.

"Why is she pedaling so fast up that hill? She's going to give herself a heart attack."

The village dogs chased after Valeria, lunging at her back tire and barking. Young boys threw chestnuts and laughed. Valeria ignored them all. She rode the five kilometers to the potter's with her knotted legs pedaling as hard as they could. Her flowered skirt, meanwhile, flapped and fluttered behind her like a banner. She was triumphant—Joan of Arc's grandmother on a bicycle. Her skin never broke into a sweat, her lungs never had to stretch for breath; over and over, in her mind's eye, she replayed the image of the white-haired, white-moustached man gobbling a banana and tearing the heads from mushrooms. She smiled to herself. He seemed so comfortable, so satisfied, so at ease. It struck her that something spectacular was revealing itself. It was as though she had stepped into her familiar yard when the sun was at a certain angle, and there, right in front of her, at the base of a tree she had looked at countless times, a precious stone that had always been there glinted and caught her eye. The best she could explain it to herself was that seeing the potter was a trick of light. She had certainly seen him hundreds of times in the village, but it was only this particular time when she paid attention to him, and having paid attention, she decided she wanted to know him better. Anyway, she was proud of herself for acting and, as she rode up the hill toward his workshop, couldn't help but feel a little hopeful.

Save for an apprentice who worked alongside him, the potter

was a widower who lived alone. When Valeria arrived at his home, she unfastened the cords that held the milk canister fast and hoisted it off her bicycle. She let the bicycle fall to the ground and carried the vessel of milk inside. The potter and his apprentice looked up, startled first by her imposing shadow and then by her harsh voice, which announced, "I have brought fresh milk for your coffee. Where shall I put it?"

The potter blinked a couple of times, then shrugged. He motioned to a door. "I have an icebox in the kitchen," he volunteered. He looked to his apprentice.

The young man, recognizing Valeria, shrugged.

Valeria grunted and marched past the two men with the milk canister balanced precariously on her shoulder. Her key ring jangled at her side.

"I think you're being arrested," the potter's assistant whispered.

"Shh," the potter responded. Then he rose to assist her, but she stopped him with a wave of her free hand.

"Just go about your work," she commanded.

He nodded and did not move. His young apprentice, however, took off his smock.

"Why don't you ask her to leave?" he said.

"Why?" the potter answered. "She just brought a month's supply of milk. She's all right, don't you think?"

"Are you crazy? She's an old hag. You'll have to drink milk three times a day to finish that in a month. It will spoil in two weeks."

"Bah. She's not as bad as all that. She just looks lonely. Besides, I think she likes me. Do you think she has an interesting face?"

The apprentice shook his head. "Maybe you are crazy," he scoffed as he exited the workshop and left the potter sitting alone at his wheel. "Ibolya is going to have your head when she hears about this. It might serve you right. Old age is making you greedy. I'm going to get a drink. Any messages?"

At the mention of his lady friend's name, the potter made a face. "Tell her I'm busy but that I'll stop by later."

The first thing Valeria noticed upon entering the potter's workshop was that except for the open studio entrance, there was not a lock anywhere. Why make plates and teapots and then not lock them up? She became a little concerned. Perhaps this man wasn't her type after all. All those valuable items he made, anyone could have walked in at any time and taken anything they liked. He was a little bit reckless. Perhaps he would be open to her suggestions. She would mention it to him, she thought. Valeria relished never having to worry about where things were. In her cottage, every item she owned was in its prescribed place and she never had to look for anything. The only thing she needed to keep track of was her key ring, something she couldn't mislay if she tried.

Valeria had a key for the chicken coop at night, a key for the padlock on the chain that was attached to the goat, a key for the front door, another for the back; there was the key to the front gate, the side gate, the windows, the woodshed, and finally the pigsty. There were even keys to unlock the cabinets in her kitchen, though sometimes Valeria succumbed to laziness and forgot to lock her icebox.

The potter's kitchen was filthy. She sighed. The wall behind his oven was black with grease. Next to a waist-high refrigerator, on a small card table, were the remnants of a meager meal long past—a slice of molded cheese, a sliver of wax pepper, and a half-eaten roll. The table was underneath a window, and resting on the windowsill were two glasses and a plastic bottle of homemade brandy. Valeria wondered about the two glasses, but the thought was cast aside by the smell of the alcohol. She shook her head at the scene. Valeria only drank sherry. It worked just as well at keeping a person warm in the winter and wasn't as harsh on the throat. A half-empty bottle of brandy could only mean that the potter was a potential drunkard.

She set the milk canister down beside the refrigerator and rummaged through the potter's unlocked cabinets until she found an old paint bucket. She wondered what a paint bucket was doing in the kitchen cabinet but decided it was best not to think about it. She used it for trash. She cleared the card table, poured out the brandy, and when she had finished, she washed what dishes there were. Finally, she scrubbed the grease off of the floor and walls, washed the window, and polished the silverware.

At his wheel, the potter heard the noises coming from his kitchen but was too apprehensive to go and see what Valeria was doing. Instead, he cleared away what he had been working on, threw fresh clay onto his wheel, and began to spin it. When Valeria finally stepped out into his workshop—an hour and a half later—wiping her hands on an undershirt of his that she had found under the sink, unsmiling, severe, he looked at her and, unsure of what else to say, said quickly, "I see you like flowers."

Valeria looked down at the skirt she was wearing for the first time and shrugged.

"I'm going to do better than a pitcher for you," he said, "I'm going to make you a ewer. A big one. To thank you for the milk."

She stared silently. Her heartbeat quickened. He was decisive.

"I thought you might need it to water your flowers," he said. "Or just for decoration. It will probably be too heavy to use. Your name is Valeria Patko, yes?"

She nodded.

"You have that beautiful garden on the other side of the village," he said. "I've been past it. You have the two cleanest pigs I have ever seen."

Valeria wanted to smile, but she didn't. Instead, she put her hand on her key string.

"It's odd how we've never been introduced," he continued. "I've lived in the village now for many years. This was my wife's home. Did you know her? She grew up here as well."

Valeria nodded and remembered the potter's wife. She hadn't liked her much—not as a child, even less as an adult. The woman was coquettish. She was silly. She was a peasant girl, simple, smiled at anything with a beard, and she was always playing with her collar, always putting things in her mouth. She was the kind of woman who needed a man to take care of her. They never spoke, never had a reason to.

"You don't leave your garden much, do you?" the potter said. "Except to go to market? I've seen you there selling peppers in the fall sometimes. I don't think I've ever bought one from you, though."

"No, you haven't," Valeria answered, suddenly remembering something she had seen and didn't like. "You buy them from the slut with the unbuttoned blouse. Her peppers are horrible. I think she fertilizes them with cat shit . . . or maybe her own."

The potter winced. "Perhaps I understand now why we've never met," he said. He looked at his wheel as though he were considering something. "No matter. You were kind to bring me the milk, and you still have a lovely garden. Aren't you lonely, though, with your hurt feelings, clean pigs, and pretty flowers?"

Valeria felt her head spin. "There are no flowers in my garden," she snapped. "It's a vegetable garden." Then she added, "You didn't really care enough to pay attention. You're trying to flatter me."

The potter nodded and laughed. He turned toward his wheel and resumed spinning his clay. He looked up a moment later. "It's true," he said, motioning to the mess in front of him. "I only know clay. Pigs and vegetables aren't that important to me, except for when they're on my plate."

Valeria smiled despite herself.

"I can understand that."

She took a step closer to him and watched him. His hands looked strong. The spinning clay yielded easily. Form was taking shape under his palms as if by magic, as if he were willing it.

"I think you will like this when it's done," the potter said. "It will be a meter tall. Do you have any pieces at home that you would like it to match?"

Valeria looked around his shop. There was an assortment of ceramics, most of them functional. There were figurines here and there, tea sets, plates, bowls, vases. She saw a couple of ornamental plates on a shelf that were similar to ones she owned that were hanging in her kitchen. She pointed to them.

"Like those," she said. "The black ones."

The potter smiled.

"Excellent taste. I will make you a black ewer then," he said. "And I will etch lilacs into it. Do you like lilacs?"

Valeria shook her head, then said hopefully, "I like peppers. Can you make it with peppers?"

The potter nodded. "I'll bring it to you within a week," he said.

Her right eyebrow arched. "You will make me a black pitcher?"

Blackened pottery was a valuable thing, and Valeria knew it. It required great skill to blacken clay. Oxygen had to be withheld during the firing process and the clay had to carbonize. It was a different chemical reaction from open-air firing. Valeria knew that the potter was doing something special for her. She was smitten again. Their brief unpleasantness had wafted away. There wasn't a hint of it left in the room. She felt her heartbeat quickening. He was watching her. She avoided his gaze by watching his big hands massage the clay into form. She absentmindedly touched her throat.

"Bah," she said aloud, shaking her head.

The potter smiled.

"If you promise to take that kerchief off of your head and let your hair loose, I'll also bring you fresh flowers," he said. "It looks like you have beautiful hair."

Valeria said nothing in return, but she felt her face flush and her hand reached up to the kerchief. She suddenly felt silly. She wondered what he must think of her. That she had acted so brazenly. That she should come to his house this way, dressed in a flowered skirt and kerchief like a young girl, cleaning out his kitchen, and bringing him—what was it? Milk? Milk. Mortified, Valeria turned and hurried away. She did not say good-bye; she did not acknowledge him when he stood up. She left his studio, lifted her bicycle from the ground, and rode away.

"Valeria, wait. Where are you going?" the potter shouted after her. "I hope I didn't offend. Your kerchief is lovely. I'll bring the pitcher to your cottage in a week. No, three days! I'll work on nothing else. I'll bring it in three days!"

Valeria was not the kind of woman who shouted in the street, so instead of responding she raised her hand. It looked like a salute, and the potter could do nothing but repeat himself and wave at her back. He returned to his spinning wheel. All the while, though, he thought of his dead wife—a woman who was like sweet grass to him. He had protected her for years. He missed her. She was an enchanting woman who one day long ago bore him a stillborn child of indeterminate sex and died thirty years before he buried her. The potter then thought of his current friend. She was enchanting in a different way, but now that he'd met Valeria, he wondered if his apprentice's comment was true: He was becoming greedy. The potter considered it, but he couldn't decide.

He had examined Valeria closely at the market and again in his studio. Her body seemed knotted. She had a mean disposition. Surprisingly, she had a nice bum. Valeria was nothing like the potter's dead wife. He could see that easily enough. She wasn't anything like his current friend either. He took a deep breath. He was relieved. Finally, here was a woman he wouldn't need to take care of with his every breath. Maybe she was a woman who could challenge him.

Valeria rode to the tavern just down the hill from the potter's workshop. She stopped and considered entering. Why not, she decided. This had been a day of why nots. When the patrons sitting and drinking recognized her in the doorway, they put down their glasses, looked at one another, and shrugged. Valeria ignored the stares. From the moment she had left the potter's, her heart had fluttered as much as her skirt. She was certain that her face was still flushed. She managed to march straight toward the bar.

"Hello, Ibolya," she said to the bartender. Her tone was clipped. She did not like being there. "I'm thirsty. May I have a tumbler of sherry?"

The bartender smiled and poured the drink.

"A tumbler. My, my," she said. "You are thirsty. It must be all that cycling you're doing today. Practicing for a race, are you? What were you doing at the potter's anyway?" Ibolya's words came out like a song, but there was something threatening behind it. Valeria looked over her glass.

"His apprentice was here," she continued. "Said you brought him milk and started rummaging around in his kitchen. Why don't you leave the potter alone? He's a nice man. He's a friend of mine."

Valeria remembered the brandy and glasses on the windowsill. She put her drink down, threw a few forints on the bar, and turned. Ibolya snickered and spoke loudly enough so that her voice carried around the room.

"I said, he's a friend of mine."

Valeria looked back.

"Oh. You didn't know?" the bartender asked. "You silly, blue-stockinged spinster, you can wear all the printed daisies you like.

You'll have to do more than change your clothes if you think you're going to get your claws into him. Really, how long do you think you could interest a man like that?"

The patrons of the bar, who had been silent up to this point, began to titter. Those out of earshot of the two women began making wagers.

Valeria considered the question. Then she smirked. "Until I bury him." She said it so that only Ibolya heard. Then she turned to the patrons and scowled. They quieted down. "Peasants," she said. "You're all, to your last ringworm-infested child, peasants. Even your dogs are peasants. How is it possible?"

She marched out. Ibolya smacked the bar with the flat of her hand and followed her. She watched her ride off down the hill. It was a beautiful day. One of those days with blue skies and chirping birds. She smiled.

"I've got outfits too, you know!" she shouted after Valeria. "He likes my birthday suit best! In fact, I'm going to go show it to him right now."

The villagers tittered. They waited until Valeria had ridden away before they drank or spoke again. Then it was only to curse her. And of the people cursing her, none were louder or harsher than the sole bartender and proprietress of the tavern.

Three

Ibolya Nagy was a widow of Valeria's generation. That is, she was at least fifty-eight years old. However, no one knew for sure exactly how old Ibolya was, because Ibolya was never one to bore a man by talking about herself. Like Valeria she was a willful woman, but unlike Valeria she was loved by the townspeople. At least, the village's men loved her. This despite the fact that she bawled them out with ease and despite the fact that she was not exceedingly comely.

But what Ibolya lacked in beauty and disposition she compensated for with a heaving bosom, a heavy hand when dispensing cheap wine, and a generous line of credit.

"You have thirty days to pay for this. What could be so hard about it?"

Also, word in the pub maintained that Ibolya would just as soon ravish a man in the wash closet as bludgeon him unconscious with a heavy glass bottle for not paying his tab on time.

She'd ravished the potter, anyway. That much was fact. Months ago. Everyone in the village knew that. How Valeria hadn't gotten word, no one could say. Ibolya had had her way with him one afternoon when he had stopped in for a cup of tea, and they'd been at it together ever since. Ibolya maintained early on that there was nothing going on. They were only enjoying one another's company. Why not?

Nobody had ever ordered tea, not at Ibolya's, and while the potter never really drank tea, for some reason he had a craving for it that day and wandered in looking for some. He'd spent the previous quarter of an hour in his studio searching for an old tea bag, or at least some ground-up leaves in a tin.

"Good afternoon, Ibolya. Do you have any tea?" he had asked when he sat down.

Of course Ibolya thought the whole thing a joke.

"Are you flirting with me?" she said.

Still, she thought the strange request and his manner of asking so charming and clever that she went to her quarters behind the pub and brought back a whole tin of Earl Grey.

"Is this what you had in mind?" She shook the can in his face playfully and cooed at him when she returned.

The potter, ever the flirt, oblivious of the effect he was having on her, clasped his hands over hers and thanked her effusively.

"Marvelous. Exactly what I was hoping for." He kissed her knuckles.

She blushed at that, but only for a moment. She was flattered. Fifty-eight years and she'd never experienced a come on like this. She wondered what other tricks he knew, what those big hands and tapering fingers could do. She boiled water and steeped the tea herself. Men around them sat bewildered.

"Would you look at that?" they marveled.

Ibolya had even found a teacup. A porcelain teacup. Not made in a small village studio but from one of the big porcelain houses in the country. She wiped the dust off of it and set it in front of him.

"Where did you get that?" one of the men asked.

"Do you like it?" she asked the potter. "It's from one of those big houses. I got it as a wedding present. It was part of a set. This is the only one left."

"What happened to them?" the potter asked.

"My husband," she replied. "I threw them at his head. Beaned him with every last one of them. The teapot too."

Ibolya poured the potter his drink. He drank it and then downed three more cups in quick succession.

"You're a thirsty man."

The potter nodded and exclaimed after the last cup, "Ah." Then he smiled at Ibolya. "Thank you, dearie. You're a vision come true. I've never seen a lovelier woman."

He excused himself to go to the wash closet. This was all too much for Ibolya to stand. She ran from behind the bar and straight into the WC after him. She locked the door behind them. The patrons jumped up and ran to listen. They smiled at one another and tried peeking through the keyhole. They heard the potter gasping in astonishment.

"What? My word. Ibolya, what are you doing?"

"You old goat. Like you don't know? Of all the crazy lines. Tea. You're so charming!" They heard her laughing.

The potter was stammering. "I was just thirsty. I was thirsty."

The patrons shook their heads.

"Don't fight it, old potter," they said to themselves.

"What man could resist a courtship like that?" one of them ventured.

"I don't get it. I've been coming here for years," a redheaded man complained. "I always order the biggest drinks. I always leave a large tip. She has never followed me into the wash closet. Not once. I've even left the door ajar on occasion thinking she was shy, thinking that she didn't realize I was interested. I'm crazy over her. I'm madly in love with her."

The other men laughed and smacked him on the shoulders.

"Don't be daft, Ferenc!" they shouted. "You have a nice fat wife at home who cooks whatever you want."

"That's not true. She only cooks pork. A man get sick of eating a pig's ass."

Men laughed and smacked him on the back some more while others shushed them and pressed their ears against the wooden door.

"I really do love her."

"Shhh. Shhh. Be still, Ferenc. I think the old potter is about to blow."

They hoisted their mugs in anticipation. A moment passed. The men at the door nodded to the small crowd.

"Hoorah." The men erupted. Beer spilled around them. "Hoorah for our old potter."

Ibolya's muffled smooches and compliments came through clear enough for them to hear.

"You are a prince," they heard her say. "So charming. So kind. I could just eat you up."

The patrons giggled and stepped away from the keyhole. The door opened and the potter emerged. A second cheer went up. Men patted him on the back. They handed him a mug of beer and a cigarette. Despite himself, he grinned sheepishly.

"Better than winning the lottery, hey, potter?"

The others laughed.

"What kind of tea was that?"

"Does she have any more?"

"I saw her bring a whole tin. You know, one of those tins from England."

Ibolya followed behind the potter, looking exactly as she had when she entered the wash closet, sweaty. She shot them all a look that silenced them right away. She went to her space behind the bar and wiped the sweat from her temples with a dish towel.

"I'd like some tea," the man named Ferenc announced.

"Me too," said a second.

"A round of tea for everyone," said a third.

"You're all pigs," Ibolya scolded. "All of you except my little rabbit here."

She gave the potter a loving look. He was sitting. His fingers trembled around his cigarette. He tried to smile but it looked half-hearted. He shrugged instead.

The other men grew silent but watched her. She arranged her top right in front of them. Her pillowy breasts shook while she adjusted her blouse. The men were mesmerized. When she had finished and looked up again, there was a line of supplicants in front of her. They placed fresh bills on the bar. They ordered fresh drinks. Ibolya smiled and collected their money.

"My darling little piglets." She relented, hopped a little, and cooed. She poured the shaking potter a fresh cup of tea.

"There, there," she said, patting his cheek. "My sweet little rabbit dick. You can have tea any time you want. It's all yours. I'll keep the cup right here and a warm kettle waiting whenever you like."

The men in the pub snickered. "Rabbit dick," they whispered.

The potter had returned several times since, but it must be mentioned that he did not like the nickname.

Valeria's visit to the potter's had elicited more than a little curiosity in Ibolya. When Valeria had ridden away and was out of sight, Ibolya decided that she really would pay her own visit to the potter. She asked one of her regulars to watch the bar and then left the pub. She walked up the hill to the potter's studio. When she walked in and found him spinning a large mass of clay on his wheel, she smiled. Sometimes Ibolya liked to watch him work. She liked the look of concentration he got, the little furrow that grew between his brows. She lingered a moment.

"Darling," she said in her sweetest voice. "Would you like something to eat?"

The potter looked up and smiled at her. He nodded. Ibolya smiled at him and walked into his kitchen. When she saw what Valeria had done, she pinched herself to keep from storming out and attacking the potter for allowing the other woman in his private quarters. However, she knew she couldn't, because it was her own idea that their relationship not be exclusive. Of course, when she had communicated to the potter that they weren't exclusive she thought it was her way of keeping herself unattached. She had fully expected to grow bored with him. She usually grew bored with her lovers. Sooner or later it was bound to happen. She liked to keep her options open. Still, she was furious when she saw his kitchen. It was so clean, so sparkling, it was as if all memory of her visits had been scrubbed away.

"What happened to the brandy?" she called out in a practiced, unconcerned voice.

"It should be on the windowsill where we left it," he called back.

Ibolya looked around. She found the empty bottle in the paint bucket.

"Bitch," she muttered.

Ibolya opened the fridge and saw the canister. She scoffed at it and pulled it out. She opened it and poured the milk down the kitchen sink.

"Oh," she shouted. "This milk is bad! Have you tasted it?"

The potter didn't answer.

"Oh!" she shouted again. "Really bad. I'll have to pour it away. Terrible. What a waste."

"Yes, a waste," the potter repeated absently.

There was no food in the refrigerator. It was empty. Ibolya left the kitchen and returned to the workshop.

"I'll run down to the pub and make us toasted sandwiches," she said. "Did you know your fridge is empty?"

The potter nodded. He was concentrating. His lips were screwed into a single point.

"Rabbit dick?" she called out.

He looked at her and frowned.

"I'll be right back. Why don't you put the clay away for me for a little while?"

"I have an idea," he said. "There's something I want to try."

"That's nice," she said. "But let's have lunch together and lock up for a while. I have a new negligee I want to show you."

The potter smiled at her and nodded.

Men.

Ibolya returned with sandwiches and cold drinks. The potter had stopped working and covered everything in a wet cheesecloth. He was washing his hands when she came in. They went to his kitchen, where she set the food on the table. They sat and ate. She tried to feed him by hand in a sort of game, but he wouldn't take it from her. He moved his head and took a bite from his own sandwich.

"Just taste it," she said.

He shook his head and made a face.

"Please. I'm eating."

"Rabbit dick, just let me feed it to you. I can sit on your lap if you like."

The potter shook his head. He was thinking about the ewer he was making. Something about it was different and he couldn't figure out exactly what. He appreciated the food, but his mind was somewhere else, and Ibolya's craving for attention was disturbing him.

She offered him another bite of her sandwich. Again, he shook his head.

"Please, for me," she entreated.

"No," he snapped. "Would you stop? I'm thinking."

"About what?" Ibolya snapped back.

"That pitcher," he said. "How to make that pitcher for Valeria. There's something about it I can't put my finger on."

Ibolya stopped chewing. Her bile rose in her throat. She put her sandwich down and stood up. The potter looked at her.

"That thing on the wheel is for Valeria?" she asked.

"Yes," he answered. "I promised to make it for her because she brought me the milk."

"But the milk was bad," Ibolya said. "Her cow must be ill."

The potter shrugged and looked around. For the first time, he noticed how clean everything was.

"Well, still, she cleaned the kitchen."

Ibolya's nostrils flared. She walked out of the kitchen and into the workshop. She approached the wheel and snatched away the cheesecloth. It was just a mess of wet clay, barely anything at all. Still, she was furious. She didn't care who'd said what to whom. This was her space.

"You shit," she said to the potter. "Who do you think you are?"

The potter was standing in the doorway.

"What?"

"Don't be stupid with me. You think I don't see what's happening?"

"About what?" the potter said.

"In front of my eyes!"

"A pitcher," he said.

Ibolya screamed. She balled her hands into fists and hammered the clay. She pummeled it until it was just a mashed clump.

"What did you do that for?" he asked.

"Don't you dare," she said. "You know exactly why!" She pointed in the direction of her pub. "I can have any man I want. Any of them."

The potter shrugged.

"Ferenc would lick my feet."

"Yes, but why would you make him do that?" the potter said. "I think you're overreacting."

Ibolya screamed again and hammered the clay one more time.

"You want to make a gift for that old hag, go ahead. But you won't see me again if you do."

The potter considered this a moment.

"Ibolya, we spoke about this. You told me yourself that you're not my wife, you're not my fiancée, we're not even courting. What is the matter?"

"Don't you dare tell me what I said," Ibolya said. "If you make this pitcher, it's over."

"Well, first off, there's nothing we have together that could be over," he said. "And I am making the pitcher because I have an idea I want to try."

Ibolya nodded. She did not look in the potter's direction again. She brushed her hands together and walked out of the studio. She walked away.

"Good-bye forever," she said.

The potter shrugged. It was a strange day.

Four

In many regards, Ibolya looked more like a horse than a woman. It wasn't entirely the fact that she sweated so much, either. The fluorescent lights above the bar had a tendency to catch her unfavorably; when they did, it was easy to imagine her bursting through stable doors and trampling over indigents and small children that happened to be in her way. Her face jutted outward. Her nose and mandible were almost a physiological deformity. Besides the swell of her bosom, the lower half of her face, beginning with her nose, was her most distinguishing characteristic. She had a long nose, sharp and hooked. Men gazed at her face, then gazed at her bosom, and then dozily ordered liter after liter of cheap beer.

"She's all natural, though, a thoroughbred," they remarked as they drank and stared at her chest. Ibolya scoffed. She liked the power of inducing her customers' imaginations. It kept them thirsty. She liked to watch the effort her more pea-brained customers went through imagining her sitting on their laps or fondling their ears. She bent over even further in front of those men, practically pouring herself into their glasses. They responded to her by ordering bigger drinks and more often.

Ibolya's influence over the village men was as strong as the mayor's. Had she thought of it, or put any effort behind it, Ibolya could have been mayor. She could even insist on a recall and have herself installed as mayor. With a snap of her fingers the mayor could be tarred, feathered, and chased out of town. Luckily for him, Ibolya wasn't interested in politics.

Her tavern was the only one in the village and the only watering hole within forty-five kilometers. It was natural to see men from the countryside laid out on the street in front of it after they had tripped off the curb or over one of the village's ubiquitous dogs. It was a twenty-four-hour establishment and had been since the day she buried her husband. After she had buried him, she ordered the men who attended the service to follow her back to the pub.

"Tear down the front door."

The men behind her hesitated.

She turned on them. Her anger flared.

"I said, tear down that door. Do it now or I'll set the whole place on fire."

The men standing behind her had the door off its hinges in a matter of seconds.

"Now tear out that front wall. The one facing the street."

"What do you want to do that for?" some of the more courageous men protested.

"Just do it," she responded. "It's my pub now and I'm going to run it my way."

"But it's a support wall. It's holding up your roof."

Ibolya thought about it for a moment.

"All right, all right. Tear down half of it."

The men shrugged and did as they were told, and since that day, the day of her husband's funeral, the door and a portion of the wall had never been replaced. She had a man paint a sign in English—IBOLYA'S NONSTOP—and during the winter she put up a sheet of heavy plastic. The villagers had witnessed their first marketing campaign. Now, citizens who happened by on their way in or out of the village could look through the gaping hole and see who was sitting down drinking. More often than not, those citizens would spot a friend or relative, who would call out, "Hey. Come on and join us. Where are you hurrying to?" Of course, the passerby could not be rude, and whether he was leaving the village or just entering it, he would inevitably join whoever had called out. He would sit. He would order. He would drink. More men would pass by. They would see their friends. They too would sit and order. What it meant was that Ibolya's pub always had a customer. She hired a young girl to handle the overnight and early morning shifts, but for the most part, Ibolya herself poured the drinks and kept the bar stocked. Years ago, her husband had planted a few hectares of grapes, and so she had plenty of homemade wine. She had also worked a deal out with a Ukrainian truck driver, and when he passed by, she met him on the highway with a borrowed diesel truck and stocked up on beer and cheaply made Russian liquor.

There were no television sets in her tavern. No stereo. No news-papers. Entertainment consisted of men beating up on the occasional wandering Gypsy or one another. There was also the hope that Ibolya would follow someone into the wash closet, but that honestly had only ever been a rare occurrence, and once she started enjoying conjugal visits with the potter, it hadn't happened again.

The tavern was a cheap-looking place, made of cheap wood tacked together with cinder blocks for support. The scent of alcohol belches and cigarette smoke saturated the air. The men there drank and smoked with few pauses. When they did, it was only to shout at each other or crack ice cubes between their teeth.

The shabbiness and despair of Ibolya's pub were reasons enough to keep Valeria from ever frequenting it. She despised the place, but the trip to the potter's had been special, after all. Valeria didn't want to wait to get home before she took her nip. She tried to imagine the potter and Ibolya together. The thought sickened her.

"Why did I stop in there?" she asked herself. "The mayor should have made her put that door back up when he came into office."

She had contacted the mayor herself on account of Ibolya's pub, asking him to make her replace the door. She even sent him a letter about it. It just so happened that in this instance they were of a like mind. The mayor—who as a younger man had spent more than a night or two reveling in Ibolya's tavern himself—did indeed try to coax Ibolya into putting a door up and replacing the wall, but Ibolya scoffed when he broached the subject with her.

"Do you know how that would hurt my business?" she grumbled.

The mayor—a New Christian Democrat—responded, "It's disturbing to the community. I've been getting complaints. I have a letter right here, in fact."

"Don't be such an ass," Ibolya shot back. "This pub is more like a community center anyway, or don't you remember that? In fact, I remember you coming in here begging for votes. Have you forgotten that already? I daresay you'll be coming back again."

"Ibolya," the mayor asserted, unaffected by the bosom she had perched upon the bar for him to stare at. "Put a door up or I will shut this place down. It's a new day. The country is changing. Do you think foreigners will invest here if they see this kind of shiftless behavior? The Germans will go elsewhere—maybe into Romania. I'm trying to get the Transportation Ministry to put in a rail line. If they were to come and see this, why, we'd be a laughingstock. They wouldn't take us seriously at all."

Ibolya laughed. She shouted out to her patrons, "Do you hear this imbecile? Do you hear this . . . ass? Do you hear what he is saying? Why, it wasn't that long ago when he was fucking the retarded Gypsy behind the tree, was it?" The men laughed and nodded. "They humped like dogs all night, remember? The whole village could hear you, mayor. It was your first time. Do you remember that? She was fifteen, wasn't she? Mind like a five-year-old. Always had her hands on her muff. Well, listen to this, everybody, Mayor Ass is all grown up. He's full of shit. He wants to shut down Ibolya's Nonstop Tavern. He wants to shut down your pub so that the minister of transportation and the Germans won't be offended. As if Germans aren't offensive in and of themselves."

A chorus of moans and curses arose from the men at their spots.

"Fuck the Germans."

"Fuck the French."

"Fuck the EU."

"Fuck the minister."

Ibolya looked at the mayor. He was red faced. He shrank bank. "The people have spoken, mayor," she said. "And democracy has given you its answer: Everybody's fucked. What do you say now, ass? You're not Khrushchev, you know. This isn't Moscow. You should tread lightly or you'll end up like Ceausescu. This is a new day, mayor. You're right about that. The will of the people. I mean, honestly, if the Communists dared not shut us down, *dared* not— Communists, real men—what can you and your limp-dicked Christian capitalist cronies do? Put your Germans and your rail line somewhere else. We don't need them here."

"Would you consider a curtain?" The mayor acquiesced. He knew when he was beaten.

Ibolya shook her head and poured him a shot of pear brandy.

"Not even a curtain," she sighed. "Have a drink, though. On the house."

Respiration. That is what Ibolya's pub meant to the village. Respiration. After a day toiling in the fields, ferrying wood, fighting the earth, fighting goats or cows or pigs or one another, after a day of backbreaking chores, Ibolya's pub was the one place where the villagers went to take the edge off, where they could rejuvenate. Ibolya did not really control that. The mayor could not contain it. Valeria could not scare it. It was bigger than all of them. If men wanted to sit and drink, then that was their will. If women wanted to join their husbands and lovers and boyfriends and secret paramours, then that was their will. Winter, spring, summer, autumn—every season, the tavern, like the growing attendance at the great temple on Sundays, was a place of rejuvenation. But unlike church on Sundays, which the Communists had managed to smother, the pub was fully active. Every night of the week Ibolya's pub re-created the masses and sent them out again, bleary eyed and cirrhotic, certainly, but willing to struggle and toil at least one more day.

So the mayor acquiesced. He quit waving Valeria's letter around and stuffed it in his pocket. He wasn't interested in fighting a battle he couldn't win. He'd leave them their pub, for the time being. In fact, he had often used it for his gain. He knew he could use it still. The mayor had plans. Great plans. He told his wife all about them any chance he had. Once the new hotel in the centrum had been constructed, Ibolya's pub would be torn down. Until then, he would work with her. Use her to his advantage.

The mayor was that most dangerous of individuals. He possessed, in equal amounts, unhealthy doses of charm and ambition. He was a driven opportunist.

Often he arrived home from work angered by the slowdown at the train station or by something that had happened in the office.

"These people can't see the future," he complained to his wife. "They just don't get it. The old days are over. Why do they fight me?"

His wife shrugged and massaged his shoulders.

"It's hard to be an eagle when you're surrounded by hens," she said.

"Exactly," he said. "That's exactly right."

The villagers liked him immensely. He seemed cosmopolitan and sophisticated. He had traveled more extensively than any other citizen of the village, ostensibly on missions of economic development. Those travels around the world—to destinations as far-flung as Auckland and Oslo—had never yielded a single result, save for a Dutch dog food company. Yet he always returned from his trips more elated than when he left. And beside him on all of these jaunts, smiling the entire time, her bow-shaped lips wet and fleshy, was his wife, that siren from the banks of the northern Danube, a willowy vixen with the longest, shapeliest legs many of the villagers had ever seen. She accompanied the mayor, and when they returned, endless bags returned with them, filled with shoes and perfumes, blouses and jewelry from shopping centers around the world. The people loved it. It was glamour, after all.

Inevitably, it turned out that the Australians, or British, or South Africans, or Brazilians would change their minds at the last minute. And just like that, the fish farms, the call centers, the pharmaceutical factories would fizzle into nothing. It wasn't the mayor's fault, though. The villagers all agreed on this. He'd tried. It was the shiftiness of those damned foreigners and Far East competition.

The mayor began his political career after university—where he had started out as a conscientious and vocal supporter of the Communist Party. He had been a terrible student, but he was a party member and turned radical students in with such zeal that his grades never showed anything but the best scores. He became an aide to the regional assistant to the minister of the interior's subdirector, but when he read the writing on the wall, saw that the Socialists would no longer be carrying the country, heard the rumblings of democracy, he made a great show of supporting democratization. He jumped on cars and smashed windows. He made reform speeches and listened to American rock and roll.

He did all of it in hopes that he would be given an appointment once the New Democrats took power. It didn't exactly happen as he planned, however. In his youthful zeal, he had been too eager. He had abandoned the party before the leaders themselves had their chance and even before they had agreed to abandon anything. The mayor found himself isolated. The promise of his youth had passed. He was stuck having to fend for himself back in the village where he grew up. He was the last to understand that except for international window dressing, power stayed with the people who had it to begin with.

But the villagers liked him in Zivatar. He had been the mayor for six years already. He had started the railway and hotel like he said. He kept trying to bring in new projects and business. Now, when he returned from those trips abroad, when his Mercedes passed the hole in the wall, the mayor beeped the horn and even his wife waved, the two of them together like a pair of peacocks.

"You look splendid, mayor," the citizens remarked on his first day back at work when he drove his way the few hundred meters along Market Street to his office.

"I feel splendid," he called out the window. "We all will. You will see."

The villagers nodded and spoke about him in hushed whispers, anxious to hear the news that was obviously good and would benefit them all.

The usefulness of Ibolya's pub clear to him, the mayor began making announcements and proclamations in her tavern. First he ordered a round of beer for the men. Then he passed around pictures and everyone grabbed them to take a look, and then he would sit on a stool among them with a mug in his hand. With Ibolya and his wife standing directly behind him, he would regale his constituents with the oddities of the world outside their village.

Men and women listened, shook their heads, and laughed. They commented on the strangeness of foreigners.

"Thank God we live here," they agreed.

"How can they stand it?" They shook their heads.

The mayor would watch them and motion to Ibolya. Ibolya would nod and immediately begin pouring another round of beer. A lot of money was spent on these nights. Maybe four or five of them a year. She had a good thing going with the mayor.

"I need them drunk," he would tell her. "Drunk enough to agree to anything. I'll buy three rounds for everyone in the tavern."

"Agreed," she'd say. Ibolya quickly learned to empty out the tables and fill up the room with extra chairs she borrowed from the church.

Recently, after a third round of drinks, the mayor had cleared his throat and looked up at the lights above them. He looked like he was meditating. He smiled slightly and shook his head. He nodded at the room.

"What is it, mayor?" the men asked. "What kind of deal did you make this time?"

"I have successfully sold all of the village's fallow fields to the Koreans!" he announced. "There is going to be a television factory. They offered us one million dollars for all the land and promised forty-seven jobs. This is a very good deal. In fact, my contracting business will need to hire fifty-two of you on a temporary basis to build the factory."

The citizens of the hamlet became excited. Ibolya shook her head. She knew that one million dollars was not nearly enough money for the land. She knew that the mayor had probably made more, had probably worked out a deal on behalf of his own contracting business—a business that was already raking in cash because of that damned train station. This kind of thing made Ibolya mad, but the mayor seemed to sense that, and in the end he ordered a fourth round of beer for the house and that placated her a bit. But Ibolya decided that she would have to have a talk with the mayor at some point. She was a partner, if anything. She should be paid like a partner.

Her customers were good and drunk, though. They blew smoke and slapped their friends on the backs. Eventually they started ordering their own drinks and even began arguing over which forty-seven of them would get those factory jobs the mayor had promised.

"I should. I've been a machinist most of my life," said a burly fellow.

"You're a drunk. The Koreans don't want to hire drunks. Everyone knows that they are hard workers who want hard workers like me. Besides, you don't even own a television."

"You're a little thief and everyone knows *that*," the burly man responded. "The Koreans would be daft to hire you."

The mayor raised his hands and shushed them.

"Gentlemen, now isn't the time to argue. We must prepare the fields for construction. See, there are those construction jobs as well. I'm always looking out for you."

The men roared their approval and ordered Ibolya's more expensive beer. They could afford it now. She smiled and poured, her loose blouse fluttering open as much as she could remember to make it.

To the last male villager—and the men proudly ran this village —their mayor was a man of vision and great perspective. He was nothing like those old appointees who came from the government. With this new breed of mayor, things *happened*. Their village was livelier, more energetic.

And there was also that first lady to consider. Standing there behind him. Smiling. Lean legged. What a woman.

She was young and thoroughly modern. Fashionable clothes and car. The mayor must be some man, the villagers remarked. Why else would she agree to leave the big city? Why would such a woman, who bought bags of expensive oranges because she wanted to, never lifted a finger if she didn't have to, never experienced sweat on her brow or the sun on the back of her neck, why else would such a resplendent woman come and live in their tiny village, in a remote part of the plain, in the middle of nowhere, if not for the singularity of this renowned mayor? One of their own. He was some man, indeed.

They didn't know that the mayor had met her in a disco. That she was a bartender from a small village in the north near Slovakia and had only been living in Budapest for five months when she met the mayor. They didn't know that the mayor took one look at her and felt *something* tug at him. He told her who he was, what he did, and what his plans were, and asked her to marry him on the spot. As she had come to the city for exactly that reason, she agreed on the spot. They went shopping the next morning and he brought her back to the village, where she promptly made herself at home.

"It pains me to say it, to even think it," said Ibolya a few days after the mayor had announced the latest deal with the Koreans, "but couldn't it be possible that the mayor really is an ass?"

She announced this to her patrons apropos of nothing at all. She had been opening a bottle of beer when the idea struck her suddenly. She had been fuming over him. She had gone to see him to talk about either increasing the number of rounds he ordered or cutting her in on the larger take she was sure he was getting. The mayor balked and refused to order anything more than what he had been ordering.

"You should be thanking me," he'd said.

"You should be thanking me," she'd answered.

The two stared at one another for a moment and it became clear to both of them that from that point on they were enemies.

She would tear the mayor down.

"You know, I've been reading that the flaw in democracy is that a country ultimately gets the government it deserves," she said to her patrons.

The men looked up from their bottles.

"Huh? What are you saying?"

"Well," she continued, "you say you want a man with vision, but how hard is it to notice that the streets need a little paving, that the sidewalks and building facades are cracking and black with soot from car exhaust and could use a whitewashing, and that every postbox, phone booth, every public thing in the centrum needs fixing. It doesn't take much vision to see that."

"What are you saying?" The men fidgeted. "Why are you speaking this way?"

"We're paying taxes to send him on vacation. At least, I have a suspicion that that's what we're doing. Don't you see it?"

The men started to shout.

"Bah!"

"You're crazy."

"Stick to pouring drinks. That's all we want to hear from you."

"You all go on like that and I won't pour another drop," she answered. "I'll have Ferenc throw you out. You'll throw them out for me, won't you, Ferenc?"

The redheaded man named Ferenc rose and nodded. Ibolya knew she could count on him, that he was madly in love with her and would do anything for her. She liked him being around. It was good to have some muscle to appeal to when things in the pub got a little out of hand. Still, she wasn't interested. Ferenc was married to a fat, redheaded woman. They had fatter, redheaded children.

Some said that Ferenc was as simple as a toddler, but he was nearly seven feet tall and was known to react violently when provoked. Once, he had broken a Norwegian trekker's arm. Ferenc seemed fidgety already, like he was looking around for someone to hit. The men quieted down. They looked at their feet.

"Now listen," Ibolya continued. "Six years ago we elected him and in that time where has he been?"

The men thought about it, argued over it, and then answered.

"Well, that's twenty-six trips in six years. Tell me, Ferenc, how many trips have you taken in six years?"

The man named Ferenc looked up at the rafters.

"None," he said.

"Think hard."

"I went on a hunting trip. But that was just over in the next village. That was three years ago."

"Anybody else?"

Nobody answered.

"The mayor has traveled abroad four times every year. He hasn't brought a single thing back for the rest of us."

A man sat up. "That's not correct! We got the dog food company."

Another man answered. "That only employs sixteen people, and the dog food is too expensive for us to purchase."

"But he brought it. The mayor brought them here like he said."

"And now he got us the Koreans. They're bringing a television factory!"

The men nodded and began chatting hopefully. Not even Ferenc's glaring could contain them. Korean televisions. Made right in their village.

Ibolya was deflated. Between the potter, the mayor, and her customers, the men in this village would drive her crazy.

Five

Why he had decided to make a ewer for Valeria, the potter couldn't say. It just happened. Why in the several months he had been in a relationship with Ibolya he hadn't made anything at all for her, he also couldn't say. He simply hadn't been inspired to.

"Am I trying to impress this woman?" he remarked to himself. He couldn't answer. He accepted the possibility, however, that he was.

Constructing Valeria's pitcher had been a time-consuming affair. The pitcher was black and garlanded with one-inch peppers that had to be made and attached individually. To attach the peppers to the ewer, the potter prepped them by scoring the back of each of them with a knife and then scoring each place on the pitcher where he would position them.

Then, when the ewer and peppers were almost dry in the open air, the potter applied a creamy solution of wet clay slip to the scraped sides of the vessel and pressed the scored sides of the peppers against it. He attached the peppers, every single pepper, to the pitcher's body. Then he worked the leathery clay against the vessel and hid any visible seams he could find. Afterward, he attached clay threads to the pepper stems, creating a garland. It took him hours. With the peppers added, the full beauty of the ewer began to resonate with him, and at times the potter stepped back and gazed at his creation. He placed his hand on its cool hip. He stroked it. He caressed the neck with a finger. He dusted its throat with a fine-hair brush. He squeezed its lip. He thought of the woman he was giving it to.

"Marvelous," he sighed to himself. "Maybe I am trying to impress this woman. Maybe that's not such a bad thing."

He placed one last pepper beneath the spout. Then he yawned and stretched. The day had passed. He went to sleep.

The next morning, when the potter awoke, he went straight to the ewer and pressed his finger against it to check its consistency. He tapped it with a pencil. He brushed off some dust, and certain that it was dry, he placed the ewer in the kiln.

If he was to make a piece of black pottery for Valeria as he had promised, he needed enough coal to burn, the key to black pottery being in the soot and lack of oxygen. Smoke had to swirl around the ewer. Ash had to envelop the piece. He started the fire and watched it grow underneath. The black smoke took time to come, but within ten minutes, he was certain that the ewer was shrouded under a black curtain. Convection currents sent sooty smoke swirling and spinning around the pitcher. He looked at his watch. He would let it bake for several hours. He would let the fire die down underneath it, and then he would leave the ceramic piece to cool off.

When it was time, he pulled the vessel out of the kiln and carried the warm piece of pottery to his workbench. He brushed the soot off and examined the pitcher. Perfect. Inside and out, the ewer was black, the color of dull coal. The potter brushed the pitcher again, with horsehair this time. In between brushstrokes he blew on it. Soot exploded like gunpowder after every breath and drifted down onto his workbench. When the pitcher was thoroughly cleaned, he stepped back and looked. He shook his head. It might have been the best ceramic piece he had ever sculpted. He searched his workshop looking for something that came close. Some piece that he could look at that would sum up the fifty-odd years he had been doing this. He found nothing. Not a single thing in his workshop came close to the ceramic piece he had just made for Valeria.

Certainly there were fine pieces all around. Good examples of quality craftsmanship. He had made the odd wine cistern or candle-stick holder, but those were merely solidly constructed objects intended for use in middle-class homes. In completing this ewer, the potter felt transported. He had transformed himself into an artist. An artiste! As far as he was concerned, this work was gallery or museum quality. That was no hyperbole, either. He looked at it and nodded.

The potter's apprentice entered later in the afternoon, opening the door noisily and breaking the potter's concentration. The potter was watching the ewer. Just watching it. Not brushing it or wiping it down. He just watched it. The apprentice made a face and tried to catch the older man's attention. When he saw the ewer, the young man whistled.

"My God. That is beautiful."

The potter smiled and nodded his appreciation.

"You made that for Valeria? You're crazy. You should take that to the city and sell it for a lot of money."

The potter looked up. The young man was surveying the piece, calculating how much he could ask for it in the city. The young man was always talking about taking their work to the city and selling it at tourist traps.

"Promise me you will keep your mouth shut about this."

The apprentice shrugged. "Why? This could fetch a small fortune."

"Promise me," the potter said again. He had become angry.

"Or I will send you back to your family of locksmiths. This is for Valeria."

The apprentice blushed. "I promise. I won't say anything about it."

The potter changed his tone.

"Anyway, you have an assignment. Zsofi Toth has been in to see me. She has ordered a teapot and platter. I won't have time to finish them, but she insisted that you do them anyway."

The young apprentice nodded eagerly.

"By myself? Did you want to assist me?"

"Alone," the potter said, motioning to the ewer. "I will be working on this for the next day or so."

The apprentice sat down.

"Take the work home with you," the potter commanded. "I need quiet. I need to concentrate."

The apprentice looked up. "What if I need help?"

"It's only a teapot and a platter, and by all accounts, you're a mighty fine journeyman at this point. You should be able to do this easily enough."

The apprentice smiled and grabbed a bag of clay.

"And the platter? What kind?"

The potter looked at him. "She wants the wedding platter."

"Zsofi Toth?" the apprentice scoffed. "What does she need with a wedding platter? There's nobody in the village who would ever marry her. No man in the village even looks at her."

The potter shrugged. "Why not? She's a pretty girl."

The apprentice nodded. "Yes, that's true. She's very pretty— and kind, to boot. It's her mother. Have you never seen her mother? Frightful woman. Mean as a weasel and fat as a cow. I think all the men are afraid of having to feed her. I'd be afraid of that."

The potter smiled.

"She was odd when she came in. She asked for you. She seemed disappointed to see me. Anyway, I think she has her mind set on someone."

The apprentice raised an eyebrow.

"Maybe it's just wishful thinking," the apprentice said. "I wonder who it is? She didn't give you a hint? Not many our age left around here anymore. Everyone else is gone. Abroad, to the city, or they're married. No bachelors left, really. Poor thing. I wonder who it is? I see her all the time. I'm surprised she hasn't mentioned it."

The potter shrugged. He motioned to the door. The apprentice nodded and turned to leave. "I am very happy you're letting me make these on my own. Thank you."

The potter shooed him away. "Thank Zsofi next time you see her. Like I said, she requested that you make them. Bring them by in a couple of days when you're ready to fire them."

The apprentice left and the potter smiled at his back. He was happy the young man had come along. The potter was getting older and taking more time to finish his orders. His slowness might have been a problem had it not been for the cheap imports flooding the country from China. Even in the village markets, plates were being sold at a fraction of the potter's costs. They were flimsy things. They chipped and broke when they were washed. Still, the Chinese, along with the apprentice, eased his burden. Soon, the potter had begun thinking, the apprentice might even take over the workshop and business, meager as it was sure to be. The potter was more than ready to retire. He laughed when he thought of the effect this news would have on the apprentice's family. He was certain that they would be upset. The potter didn't mind giving his shop to the young man. He'd have no use for it. He had no children of his own. Why not?

The apprentice was from a family of locksmiths. His father was a locksmith. His uncles were locksmiths. His cousins were all locksmiths. They owned and operated the only locksmith business in the village, had a key to every lock in town. When the apprentice was growing up, he spent every day by his father's side, going from house to storefront to city office, changing and fixing locks. There was even the summer after the Soviets left when the family made huge profits installing safes.

"I wondered who they were protecting themselves against," the apprentice had said when he and the potter first met at Ibolya's tavern two years before. "Everyone in this village either knows everyone else or is related to everyone else. It doesn't make sense, the safes."

The villagers figured that out, it seemed, because the very next summer the apprentice spent his days removing those safes. People had forgotten their combinations or had lost their keys.

"Again with the safes," he told the potter at Ibolya's tavern the following summer. "I tell you, I hate it. I just hate it."

Zsofi Toth rode by on her bicycle. She called out to the young man and waved. He smiled and waved back. She was such a comely girl that the men in the pub stopped what they were doing and congratulated the young man. He shrugged innocently. *Just friends. We were in the same class.* Even the potter nodded appreciatively.

"Why don't you come work for me?" he said. "I'm getting old. I don't have a son. I could use the help."

The apprentice did not need to consider it very long. He agreed right at the table. He thought it was a brilliant idea. He jumped up and shook the potter's hand. Then he ran straight home and told his family that he was leaving the family business at the end of the summer.

"Business has grown slow," he announced to his family. "And all we ever seem to do is copy keys. How long do you expect me to sit in front of the key grinder? And the only person who ever comes here anyway is that crazy old lady, Valeria. I'd swear I've cut over a hundred keys for her alone. The whir of the machine grates on my nerves. The smell of the grinding metal makes my nostrils burn. I'm starting to get headaches. I want to apprentice with the potter. So I'm telling you all today that I'm leaving the family business for good."

His parents shook their heads. His mother wrung her hands, while the vein on his father's forehead began to tremble and his eye twitched.

"A potter? But you're a locksmith," his father argued. "It's even your name."

"There are more and more Locksmiths in this village and less and less work for them. There is only one potter. And he is old. I can have a good business."

"But a potter? Potter Locksmith? That's no name for a man. It doesn't make any sense. Tell me, who will inherit my share of the business?"

"What business?" the apprentice said. "That's what I'm talking about. All we ever do anymore is cut keys. I won't do that for the rest of my life. I couldn't do that for the rest of my life."

At this point, the apprentice's grandfather tottered in. He heard the shouting, and never one to miss a fight, he came to draw blood.

"What's wrong with it, eh?" he butted in, not missing a beat, seeing his grandson backed into a corner and knowing exactly who and how to attack. "I did it. Your uncles do it. Your father does it. My grandfather did it. Generations, by God. Generations! It fed all of us. Think of the service we provide. Without us the world would sink into chaos. Peasants and Gypsies walking in and out of places they don't belong. Imagine it! Frightful, I know. Well, there was a time when exactly that sort of thing used to happen. And then they invented locks. The Carthaginians, it was. In Carthage. To keep out the peasants. Well, Gauls really, but peasants just the same. And they've been around ever since. Everyone needs a door to lock. That's just the way it is. Not like your pretty plates."

"Not just plates," the apprentice argued. "Ceramics! Plates, pots, cups, ashtrays. All of it. Everyone uses plates. I bet the Carthaginians had plates before they had locks."

"Plates! Never heard of 'em. I've never used one."

"What are you saying?" The young apprentice shook his head. "Of course you have."

His grandfather shook his head. So did his father. His cousins —who had heard their screaming grandfather and wandered in— shook their heads. All of the men in that family were standing in front of him. They shook their heads and denied ever having used, needed, or even seen a plate. They also, to the dismay of the Locksmith women, stopped using them from that point on. The Locksmith women never forgave the apprentice after that.

The young apprentice shrugged. He threw his hands in the air.

"I will be a potter and make plates," he said.

The men smirked at him. The women held their hands to their mouths.

"Will you wear ladies' bloomers also?" his grandfather shouted.

"He will. He will wear bloomers."

"Just like my uncle Fridi," his grandfather said. "He wore bloomers and a corset, if you can believe that, but damn it all, he made keys!"

The apprentice shook his head and left them reminiscing over great-great-uncle Fridi. He'd been the potter's apprentice ever since. He was forbidden to bring anything from the potter's workshop into their house, and in their anger, they banished him to a shed in back. Things had quieted down in the year since. One of his cousins even became an electrician; another became a professor.

With the apprentice gone, the potter relaxed. He examined the freshly brushed ewer. It was rich looking but still lacked something. The potter meditated a moment more and then went to a drawer.

He pulled it open and rifled through the contents. It was a drawer full of rocks, mostly river stones. He found the smallest stone he could hold between his thumb and his index finger. It was really no more than a pebble. He carried the pebble back to the ewer. Then he rubbed the peppers with the stone. He rubbed the peppers until they became lustrous. They began to glow. He continued on in this way, rubbing one pepper after another. When he was done with the peppers, hours later, he rubbed the stone on the inside of the ewer's lip, defining it, moistening it.

The peppers were like sapphires. The ewer's lip was puckered, like a woman about to whistle. The potter smiled at the pitcher. He brushed it with a fine-haired brush one last time, then he wiped it with a cheesecloth and spent the rest of the afternoon and evening sitting in front of it, smoking, and looking at it from different angles. He waited like he expected it to come to life, walk toward him, sit on his lap, and kiss him on the mouth.

Then the potter thought about Valeria. He wondered if the pitcher would mean anything to her, if she would even appreciate his work. Then he remembered the look on her face when he told her he would make her something special. He remembered the way she had pursed her lips and said *peppers*, the way she had almost smiled but stopped herself. She had seemed lovely to him just then. She had seemed shy, and sincere, and lovely. That was the reason he promised to make in three days what would normally have taken six. Since then, he had sat awake, without food or drink, in order to mold clay, polish peppers, and fall in love.

On the third day, with this realization fresh on his mind, with the thought of what more he might create at her prodding, the potter stood up with a start and rushed inside his living quarters. He jumped into his shower and washed the dirt and clay from under his fingernails. He clipped them. He shaved the three-day-old stubble that had grown on his face and under his chin. He pomaded his hair and moustache until his hair was as shiny and white as silk paper. He looked at himself in a mirror. He felt resplendent.

Bathed, clean-shaven, and wearing his nicest suit, a tailored one of blue gabardine with broad shoulders and three buttons down the front—he had bought it for his wife's funeral—the potter grabbed his satchel and put it on across his chest. He ran out of the workshop, grabbed some wildflowers, and wrapped the stems in wet toilet paper. He put them into the satchel.

He grabbed the first wrapping paper he could find, green tissue, and wrapped it around the ewer. He wrapped and rewrapped the ewer, and then hoisted it up. It was thirty kilos, easy. He carried it to his bicycle and attached it to the rack above his rear tire with cords and twine. When he was sure that it was tightly secured, he got on the bicycle and pedaled toward Valeria's cottage.

Six

Valeria had spent three days preparing her cottage for the pitcher's arrival. She had decided to give it a deep cleaning. She bathed the pigs and brushed the cow. She dusted and polished her furniture. She cleaned all of her windowsills and mopped around the hearth.

Now she finished up by scrubbing the tiled portico and her concrete stairs for the second time in a week. This was a meditative activity and she never hesitated to clean them when she felt a need arise. She was soon enraptured by what she was doing, completely absorbed in the motion of her arms. Her mind was blank. It became so still that very soon after beginning her chore, she began to whistle. An old love song. Something from her childhood, some melody heavy with longing. A heart's deep and terrifying longing. Insatiable. Unyielding. Desperate, even. Desperate like a hungry child at its mother's breast or a dying man rattling for air. Valeria's mind was blank and her heart took over, and her heart was desperate. She scrubbed an entire stair before she heard herself, looked around, and stopped what she was doing. She put her tongue to her lips and realized that they were warm, wet even. They had been pursed. She could tell because they were tired from it. Her lips ached. It was the sweetest feeling. She touched them.

"My word," she whispered to herself.

It was an odd sensation. Valeria experienced a hungry wish that someone—anyone—would lay on top of her, press against her, press her into the ground, tug her hair. She remembered and longed for a man's touch. Valeria squeezed her arms. She hugged herself. That seemed to help. She sat on her ample backside. She wiped the perspiration from her forehead with the back of her hand. She fanned herself with an open palm and breathed a long and deep breath. Then she sat a moment more and concentrated. Her senses returned. Just as quickly, the whistle threatened to return, but she smothered it under the weight of her tongue. She barricaded the emerging melody behind a wall of clenched teeth. She shook her keys. In a moment, her body's longing was crammed back into her heart, locked in the cupboard that was her left ventricle.

Valeria retrieved the brush from the pail of water and resumed her housework. It must have been inattention that caused her mind to wander. Nothing more. She had simply allowed the late-May sunshine to affect her. It was an innocent enough thing to happen, she thought. Such a long winter. The warm sunlight had merely pricked her brain. She had only experienced a momentary lapse of concentration, a momentary, uncharacteristic disregard of self-control. It wouldn't happen again. She had regained herself now, and her heart did not flutter, and her lips were not moist. They were certainly not puckered. As for their searing ache, her body's searing ache, that too would pass soon enough. This kind of lust was distasteful for a woman her age.

With the stories of Valeria's recent behavior circling town, with what the villagers had heard from the potter's apprentice regarding her impromptu visit and then his subsequent disappearance from the pub for several days, with the new warmth and late-spring clothes that were being brought out of chests and closets, the citizens of the tiny hamlet sensed that some strange gravity was tugging at them, tugging at that spot in the chest where the solar plexus resides. Tugging like they were being fished out of their habitat and pulled into space on a string of desire, only to be left dangling. Dangling there, unfulfilled, in that heady orbit of pheromones and springtime yearning. For something. Anything. A touch. A whisper of lips against an ear. A bite on the back of the neck. A nuzzle of a throat. A hand slipped inside a blouse. The warmth of their lovers' bodies. An orgasm, damn it. Even the animals felt it. The stray dogs began to rut in the street. Children threw stones to stop them. Pigs rubbed their rumps against posts. The village was awake. Hot and awake. And somehow all of its citizens sensed that it had something to do with Valeria and the potter. Three days after Valeria's visit to the potter, almost instinctively, villagers arrived in front of her cottage as she was brushing the final stair. They crowded around her locked gate in anticipation.

"What are you doing today, Valeria?" they asked. "What are you up to?"

"Are you and the potter lovers?"

"We saw you making eyes at one another in the market."

"I heard you visited him by yourself and that you stayed over an hour."

"He's a nice man, the potter. You should leave him alone."

"He and Ibolya are lovers, or don't you know that?"

Valeria didn't turn around but kept scrubbing.

"You'd be wise to leave me alone today," she warned.

The townspeople had heard about how she'd pedaled furiously up the steep hill on the other side of the centrum, and about how later in the day she had stumbled into Ibolya's pub wild-eyed and looking for a tumbler of sherry. It had even gotten around that she had called all the village children dogs.

"As I was hunting pheasant out in my field," one man volunteered,

"I saw a fearsome shadow on the road. When I took a closer look through my binoculars, I saw that it was Valeria. She was on her bicycle. You should have seen her face. It frightened me. She looked wicked."

The villagers nodded understandingly. They all pitied the potter. They knew him as a kind man. He wouldn't have had anything to do with a harsh misfit like Valeria if he really knew anything about her. She was a spiteful old woman—wholly incorrigible. She had no use for any of the village's denizens, and in fact, they couldn't understand why she remained among them. Surely it was out of spite alone. They all agreed. The kind potter should never have anything to do with Valeria. It wouldn't be good for the village.

The potter, after all, had made those nice platters. For as long as many of them could remember, every newlywed in town had received a platter and a stein from him as wedding gifts, and none of them were ever alike. They shook their heads. If the potter and Valeria were to become involved, the villagers were certain that no serving platter would ever display a tasty morsel and no stein would ever be hoisted again, at least not unless they had been paid for, and the villagers were well aware of Valeria's prices from when she sold vegetables at the market.

"Imagine if she were to control his purse strings."

One of the village children came running toward them. "The potter is coming. The potter is coming."

The villagers became agitated.

"Valeria and the potter. Can you believe it?"

"The poor man. She must have bewitched him. Surely he is confused."

"He's a widower. I knew his wife. She was a lovely woman. She was always selling wild mushrooms in the market. Don't you remember?"

The others nodded and remembered the potter's wife.

"That poor dead woman."

"She was a saint!"

Valeria watched pensively from her portico as the crowd grew. She picked up a handful of pebbles. She hurled them.

"Get away from my house!" she shouted. "Get away. There will be no trouble today."

But the villagers would not move. In fact, the more Valeria shouted and the more stones and chestnuts she threw, the more quarrelsome they became.

"Look at her. What could the potter possibly want with her?"

"She's so plain. I can't understand it."

"Ibolya certainly won't put up with this."

The women nodded.

"You know, Valeria wouldn't let me taste her peppers, not even one. She charged me five forints for it."

"She called the children animals."

"She called them dogs."

"She's always throwing chestnuts at them."

"She wants to kill the children. She wants to stone them."

"And what about the potter's dead wife?"

"She was a saint!"

While they spoke, the potter arrived. He rested his bicycle against Valeria's fence. The villagers could see that he had combed his moustache, that his cheeks and neck were clean shaven and rosy, and that he was freshly bathed. In the satchel across his chest rested a bouquet of wildflowers. But what incensed them was the near-meter-tall object strapped to the back of his bicycle and wrapped in green tissue paper.

He smiled good-naturedly at the villagers, his neighbors, and he held out his hand.

"My platter wasn't that big," a woman shouted at him straightaway. "What kind of platter is that?"

"Silly woman, that's not a platter," said a man. "It's a beer stein."

"Look here, potter," a burly man said. "What's this all about, anyway? My stein was only big enough for half a liter. That looks like it could hold at least seven liters." The crowd began to shout at the potter and at each other. They argued with one another over whether the package was a stein or a platter, and they argued with the potter over his bringing whatever it was to Valeria.

"But why does this matter?" the potter argued. "I have never given anything to Valeria, and three days ago she brought me a canister of fresh milk and helped clean my kitchen."

The crowd wasn't interested, and slowly the potter felt himself being pushed against Valeria's gate.

"Likely story," they shouted at him.

"What about your poor dead wife? Have you forgotten her so soon?"

"She was a saint!"

"And what about Ibolya?"

"Are you two-timing Ibolya? Tut, tut, I thought you were a nicer man than that."

The potter was wide-eyed.

"How dare you," he said. "What do you know of my wife?"

"We know that she was a saint!"

The potter was angry.

"You get away from me this instant," he said. "Get away."

The men started to jostle him.

"Enough!" Valeria shouted. "Or I will call the chief inspector."

The villagers parted at her rough voice, but when they saw that the inspector was already there, that he was as red-faced and angry as the rest, they became emboldened. They shouted curses at her and pushed the potter around. Valeria opened her gate and pulled the potter in. Together, they ran into her house as curses, chestnuts, and pebbles rained on top of them. Valeria and the potter locked themselves inside and peered out her window.

"They're crazy," the potter exclaimed. "I've never seen anyone act like this . . . over nothing."

"They're all sons of bitches," Valeria said, then shouted out her window to the crowd, "You're all sons of bitches!"

The mob cursed back and then attacked the potter's bicycle. They set the pitcher on the ground and tore the paper off.

"Let's see what that scoundrel has made for her!"

When the paper had been torn completely away and the massive ewer was exposed, the villagers grew silent. It was the most beautiful piece of pottery they had ever seen. Even Valeria, seeing it through her window, gasped.

"Oh. But you made that for me?"

The potter stared at his creation with moist eyes. He was nodding.

"It is a masterpiece," he said. "I think it's the peppers."

Valeria looked again. Peppers. She could see them around the pitcher, garlanded around its hip, its neck, and even one dangling under its lip.

The villagers gawked. The ewer was tall and black. It was as black as a cellar broom closet. And though it wasn't glossy or enameled, it glowed. A few people threw up their hands, shook their heads, and walked away. The rest were silent.

A village mutt approached the ewer, and he lifted a rear leg. He made water on it. The man closest to the mutt kicked at him to make him stop; the dog, seeing the foot, jumped to the side, and when he did he hit the pitcher and tipped it over. There was a crunch. The potter flinched.

Valeria opened her door and rushed out. Her kerchief flew off her head as she bent over to grab a handful of pebbles.

"My pitcher!" she screamed.

This time, the inspector was nowhere to be seen. Without him, the crowd dispersed quickly. Pebbles stung them as they ran. The dog yelped when a stone hit him on the ear. Valeria opened her gate and stepped out. The pitcher's handle had broken off and when she stood it upright she saw a hole in its side.

Nobody watching would have noticed, but Valeria felt her lower lip tremble. She thought about gluing the handle back on and using plaster of paris for the hole. She thought about doing any number of things to fix the pitcher, but all she could manage was a sigh.

"My pitcher," she murmured. "My beautiful pitcher."

She felt a hand on her shoulder. It was a strong hand. She turned to look. It was the potter. He was smiling, concentrating on her. He caressed her cheek. The world started to spin. The tug in her heart returned. The yearning returned. Her lips ached again. He was reeling her in.

"I'm glad you let your hair loose," he said. "I've brought you flowers."

Seven

The potter was not really a passionate man. Certainly he was easy-going and gregarious, but stormy outbursts, in any direction, could not be sustained by any predilection of his personality. He was generally undemonstrative with feelings of anger, love, or compassion. His emotions were doled out moderately—some might have argued meagerly—but always purposefully. When the potter felt something, he meant it. So it wasn't with haste that he made his way in the world. It was purposefully and slowly. Carefully and thoroughly. Discerningly. Exactly like an ox. Even his relationship with his deceased wife was something he had eased into. Yet still, for all his striving for a steady ship to sail through life on, few men in the village had a more dramatic personal story than the potter. It was as though the world sensed his surefootedness and sent circumstance encroaching upon him from all angles and in the loudest volumes. It was as though a die had been cast where only a man of his naturally quiet demeanor could stomach the mourning and fury of his life's details. And they were mournful details. As dramatically sorrowful as a stringed instrument wailing in a funeral parlor, without any reason for hope, levity, or recourse.

In the end, though, it was exactly the inescapability of his circumstances that led him toward the art and craft of pottery. The potter needed to create. Clumps of formless clay were a salvation for him. The immense and immutable sadness of his life, like the sorrow of Christ on the cross, only tempered him. He was a man like heavy glass—cracked and chipped, but never shattered. That is who the potter was: a hopeful man who sublimated the tragedies of life into art.

The potter had met his wife, his darling Magda, as a young man, probably twenty-eight or so, in the city of Miskolc. She had been visiting relatives. He was friends with her cousin and had promised her family a private tour of his new workshop when they met in her extended family's home. It was his first workshop and he was proud of it. He'd been a journeyman in a different town and finally been released from his mentor and recognized by the guilds, which still exerted a bit of influence in those days. He undertook the responsibilities of his own shop, under his own name, with everyone's blessings. The party allowed it, applauded it even. He was working with his hands, after all. A true proletarian. A man for the masses. Content and hardworking. Content with hard work.

He was a very masculine young man, solidly built and handsome. He had long lashes, though, and chestnut hair that glinted in setting sunlight. He was healthy and vigorous, rosy cheeked. He was even good at sports, a kind of savant on the pitch. He was a natural midfielder who knew how to control the momentum of a football game, knew how to control his team's direction. All in all, he was a real catch: sensitive, artistic, dreamy eyed, and athletic, with his own business and a promising future.

One might easily have taken a look at him and summed him up as a rake or roustabout, but he was nothing of the sort. The young potter was decent. Hardly religious, but always kind. The type of young man who tipped his hat at older women, shook firmly when introduced, and kept himself unquestionably above reproach. He didn't chase skirts. He had once courted a young woman in his hometown and had planned to marry her, but she ran off with a Russian artillery unit commander and moved east.

So when he made the acquaintance of his future wife, the pair of them hardly spoke to one another at all. A few pleasantries were all that they exchanged. He may have taken her hand. Neither of them could remember exactly what was said between them at that first meeting. When pressed, he would shrug and claim that he barely noticed her. He certainly didn't notice any internal stirrings in the petite young woman. During that first visit, not much at all happened between them, but in fairness the summer had just begun. By the second or possibly third visit, the potter himself began to stir. He grew enamored. A season would prove long enough.

Later that summer, when shadows and objects shimmered on the horizon, caught in between the heat overhead and the heat on the ground, the girl's family went for a final time to visit their new friend at his studio and make that large purchase they had promised to make early on. *He was such a charming young man, you see. How could one resist those eyes?* His future mother-in-law had made this remark to her own daughter with a knowing wink. *And such beautiful skin for a man!*

The family purchased an ornate wine cistern inlaid with a painting of rural life. One of those romantic scenes where men in flowing robes and three-cornered hats stood straight and tall astride the backs of a pair of horses and chased down an escaped colt. He had painted that scene himself with a short-bristled paintbrush. The potter had always been an artist, you see.

However, this time, when no one was looking, when her family was absorbed with the agrarian scene adorning the wine cistern, the young girl cornered the potter and batted her eyelashes at him furiously. She had never done anything like that before, and he had never witnessed anything like it either. Her eyelashes flitted at him like the beating wings of a month in a web. Quick and madcap. Drawing him closer. The potter was flustered, but he hid it from her. He reached his hand out and touched her hair. It was bobbed at the time. Feathery and delicate. Everything about the young girl was delicate. He slid his fingers along her jawline. Then he brushed past the beaming young woman and her twitching eyelids, practically knocking her into a stack of teacups. He reached for the first thing he could lay his hands on to steady himself, a white cake platter. He gave it to the young woman with a smile and ushered her back toward her family. She thanked him and showed it to her mother.

"Well, we must pay for it."

"No-no," stammered the blushing potter. "It's a present for your daughter."

The young woman, her face flushed, reached for something to hold on to lest she swoon, and her hand rested upon a beer stein.

"Let me buy this, then," she said, her eyelashes fluttering all the while.

Her mother looked from one to the other and smiled to herself. The match pleased her.

When his wife-to-be and her family finally left his workshop, when they were about to pile into their East German vehicle and drive away, the young woman turned from where she was, put her hand to her hair, and cried out to her family, "I've dropped my hairpin. I'll be right back." Her father told her to forget it, but her mother put her hand on his knee and shook her head. The old man shrugged. The young woman bounded back into the potter's shop, where he was sitting on a stool drinking a mug of water and trying to recover his senses. When he saw her approach he spewed the water over the front of his shirt.

"Magda," he said. "What? What?"

She walked right up to him, as sure-footed as a lioness, something she would never be again or show any hint of being, and she handed him the stein.

"This is for you," she said.

Then, one last time, just in case he hadn't understood her desires, she batted her eyelashes at him for a good ten seconds, threw her arms around his neck, and embraced him. There could be no question of her motivation. The potter swallowed hard, put his arms around her waist, and pulled her close. She smelled of gardenias. He could smell gardenia oil on her skin, and he saw that spot on her neck, just underneath her ear, and he couldn't help but peck at it with his lips, right where the scent of gardenia seemed to throb with a life all its own. The pulse of her life and love resided right there on her neck. This was the extent of their courtship.

When she left Miskolc and returned to her village, the potter followed her. He spoke with her parents, proposed to her, and set to building a new workshop. At no point did he make fanciful declarations of love or happiness. At no point did he jump about like a brain-fevered madman. He never sang songs outside her window or gave her a gift of cheap perfume. He only touched her again on their wedding night. He held himself off until then. And when he finally did touch her, he started at that same spot on her neck. The gardenia spot, he called it. And the spot grew and grew until it enveloped her, and the potter was happy. His head was in the clouds. He was swept up in love with his petite, dark-haired wife and with his new life in her remote village.

Soon after they were married and settled in, whenever a wedding took place, he hurried to his studio, took a cake platter and stein from a cabinet, and presented it to the couple at their wedding reception.

"This was good enough for Magda and me," he'd say to the newlyweds. "It's all we needed to fall in love."

This, his only act of romance, became a village tradition and endeared him to everyone.

Whether or not he had been endeared to the townspeople didn't matter much in his present situation. That the potter had betrayed that love was obvious enough to the villagers. Putting in with a misfit of a woman like Valeria and forgetting those traditions would mark him an outcast. If not for the memory of his saintly wife, perhaps the townspeople might have stoned him. Perhaps they might have thrown him from his bicycle and chased him out of town.

His lovely Magda was no kind of saint, however. She was all too real a woman. All too real a person of flesh who experienced ill health, a broken womb, and finally a heavy presence. The couple had tried for years to have children. They started right away, in fact. From their first night together all thoughts were on making a family. It was impossible to achieve. They were as barren as a pile of rocks. Midwives and doctors couldn't help. Gypsies couldn't help. A countless number of concoctions, tonics, and tinctures worked to no avail. In a more modern country they might have checked the potter, but in the rural countryside it was most certainly Magda's fault. Try as they might, nothing happened. It stayed that way for years, and then miraculously, one day when Magda was well into her forties, something finally took. Something they had done together was taking root, was coming to life. All she had to do was breathe and she could feel it inside her forming. And where it had come from she couldn't say, but she felt it in her gut. The potter felt it in his too. True aim. Luck. Maybe it was just all those years of hoping and wishing. The culmination of their lives would finally bear fruit in the form of a child. For the first time in their marriage, the pair had a common hope for the future. What they never considered was that it was only a broken embryo. Chickens laid more viable eggs than what Magda had growing in her belly. The disheveled egg in her womb was the last thing in the world they could consider the fruit of their love.

Magda immediately started having fevers. She went into convulsions and chills. Some force had reached up her slip and made its way inside her. She would say so to him and beg him to stay at her side. Some otherworldly hand was shaking her entrails, shaking her baby, her hope, and squeezing it. Her insides were rotten from the start and now were being squeezed like an overripe plum. Nothing left but the pit. Dust to dust, and never did it happen that they heard a baby sigh, or cry, or scream for help.

Old nurses came by their home and checked on her. They shook their heads at him when they left her in their bedroom with a cool rag pressed against her forehead. The potter didn't know what to make of any of it. Like most men of his day, the mystery of women would remain that, so instead he sculpted ceramic rattles and mobiles. He also nursed her the best he was able. He brought her chamomile tea. Forced tonics down her throat. He didn't shed tears. The potter was not the kind of man who would.

Finally, six months into it, she screamed. The potter was sleeping in his workshop, giving her the space she needed to writhe about. When he heard her, he ran to see what the matter was. He ran to her bedside, but upon entering the room he dropped to his knees. He didn't gasp or scream, but what he saw brought him to his knees! Magda lay in a pool of blood in front of him, the coverlet thrown aside and a malformed figure between her legs. A frightening homunculus in a membraneous bag. The color of raw liver. Dead, whatever it was. Lovely, dark-haired, darling Magda dead along with it. Her eyes open, her heart beating, but dead just the same, and she never returned to him.

Gardenias, it should be mentioned, sickened the potter forever afterward. He couldn't stomach to look at them, couldn't stand the smell of them. Bushes of them grew out front and he hacked them all. The petals fell to the ground and he stomped his foot on them and buried them in the dust. So in regard to gardenias, he was passionate. He passionately despised them.

Eight

The potter's hand rested on Valeria's shoulder. He had been taken aback by the townspeople's behavior but he tried not to show it. The street was empty now. Just a few parked jalopies and a stray mutt watching them from a safe distance. The potter looked at the dog and raised his hand. The animal ran away.

Valeria stood up. She touched her hair. She looked behind her for the kerchief. She accepted the flowers from him. They lingered a moment and looked from pitcher, to flowers, and finally into one another's eyes.

"Bring the pitcher inside," she whispered. "You may stay the night, if you like."

It had been decades since a man had visited her cottage.

The pair helped each other into her home.

"I'm all thumbs," she laughed, putting her hands into her apron's pockets. "I'm sorry. I don't know what's come over me. Would you like something to eat? I made a goulash earlier today."

The potter put the pitcher down and smiled at her. The tension had stirred him. He admired the way her body assaulted its clothing, the way the fabric stretched in desperation at the seams around her hips, the way her housedress reached the middle of her thigh. In running at the villagers, her bosom had even overflowed its harness and now poured out over the top of her bodice like boiling milk in a pot. The only thing that contained her was the apron.

The potter couldn't bear it. He was wracked with longing. He stepped in and kissed her throat straightaway. Importune a woman with action, he thought to himself—without pomp or thought. He would not give her time to think. He was not thinking himself. What would be the point? What was there to think about? The potter wanted her. He could feel that she wanted him. At their ages, that was enough.

"Just relax," he whispered as he tugged her apron away and then tugged at her housedress, releasing her to his touch. "Relax."

Valeria's hands remained at her sides; she hadn't returned the embrace just yet, but she was tugging her key string. It made a delirious chime.

"Really, the goulash is no trouble at all," she said, and felt distinctly like an ass for doing so. She couldn't stop speaking. She was like a young girl. "It would only take a minute to warm."

The potter didn't respond. Or maybe he did respond, but it wasn't in any recognizable language. Instead, it was something warm and breathy against her throat and upper chest. Like a steaming kettle or an old locomotive. Valeria closed her eyes to listen, to try to catch what was being said, but when she did close them, she couldn't resist his touch anymore. It had been so long. Too long. The desire, the lust, the cabinet in her heart sprang open and she couldn't pull any of it back in. Good sense and better taste were cast aside. She thought of the rutting dogs; she understood the scratching pigs. She wanted to feel his solid body against her front and feel her back against the wall. She imagined splaying her legs and wrapping them around him. If she were younger she would have done it. She wanted him to take her. Valeria let go of her key ring, put her hands on his hair, thrust her chest out to meet his lips, and pulled him in tighter.

"I want to feel it," she moaned, and pulled him. They fell back. She was caught between him and her wall. She raised her face to the ceiling and sighed.

Then they slid up and down across one another, cupped one another's bottoms and torsos. He spun her around and kissed the back of her neck. He slipped her dress completely off and unclasped her brassiere. He kissed her back. Pinched her backside. She was shaped like a cello and he ran his fingers down the frets of her spine, tantalized her tailbone and the crack of her ass. She pushed herself back against him. She pulled at his pants, turned and rubbed his crotch. He kissed her more. He kissed his way down her body. If he was intent on showing her that she had never really been loved by a man, intent on proving to her that she had only known misuse, that she was awaiting virtuosity, she was equally intent on being his partner and showing him how deep an ocean she could be, how strong a river.

When the potter awoke the next morning, he had a knot in his stomach. He had that queasy feeling he associated with having eaten a bad meal. He wondered if it was the goulash making him feel bad. He rarely ate late anymore and it was past midnight when he and Valeria had finally let go of one another and warmed his dish.

The sun had risen and Valeria lay beside him snoring loudly. The potter looked at her plump body. He ran his fingers through his hair to smooth it down. He kicked his legs over the side of Valeria's bed and sat up. She woke up instantly and looked at the freckles and liver spots on his back.

"Do you want breakfast?" she asked pleasantly enough while caressing him. "I have rolls that I can warm. There's butter. Would you prefer eggs?"

The potter did not know that Valeria usually ate a small breakfast of salted rolls and coffee and left it at that. He did not know that she was trying to impress him, that she wanted to show him how useful she could be.

Why Valeria wanted to show him these things she couldn't say. There were enough animals to feed already. Still, she did want to. She wanted him to stay in the house with her. At least for a little while longer. There was still something stirring inside her and she wanted to let it out.

The broken pitcher stood in the corner of her bedroom. The potter walked over to it and squatted to get a closer look at it.

"I can fix this," he said. A pepper had fallen off. He picked it up and examined it. "Or I can make you a new one."

She looked at the pitcher and smiled.

"I like the way that one dangles there, under the spout," she said, pointing to it. "Thank you so much." She addressed the potter's back. He rose and turned with his hands on his stomach.

"My belly hurts," he answered sheepishly.

Valeria's anger flashed.

"You're a child. Your stomach didn't hurt last night when you were taking advantage of me."

The potter blinked at her. He laughed.

"You can't possibly believe that," he said, shaking his head. He had raised his voice at her. He was thinking of his dead wife, and of Ibolya.

"I can and do. You took advantage of me when I wasn't thinking straight. All the commotion in the yard. I wasn't thinking straight."

"I think you were just fine," the potter said. "You seemed perfectly full of your faculties."

"I wasn't."

"Valeria, you were giving me instructions. Don't you remember?"

Valeria flushed. How rude of him to speak of details to her like she was some common peasant girl who could talk about these things, laugh about them with glinting eyes and open mouth.

"How dare you speak to me this way," she said.

"I have to leave now," he interrupted. "I am sorry you are angry. I will come back to fix the pitcher later this week."

Valeria pulled her covers over her breasts. There was a nude man standing at the foot of her bed. Her eyes swept across his body. The blood rushed to his face. He looked at his pants. He was frozen, unable to reach for them, yet unable to remain where he stood.

"Forget it," she said. "Maybe it's supposed to be broken."

The potter looked closer at her. He tried to smile, but it seemed —to both of them—forced.

"It's funny," he said. "I don't think I could make something like that again."

"Poor you," Valeria said.

"No. Seriously. I don't think I could. I'm not sure how I managed that."

"I need new vases," Valeria suddenly responded. "A pair of them that can sit in my kitchen. They need to be practical. I can't lift that pitcher. Could you make them for me?"

"Perhaps I could etch peppers into them?" the potter asked hopefully.

"No," Valeria answered. "You won't do better with peppers than you've already done. Use a turnip."

She smiled when the potter's eyebrows furrowed. It was the same look he'd given her when she asked for peppers on her ewer. She knew that she would see him again.

"Turnips?"

"Yes," Valeria answered. "Don't come back until you are finished. I don't want to see you until the vases are done. I'm busy."

"Why turnips?" the potter stammered.

"I like them. They grow fast," she replied. "They have high yield. They have a lot of energy. Livestock eat them readily. They can stand the cold. I have a million reasons. But mostly it's the livestock. Do you have any idea how hard it is to feed livestock? Do you know the manual labor involved in feeding animals? There is no man around here to do that kind of work, and if there were, he'd choose to do something else. A field of turnips means that the cow, the pigs, the goat, they can all forage for themselves. I've eaten them my whole life. When I was a child, my grandfather dedicated whole pastures to the turnip. Whole hillsides would teem with the tops of them. Then he would let the animals graze. They would graze the tops and nuzzle the earth for the roots. We never lost a single calf. We never lost a single lamb. Turnips were good for them. He even put it into soup for me when I was growing up. Free energy. Now chew on that and leave me in peace."

The potter nodded and reached for his pants. He decided he would never have to see her again. He had no intention of making her a pair of vases. He could go back to his life—which is what he intended to do as soon he finished dressing and walked out her door.

"That might take a while, Valeria. I have a lot of orders to fill back at the shop. Maybe I could get to it next month. Or maybe I could let my apprentice do it."

Valeria didn't answer. She was looking around her. She was looking for something to throw at his head.

"Go away," she said. "Just go away."

The potter didn't hesitate. Like a man freed from a laager, he bounded out of her cottage and looked up at the sky. It was bright and wonderful to him. It had never been so blue, he thought. How could it be so blue? Then he thought about stopping in at Ibolya's, but he decided against that. One woman's ire was enough for a day. Ibolya had certainly heard about things by now. She would certainly be waiting for him with a pitchfork. The potter decided he would leave indiscretions like that to younger, foolhardier men.

However, by the time he made his way to the studio—having had to carry his bicycle an extra half a kilometer through fields in order to circumnavigate Ibolya's tavern—his good mood had dissipated and he was angry. Sweaty and angry. Had she only understood how much time he had spent on the ewer, Valeria would not have dismissed him to return to his workshop so quickly. She should have begged him to stay and fix it. It was only natural. What was the point of making the damned thing if it was destined to sit in the corner of her bedroom with a hole in its side, collecting dust? Who did she think she was? Besides, he did not want to return to the worktable just yet. He felt a pang, as though he might even come to hate the studio—one lonely room, one poorly lit room, one room that demanded nothing of him except that he produce. Creation was hard, discouraging work, the potter noted, then wondered if God felt the same. Once begun, never mind the suffering until the end. And what was the point? Just a bitter end. Sour grapes and a kick in the pants, the only thing left, the only reward. *No good deed unpunished*, the potter thought. He was generally bewildered. Anxiety had its place over him, while depression had its fangs in his heel. The potter shivered and kicked a table leg. He was once again alone in his studio with bags of clay . . . a miserable little deity and his more miserable creation. Prometheus depressed. Blue-funked Jehova.

He was godlike, though, and that was no blasphemy. He was godlike, and that was not hubris. In a single moment, the potter understood that he had reached a level in his craft where all the fear, anxiety, and depression in his life could be sublimated into art. He recognized this. The potter recognized that there was nothing better for a man to do—to reflect his godlike image— than create something lasting. Chastity is not God. Benevolence is not God. Honesty is not God. What is God, what is the crux and apex of man's existence, is when he reaches deeply into himself, uses his hands, his mind, his blood, his imagination, and his semen, points to a formless void, the emptiness of his surroundings, and utters the same phrase that began the entire universe: Let there be light! When a man does this, when a man really does this, and creates something new to boot—some art that is new, some thing that is new—then that man is holy. That man is living his life in God's image. That man is an apostle. He has transfigured everything about his miserable little existence and will sit at God's feet.

The potter pointed hopefully at a bag of clay.

"Let there be a turnip!"

He took a breath and put his head down. His chin rested against the top of his sternum. His anxiety dissipated. He was thirsty. He could use a drink, he thought. Maybe he could stop in at Ibolya's for a second. Just for a quick drink, you see, because he had to get back right away . . .

He *was* glad to be back. He was glad he had returned. He was glad to have been charged with a task. He looked at the bags of clay. He was desperate to begin on Valeria's vases. He was excited to see what his imagination might create. Valeria wanted vases? She wanted a pair of vases? A simple pair of vases would have been no problem, but she had said that she wanted them to remind her of turnips. She had sent him away for turnips. He had seen, at least, half a hectare of the damn things growing in her garden. He had seen their purple roots jutting out of the earth at strange angles.

But what the hell did she need with a turnip vase? The only thing the potter knew about turnips was that they were purple and had a squat oval shape. All that information she had given him was useless. She wanted vases with purple turnips on them? He thought about it. What could she have meant? Purple turnips etched into the clay? Turnips painted onto clay? Raised turnips made separately and then scored onto the vase like he had done with the peppers and the ewer?

None of those images appealed to him.

The potter paced in his workshop. He wet his hands and began working. He decided he would make the vases every way he could. He would etch them into the vase; he would make them separately and attach them to the vase. He began by making miniature models. Within a couple of hours he had produced dozens of them. He lined them up and walked around them.

None of the vases looked right. He was almost out of his mind when the door to his workshop opened and his apprentice walked inside.

"I heard about the whole thing!" the young man announced. "The village is speaking of nothing else. Did you two really attack a crowd of children? You haven't really been over there all night, have you? Some are saying they saw your bicycle resting beside her gate. Some of her neighbors say they saw you leaving and skulking around the village this morning. And Ibolya! You'll have hell to pay, for sure. She smashed your teacup and said Valeria would have to make your tea from now on."

"Ibolya is jealous?" The potter's ears perked up.

The apprentice laughed. "Ha! Is she ever. You should have heard some of the things she said. She said she hoped your malnourished prick fell off at the first whiff of Valeria's old crab cake. And that was one of the nicer things. Did you really sleep with that old hag?"

The potter looked at the apprentice. "What kind of question is that?"

"There's a wager going. Half of the town doesn't believe you went through with it. The men are all saying that no sane pecker would serve that call to arms. That your ten-hut would fall on deaf ears. But others were listening at the gate. They say Valeria's a screamer. Is it true?"

"People were listening?"

"At the gate."

"That's disgusting."

"So, it's true then? You did it?" The apprentice was disappointed. "And I'd bet that you hadn't. I've lost a lot of money because of you."

The potter shook his head. "It won't happen again. I don't know what I was thinking. I guess I should go and see Ibolya. I'm not getting anywhere here."

He noticed something in his apprentice's hand. "What is that?"

The apprentice held up his creation. "I did it. I made Zsofi her teapot. She's really nice, you know. We've been talking. She told me what she had in mind. I think she's special. She's got something. Too bad her mother is as nasty as Zsofi is lovely. She'll never find a husband. Poor kid."

The apprentice pulled the teapot from out of a bag and presented it to the potter. The potter examined it. He noticed that its shape was not unlike a turnip.

"What is this?"

"I said it's my teapot, for Zsofi."

The potter smiled; then he laughed. "What kind of teapot is it?"

The apprentice blinked. He looked at his teapot. He saw then that it was malformed, that it was not right, that he had wasted time at his parents' home, listening to the men taunt him, listening to their insults about the work he was doing. He shook his head.

"It is supposed to be a teapot. She asked for it to look like this. She said she liked it. But you're right. It looks more like a turnip. Maybe she was just being nice. I'll have to tell her that I'll start over. I'm sorry. My family distracted me."

The potter was joyful. He patted the young man on the shoulders and pointed to the clay.

"Yes. Take some clay and do it again. You're very close. Spin your wheel faster. You should know better. You're a journeyman."

"What? Can't I stay here and work?"

"No," the potter said. "I'm working on something special."

"Again?"

"Yes. I need quiet. You know how to do this. I've shown you enough times. Go and make a teapot."

"But my family," the apprentice protested. "They won't let me be. I can't make a teapot with my grandfather breathing down my neck and blowing cigarette smoke in my eyes. My father is spitting sunflower seed shells at me. Even my mother has started pinching me. You don't know what it's like."

"I also don't care," the potter answered. "If you want to make the teapot, you will. If you don't, then don't."

"What does this crazy girl want with this crap anyway?" the apprentice asked scornfully. "She isn't even engaged. Who is she pouring tea for?"

The potter shrugged. "Who knows? But she's paid us, so go and make her a teapot."

The apprentice shook his head but took a bag of clay.

"Should I take that?" he said, pointing to his creation.

"No," the potter answered. "If you don't mind, that will stay with me. It's given me an idea."

The apprentice shrugged and left. "I'm going to get a drink first. Any messages for Ibolya?"

"Tell her I'll visit her tomorrow. No, tell her that maybe I'll stop by tomorrow. No, wait. Don't tell her anything."

The apprentice nodded and left. The potter examined the teapot and laughed. It looked exactly like a turnip. His apprentice had even gotten the color wrong. He had been sloppy and let the red and blue paints mingle. But still, while it was horrible for a teapot, it was exactly what the potter was looking for.

"I can make her a turnip, easily," he said.

Nine

A market vendor motioned in Valeria's direction.

"She looks different."

The other vendors looked and nodded.

"She'll look even more different when Ibolya gets ahold of her."

The women laughed.

"She seems quieter."

"Settled?"

The women snickered.

"Relaxed."

"Softened?"

"That might be it. She hasn't bothered me in a few days. You know, we may have to thank the potter for kneading her bottom after all. Someone should have plucked her strings years ago."

"Maybe he'll keep her up so late she won't be able to make her morning rounds anymore."

"God willing."

The women laughed.

"I don't know. I heard that Ibolya had his hide. Serves him right. The potter a two-timer. Who would have believed that? My husband told me he went stumbling into the pub the very next day talking about turnips, acted like nothing at all had happened. Sat at the bar and started up a conversation."

"With Ibolya?"

"With the whole pub. Talking nonsense about free energy."

"Was he drunk?"

"Who knows? But I heard that Ibolya lunged at him. Said that no man had ever embarrassed her like that and lived to talk about it. Told him that she was so furious with him that she never wanted to see him again."

"Can't say that I feel too sorry for her. Ibolya's had it coming for years. How many men has she stolen?"

"That's true. That's true."

"Still, by the end of his visit, my husband told me she was practically sitting on his lap crying. Begging him to leave Valeria alone. She said she wanted to get married."

"Ibolya? No. I don't believe that."

"That's what my husband said."

"Ibolya wants to marry the potter? That doesn't even make sense."

"And now this one here has put her own scent on him," a woman said and motioned toward Valeria.

"What a scandal."

The other women nodded.

"And at their ages!" they laughed.

"Look at it on the bright side," one of them said. "There's hope for all of us yet!"

The women snickered. Valeria ambled down their aisle.

"Good morning, Valeria!" one of the women shouted. "Would you like to try some of my fruit today? How about some coffee? I'm selling coffee now, you know. Costa Rican coffee. A country near Mexico. The mayor arranged it for me. I'll probably quit selling fruit entirely."

Valeria stopped and regarded the coffee bags.

"Near Mexico," the vendor repeated. "Can you believe that? The mayor was so helpful. I'm the sole distributor for a hundred and fifty kilometers. I might even have to travel abroad! He even promised that I could ship by rail once the line is finished. I might even open a coffeehouse!"

Valeria picked up a bag of coffee and smelled it. She smiled at the woman and nodded. The coffee smelled good.

"It's two thousand forints," the woman said. "A lot, I know, but this is the only market where you can buy coffee like this. Costa Rican! It's special. Just an Austrian roast, but the beans are Costa Rican. I might start selling chocolate as well. Try some."

Valeria shrugged and pulled a couple of bills from her purse. She handed the money over, took the bag, and walked away.

"Did you see that? She bought it. I tell you she's been buying everything over the last few days," the vendor said. "And not a word. Nothing. She didn't say a thing. The potter really did her in good. She must have really banged her head on her headboard."

"Maybe she'll buy my kiwi," another vendor said. "The damn things are beginning to rot. Valeria! Valeria! Come back. I have a new fruit you have to see. From New Zealand. Near Australia. It's called kiwi. One thousand forints for two of them. Or try some of my new yogurt! Five hundred forints."

Valeria waved, returned, and bought the kiwis and the yogurt without a word.

Whispers tore through the market and out into the street. After a few more days passed like this even the mayor had heard: Valeria was ill. Probably insane. Her normally stark face had become tinged, slightly sun kissed. Her lumbering gait had diminished, and she was almost gliding. A stranger to town might not have noticed anything remarkable in her countenance, but to the villagers, the change in Valeria's demeanor was as obvious as a sinkhole. Wherever she walked or pedaled her bicycle, conversation stopped and onlookers gawked and whispered.

"I hear she's dying."

"She's been stumbling around the market all week. Haven't you seen her? She's out of her mind. Spending her life savings on the craziest things."

With an inattentive Valeria on the loose, market vendors inevitably grew bold. The quality of produce declined sharply. Valeria had even missed spotting furry radishes. A child could have noticed the blemishes—dots of white fur on red peel. People said that Valeria looked right at them and was smiling. The vendor, who was not at her stall at that moment, tripped over a young girl as she tried to make it back when she saw Valeria hovering over her produce.

"I am so sorry," the out of breath woman panted to Valeria as she covered the radishes with a cloth. "I really don't know how they got there. My husband arranged everything this morning before I arrived. He was trying to help."

Valeria said nothing. She did not even look at the woman. She smiled at nobody in particular and walked past.

Some of the older villagers, with nothing really better to do, began following her around.

"She's been whistling old folk songs," they told their neighbors. "Love songs."

"Well, it's either love or Alzheimer's," their neighbors remarked. "Or perhaps that fat cow of hers finally kicked her in the head."

When the mayor's wife bumped into Valeria and spilled her oranges onto the ground around them, Valeria just smiled. She didn't even notice the lithe young woman's short skirt.

"Valeria," the mayor's wife asked. "Are you all right this morning? My husband has been asking about you."

"Yes, desire. Quite. Don't you look lovely today."

And that was that. She walked away before the stunned young woman could offer to walk her to a bench. In fact, in the week following her encounter with the potter, Valeria had only snapped once, and that was at the butcher's. He had tried to slip her a piece of green meat. But even that outburst seemed half-baked compared to what the people in the market knew she was capable of.

"She's man-hungry, is what she is," the old men said, licking their lips. "Look at her. Ready to pounce. She's become a real man-eater. Don't catch her eye if you don't intend to do anything about it. Tee-hee!"

"I prefer Ibolya," other men answered. "She's younger. Valeria looks like a potato."

Still, most of the village widowers, never getting too close to Valeria anyway, gave her an even wider berth.

"Better safe than married and tossing hay for a lumpy, mean woman," they said, only half-jokingly.

"I hear the potter hasn't been back around her way, though. Maybe it was a one-time affair. I bet that's what it was. That potter. You wouldn't know he had it in him by the looks of him."

As most of the old men's conversations took place in Ibolya's pub, Ibolya couldn't help but hear their comments from behind her bar. Usually she scoffed at their conversations, but since this particular story involved her directly, she had very little patience for the topic. The potter had been to visit her the day after starting on Valeria's turnips. He was unshaven and sheepish, and while she had planned on giving him the cold shoulder for a bit, he didn't seem sheepish enough, and that drove her mad. They had argued. Well, she had argued. He had shrugged.

"It was something that happened, not something I planned," he'd said.

While Ibolya understood exactly what he was talking about—

having experienced the unplanned happenings of things herself—this was the first time she was on the receiving end of it. She didn't like it at all.

"Who do you think you are?" she shouted at him, and realized she sounded like a jilted girlfriend. The only thing missing was a rolling pin.

"Ibolya," he said. "It happened. One time. And you're not my wife or my fiancée."

The men in the pub tittered at this. Even the redheaded man named Ferenc seemed pleased. Ibolya grabbed a rag and wiped the counter. Her hair was quivering. She changed her approach.

She walked around the bar put herself into his lap. "Are you truly this cruel and heartless?"

The potter stammered. He pushed her off and stormed out of the pub. He turned to say something but cleared his throat instead and left for his workshop.

"Ibolya, will you marry me?" the man named Ferenc asked.

"Shut up," she said. "Go home to your wife."

Since that day, men watching her noticed that whenever they were talking about Valeria, all the vessels and capillaries in Ibolya's face would burst open at the same moment, and her hair began to quiver and grow more disheveled. It eventually reached the point that when she heard her customers even mention Valeria, or anything that could be misconstrued as Valeria, she'd explode.

"That's it! You've reached your limit, old farts. You have forgotten yourself. The sign out front says nothing about Valeria. It says 'Ibolya's Nonstop.' I am Ibolya. And I say that Valeria is a rotten old potato who has never felt so much as a decent pinch on her broad backside. Shut up now or go home. You're making me sick."

She even stopped pouring drinks. She cut the old men off from everything: her alcohol, her smiles, her bosom perched on the bar, even the sunflower seeds. She wasn't able to control the potter, but she could control these men. No one in her establishment would be worked up unless it was over her.

The old men stammered in protest, but being tongue-lashed in front of the others, being humiliated so, and, most of all, being cut off from her heavy-handed cocktails, they all quickly acquiesced and agreed they were not in their right minds.

"We're sorry, Ibolya," they begged. "We're drunk. Here, see? We're playing cards now instead. See? We're playing cards. Valeria who?"

Ibolya remained aloof and steadfast. It was only after their second round of apologies, when they had all but recanted, proclaimed themselves blasphemers and heretics, that she walked over to them, tossed her haystack of hair just so, so that they caught a good whiff of cigarettes, perfume, and liquor, and poured them a shot of plum brandy. They licked their lips as they reached for their shot glasses, and while doing so Ibolya leaned over ever so slightly, just enough to give them a peek at the tops of her breasts. The old men became slack jawed. They rubbed their eyes. They quickly ordered another round. Their grandsons just laughed and slapped the table. Ibolya winked and smiled.

"Valeria is a basket case. Don't you forget it. There are people in this world who are simply unfortunate, and not because they were born that way, but because they strive to make themselves that way. It's the worst of deficiencies. Valeria suffers from it."

The conversations ended, and Ibolya was glad of it. She noted that Valeria's dalliance with the potter was bad for business all around. These conversations were becoming more and more frequent and harder to stamp out. Ibolya's jealousy caused her to reason that people who were gossiping about Valeria's affair with the potter weren't working hard. People who weren't working hard, who weren't breaking their back, had no reason to drink, and people who weren't drinking weren't coming into her tavern.

While Ibolya was certainly upset that her friendship with the potter had fallen apart—he wasn't visiting, he wasn't answering his phone—what bothered Ibolya more was that business was slow. She had to wear shorter skirts and smaller blouses. She had to lean over more when she poured drinks to keep the customers she did have from going away. Her back was beginning to ache and it had only been a week.

These things bothered her because if there was one thing Ibolya understood, it was a man's attention span. At fifty-eight, no matter how short her skirt was or how far over she leaned, the men she enticed were now all older than she was. Their handsome grandsons smiled and flirted, but she could see in their eyes that there was no real interest there. There might even have been antipathy. They were just being polite, trying not to hurt an old lady's vanity. How long could she keep it up, she wondered. How long before the men who remained in her tavern were bald, toothless, and penniless? Ibolya was smart enough to know that she only had five or six years left before she would have to hire some younger women. Maybe even sooner. Maybe she'd need to hire someone right away. Someone who could wake up all of the men and bring them in. Perhaps she could find someone as glamorous as the mayor's wife. That would be something. That would make her wealthy beyond her dreams. Maybe she could even turn the pub into a striptease. Men would pay through the nose for something like that. Ibolya lost herself in this reverie and then noticed the potter's apprentice sitting with a young woman. A pretty thing. The girl was laughing and tossing her hair. Her mouth was open and she didn't put her hand over it. Ibolya looked the girl over. She had a nice figure. She was similar enough to the mayor's wife. *Yes*, she thought to herself. *I can work with that. She'd be perfect. The potter has his apprentice; I can have mine.*

Ibolya's relationship with men had not changed in forty-five years. She knew what they wanted, knew how to manipulate them to get what she wanted, and wasn't prudish about it. Not even her marriage had slowed her down. She had married a brutish dimwit and cuckolded him during the honeymoon.

Eventually, her passions faded and her relationships would fizzle, but Ibolya didn't really mind that fact. There was always another conquest on the horizon. The handsome potter with his white whiskers and wavy hair wasn't the only catch. It was true that she was frustrated that their time together was fizzling before it had really peaked. She had to listen to the gossip already about how the potter preferred Valeria to her. Ibolya could not stomach that. She would not accept that kind of talk. She could not. As long as her legs were pretty and her perfume was fresh, Ibolya could win the potter back. She was sure of it.

"Valeria might as well be walking around the village with her skirt over her head for all the attention she's getting," Ibolya said.

She looked to her patrons. They were all drinking merrily now; Valeria was a forgotten topic. Ibolya was the only one thinking about her. She laughed to herself. Farmers. That's all they were. They could only think about the weather and what was right in front of their faces. They stumbled from polished pebble to polished pebble, never reflecting long enough to understand the whys and the how-comes or the possibilities of anything except whether or not their crops would make it, and then if they did, how much they would yield. When the real question, the only question in Ibolya's mind, was, how much could she yield?

"I'll send him a note," she whispered to herself. "I'll forgive him. He'll come back to me."

Ten

Two notes arrived at the potter's home. The first was from Ibolya. It was a red envelope, perfumed and kissed. The second was Valeria's. It was a simple white envelope embossed with flowers. The envelopes couldn't have been more different in texture or style, but the content of both of them was very much the same. The two women who sent them were equally disappointed with the potter. They castigated him for his cruelty. The pen strokes dug into the paper. The potter read them and sighed. *A fine mess*, he thought to himself. He answered both women with a quick message of his own a day later. He sent them the same message: He apologized for his absence and explained that he was very, very busy. Then he placed their missives in a drawer and he tried to forget them for the time being.

Still, he felt uneasy about his situation, and when his apprentice arrived, the potter brought up Ibolya's note right away. The potter and she had spent the longest amount of time together, after all. While it couldn't be said that his heart panged with guilt over her, his conscience did.

"She forgave you?" his apprentice asked.

"That's what her note said," answered the potter. "She forgives me and she wants us to be together."

"Ibolya sent a love letter? Kissed and perfumed? I can't believe it. I really can't believe that."

The potter handed him the letter and allowed him to read it. The apprentice shook his head.

"She's not the only one," the potter said.

"What? You mean Valeria also? There's no way. What did she say?"

"She forgave me also."

"For what? Valeria should be thanking you."

"For how I behaved afterward, I imagine. I feel I've been shabby with both of them."

"But what do they want?"

"They want me to choose."

The apprentice shook his head. He smirked.

"You should be ashamed of yourselves. All of you. You're old enough to be in retirement homes. This is craziness. You're worse than adolescents. What did you do?"

"I wrote them both back."

"You did? Why would you do that? What did you say?"

"I thanked them for their friendship and told them both I was too busy to see either of them for the foreseeable future."

"And then?"

"Ibolya sent another note. She said that she would not give up, no matter what. Valeria left a message that she wants me to visit. I think I will. I'm working on her vases and that's fine, but I don't want her to think it means anything more."

"What is she supposed to think? You slept with her! You slept with them both. Anyway, if that's the case, why visit Valeria? Just finish the vases and I'll drop them off. Or don't finish them. You're leading them on, old-timer. You're a gigolo! You're confusing yourself with an Italian."

The potter shrugged. He was at a loss.

"I don't want to think about it," he said. "I have to finish these vases."

"Valeria's vases?"

"I suppose."

"You've got to get your head examined."

"She has a nice bum."

The apprentice laughed. "Who are you talking about? I'm sure I wouldn't know."

"Ibolya has a lot of fire."

"You're crazy."

"One's a volcano, the other is an ocean. It's a difficult choice to make. You can see my predicament."

"Pick your poison, old-timer. Burn or drown. Either way, you're going to suffocate."

The potter stopped what he was doing and looked up.

"No, no. Sometimes I need fire to remind me that I'm alive. You'll see what I mean as you grow older. I want to feel alive, like I've got the world by the balls. I don't feel that way much anymore. I feel something like that with Ibolya. But then, sometimes I feel like being on fire isn't really all it's cracked up to be. So what? You know? I'd rather sit in a sauna or thermal spring somewhere. Maybe just have a smoke. Maybe go swimming and feel my muscles stretching. Valeria is like that. It's a tough choice at any age."

The apprentice picked up a plate and looked at the seal underneath. He traced it with his finger. He smiled.

"So choose polygamy," he joked. "You'll just have to convince them both that it's the ideal arrangement. Somehow I think you could. Valeria during the week and Ibolya on weekends."

The potter smiled back.

"That would most likely kill me," he said.

The potter felt that his apprentice was a good young man.

He had become a good potter as well. He had finished the tea-pot and was now finishing his work on Zsofi Toth's platter. The potter had let him back in the studio to work once he'd decided on how to make Valeria's vases. What he had not mentioned to the apprentice, however, what the potter felt but couldn't communicate to any of them, was that what he especially feared regarding his winter years was a gathering sense of isolation. More and more, the potter felt disconnected from his surroundings, and what he had discovered in being with both women was that either woman helped him feel less isolated. It was as much for that reason as any other that the potter couldn't bear to choose between them.

The potter's apprentice was in good spirits of late. He had been spending a lot of time with Zsofi, but there was nothing romantic going on between them, or so he'd told the potter. Still, a half hour after they had finished their conversation, Zsofi came to visit them. She had been doing a lot of that recently. She had been thrilled when the apprentice delivered her teapot and had begun popping into the workshop unannounced. When she did, she brought food along with her and hung around the shop tidying and making the men feel pleasant and hopeful. The potter liked her immensely. A handsome young girl. Healthy and smart. She joked with them and told ribald stories about the men in her mother's life. One was a strange foreigner who hardly spoke the language and had boarded with them when she was younger. He was an engineer and her mother had fallen madly in love with him, had even gone so far as to slip a shot of brandy in Zsofi's juice cup to make her fall asleep. Then she would stay up with this boarder and carry on.

"That's what my mother calls it. 'Carrying on.'"

It turned out that the boarder had a wife, an even fatter woman apparently. She started sending packages and indecent photographs of herself. When her mother discovered them while cleaning his room, she threw him out and cried for a week.

The potter enjoyed Zsofi's stories. He joked with her in front of the apprentice that if he were a younger man he would propose and take her someplace nice.

"You're sweet," she said, and looked at the apprentice.

"Careful," the apprentice remarked. "He's not as sweet as he looks. The elderly grandfather routine is just a ruse. You'll be stuffed and hanging on his wall in no time. He's a real gigolo."

That was the extent of the apprentice's conversation whenever the topic of marriage arose. He didn't allow himself to be drawn into conversations about that particular topic. He worked at the base of her platter with a wooden clay knife.

"Well, I'd like to get married one day . . . and soon," Zsofi said.

"Of course you would, my dear," said the potter. "You have a lot to offer. Any man would be lucky to have you,"

"Why?" the apprentice chimed in. "I'll never marry. Not me. Too many headaches. Too much nagging. I'll stay a bachelor as long as I can."

The potter thought he noticed a flash of anger on Zsofi's face. She grew suddenly chilly. She stormed out for what the potter figured must have been the millionth time. Whenever the apprentice made comments like that, she took up their food—finished or not —said good-bye, and walked out the door. The potter had recognized this early on and learned to eat quickly. He didn't mind it so much now. The apprentice, on the other hand, had never learned and was never finished. He would whine and complain, but it was useless. Her only response was the swish of her skirt and the slap of her flats as she walked out.

"You're a very nice boy," the potter said to him. "Not too bright though."

The apprentice looked at him.

"Why does she always storm out? I'm just telling her how it is. She's like my sister. I want her to know what men are really like."

When the potter heard this, he thought of Valeria and felt guilty again. Notes and a message had been their only communication. He decided it really was time to see her. He couldn't put it off any longer. He shouldn't, really. It was nearing ten days since their encounter. He had to admit that he was behaving childishly.

"I'm going to visit Valeria," he announced. "Put an end to all of this."

The apprentice shook his head.

"Good luck to you."

The potter rose from his spot and went to his living quarters. He showered quickly and dressed nicely, but not too nicely. He didn't want to seem formal. In fact, he wore a blue cap because he thought it made him look casual. That's what he wanted. A casual visit. The kind of visit a friend might make when calling on another friend. Nothing heavy. Just a casual visit to inform a person that he's not romantically interested.

The potter left the apprentice to work on his platter and he bicycled down the hill, making sure to casually wave at Ibolya on his way to the Centrum. *You see*, he thought, *just a casual bike ride through the city. It's working already.*

He reached Valeria's cottage without incident. He knocked on her door.

It took a moment, but when Valeria opened it she was wearing rubber gloves and an old dress. Her hair was pulled back and up out of her face. A bun rested on the crown of her head. Silver wisps fell and she tucked those behind her ears. She shifted uncomfortably.

"Ten days!" The words shot out at him. "Who do you think you are? Ten days and one note. You're taking your time on those vases."

The potter nodded. He was taking his time on the vases, but he was doing a good job.

"Hello, my dear. It is something special. I'm making you something special. Only I couldn't afford to clear my workshop out like I did with the ewer. I'm getting to it after-hours in the evening before bed."

Valeria seemed satisfied with this answer. She looked at herself in the window.

"You should have told me you were coming," she said. "I'm not dressed for company."

"Ah, please. Don't worry about that," he replied. "It's just a casual visit. You look lovely. In fact, I like your gloves."

Valeria took them off and put them in her waist pocket.

"I was cleaning the bathtub. It was stained. It needed lye. The water is hard here. I wish the mayor would do something about that instead of this damned station. It's all anybody talks about anymore. Never mind that the water tastes like metal and we all probably need tetanus shots. I wonder if the doctor's been seeing a lot of cases of lockjaw. What do you think? Why not fix the wells?"

"I don't know." The potter shrugged. "Funny thing about the station, though. The mayor came by my workshop last week and asked me to make him something for it. Some people told him about the pitcher. I guess he thought I might be able to help decorate. You know, he's a regular customer of mine now. He's always picking up those figurines I make. It's his wife. He says his wife has taken a liking to them and started a collection. He asked if I could make a larger one for the station."

"Like a statue?" Valeria asked.

"Yes, yes. A statue. Can you believe that? I told him I would be delighted to try but that he should not expect very much. I'm not a sculptor."

Valeria smiled at him. "You're like our very own Michelangelo."

"Hardly," he laughed.

He was relieved. This easygoing approach seemed to be working. Exactly what he'd hoped for. Here they stood, two friends enjoying a casual visit. Enjoying each other's company.

The pair shifted on her front porch. Things grew quiet.

"Still, ten days is a long time." Valeria was reminding herself. He was so charming and easy that she almost forgot she was angry. "I've got the kettle on. Would you like a cup of tea?"

She had bewildered him.

"What? Tea? Well, yes, I suppose. Certainly. Tea would be nice."

He followed her inside. They sat in the kitchen. She had moved the ewer there, and when the potter saw it he sighed.

"You should let me fix that."

Valeria unlocked a cupboard and pulled out a pair of teacups.

"I like it the way it is," she said.

"But it's broken," he said.

"What isn't?"

The potter considered this. Her voice was firm. He decided there was no malicious intent behind it, but the air between them seemed to be growing heavier. He tried to maintain his light touch. He smiled at her.

"Valeria, I've come to apologize for how I behaved."

Valeria tilted her head.

"You were right. I did take advantage of you. I'm terribly ashamed of myself. See, I got so worked up over making the ewer, and I was so proud of myself for doing it, and then your hair was loose, and all the craziness going on around us. I don't know what I was thinking. I was careless."

Valeria nodded and sipped from the glass. "What are you saying?"

"I'm saying that what we did may have been a mistake. I am

104

saying that I should not have taken advantage of you. You were right. I'd like to make amends somehow, but I don't know how. And then there is Ibolya, and I suppose I should have mentioned to you earlier that while we are not engaged or married, she and I have been friends—that is, romantically linked for a few months now. You see, it's a small village and things appear unseemly. I wouldn't want for you to be affected in any way."

Valeria swallowed her tea. She looked like she was about to laugh.

"My, you are a silly man, aren't you? I'm a sixty-eight-year-old woman. I have a brain. I knew what I was doing. I wanted to do it. I chose to do it. Are you trying to insult me?"

She stood up. The potter was aghast. He put his hands up in front of him and shook them.

"No, no. Not at all. I just thought—"

"You thought what?" Valeria's voice had risen. "You thought you could come here and smile and be charming and worm your way out of my life and that I would nod and tell you everything is all right?"

The potter furrowed his brow.

"You're a silly man if that's what you thought."

"I didn't think anything."

"Then you're a thoughtless man."

"I just thought that—"

"You thought you could save yourself from having to make a hard decision. That's what you thought. But I'm not going to let you do that. I can decide to sleep with whomever I want."

The potter was confused.

"What?" he said. "Who would you sleep with? Why would you want to do something like that?"

Valeria was walking out of the room. She went to the front door and opened it. She held it for him.

"Get out."

"I'm sorry. I'm not understanding you."

"Get out," she answered.

The potter walked toward the door.

"Will you come by the shop to collect your vases?" he asked. "Or should I call you?"

"Leave," she said. "Come back when you've grown up."

She all but pushed him out the door. While he stood there protesting, she shut it in his face.

Book Two

Eleven

The chimney sweep's bicycle was manufactured in 1902. It was the premier model of its era, dubbed the Rabbit because of its swiftness and high, wide handlebars. It was among the first bicycles in the world to feature a gearshift and vulcanized rubber tires half a meter in diameter. It was also an unlucky contraption that brought nothing but despair to its owners. All of the bicycles from that era, the chimney sweep's included, were manufactured in a Croatian factory north of Dalmatia and west of Split, in a seaside village named Trogir.

The bicycles were made at the request of Franz Ferdinand, Austro-Hungarian emperor and avid cyclist. In fact, the unlucky 1902 model was his favorite and he owned six of them. He decreed that the bicycles he distributed around the empire to mail carriers in the postal service. He reasoned correctly that they were cheaper and more efficient than horses.

One Rabbit was stolen from its owner—a prefect judge's Serbian retainer named Gabriel Csusco. Ruffians on the Vlasnyet Bridge, on the outskirts of Belgrade, bludgeoned the unfortunate retainer over the head and threw him in the river late one winter. These men—young anarchists, mostly, though one documented homosexual was among them—were later apprehended for the crime after one of them, in the middle of the day, apparently forgetful as to how he had acquired the bicycle, used it so that he wouldn't be late paying a fine at the courthouse. The policemen standing outside the courthouse said later that they were astounded by several facts: first, that a documented anarchist would pay a fine at all, and second, that he tried to park his bicycle in the prefect judge's retainer's space with the livery still intact.

The band of anarchists and the homosexual were captured, and the bicycle was held as evidence. That would have been the end of its story except that a corrupt policeman sold it to a mail carrier whose own bicycle had been lost in a card game and who needed a replacement before his superiors discovered it. The mail carrier was a German immigrant named Von Kleist. He was a self-indulgent man, overweight and asthmatic, and since the switch from horses to bicycles, delivering the mail had become a life-threatening chore. In a stroke of brilliance he devised a system of delivering the mail that worked out well for everyone along his route: he left all the mail he was given at either the church or the tavern. Nobody ever complained. Attendance at both increased. All parties concerned were happy. People picked up their post when they felt like it.

Von Kleist died in his mistress's bed the next spring with a bag of mail resting at their feet. The distraught woman reported it to the police and for months afterward citizens were coming to her cottage looking for letters or packages from abroad. When the post had finally all been collected and the woman was left in peace, she breathed a sigh of relief and immediately took up with a married brick maker. Due to a bureaucratic mishap, the empire never came to collect Von Kleist's belongings, and the bicycle was left unclaimed, on its side, in front of the woman's cottage. Then the First World War erupted and Von Kleist's mistress's home was set ablaze by a band of roving Slovenians.

The bicycle was buried in shingles from the unlucky woman's collapsed roof.

Long after the war the bicycle was discovered by a group of Gypsy children who took it back to their father, a tinker of some renown. He fixed the old bicycle, but before his children could learn to ride it, the Second World War erupted and the entire family was taken away by German soldiers who confiscated the bicycle and presented it to the children of a well-connected family in Budapest.

Suffice it to say, the children in that well-connected family all drowned in the Danube when a retreating German army shot holes in the family's pontoon to slow down the British who were arriving via river patrol. Afterward, the distraught parents offered the bicycle to a chimney sweep, who, when tearfully told of its history, remarked: "Well, I'm looking for something durable. If it can survive all that, it was surely built to last."

Quite a few years later, an accident in an asbestos factory rendered the chimney sweep blind. He passed the bicycle on to his young apprentice.

For five years the young apprentice and the chimney sweep criss-crossed the land traveling from village to village. For three weeks during the holidays, the young apprentice visited his mother. He had been a severe child. Over the years, his severity developed into a full-blown melancholia. He was bilious to the point of belligerence. When the chimney sweep went blind and soon after died, he left the adolescent his small cottage and all his belongings. The young man collected his mother and moved her there. He visited her more often after that, but by the time he was thirty, his ennui was full-blown and he set fire to the house, sold the land, and put his mother in a rest home.

"Funny," she said one morning at the rest home when he had come to pay her an infrequent visit. She was looking out the window as they breakfasted together on toast and jam. "You were always so short. It's really marvelous that you became a chimney sweep. Don't you agree?"

The chimney sweep cursed and threw the butter dish at her. Knowing him like she did, the old woman had only portioned out a few tablespoons. The rest of the butter was safe in the icebox.

"I meant it as a compliment. You have a profession. Little Tibi's mother is heartbroken over him. He's in jail, you know."

"Little Tibi is irrelevant, Mother," the chimney sweep said as he put out his cigarette in the jam.

"Oh! That's not true. He was such a nice boy. He brought his mother flowers all the time. He even sends her paper flowers from jail. He's thoughtful like that."

"Mother, Tibi, his flowers, you and me, we are completely irrelevant in the grand design of things. Irrelevant, even to the lives of our fellow men. If I die cleaning a chimney tomorrow, a Chinaman in Peking won't make the slightest shudder. Not even a fart for me having lived."

The chimney sweep's mother clucked at him, and then her eyes grew wide.

"You've seen a Chinaman?" she said. "What was he like? Did you clean his chimney?"

The chimney sweep moaned.

"No, Mother. I haven't. I'm saying that you and I are irrelevant. I couldn't care less about little Tibi, his paper flowers, his mother, or you or me, for that matter."

"I saw Arabs once," his mother replied. "Or maybe they were Negroes."

"Mother, do you hear me?"

"At the Western Train Station in Budapest. I was a young girl. It was 1923. I'll never forget it. They were sitting together and eating soup in a restaurant. They seemed so normal. Everyone stopped to stare. When they finished and wiped their mouths, we applauded."

"Mother, we are irrelevant."

"They seemed happy too. They smiled at us. They were very charming. One of them was carrying a trumpet. I do remember that."

"I don't care about the Arabs, Mother."

"Negroes. I'm certain now that they were Negroes."

The chimney sweep flicked his cigarette butt at her. It landed on her macramé.

"Oh, dear," she said. "You've ruined it!"

"Well at least I'm capable of something," the chimney sweep muttered.

The woman looked in his direction. She put on her eyeglasses. She shook her head.

"I should have had a Negro son."

"What?"

"I'm certain a Negro son would never ruin his mother's macramé. Oh, but you should have seen how nicely they had their soup."

The once young apprentice was now a chimney sweep nearing sixty. His mother was long dead, and he was resigned to his fate. He arrived in the village of Zivatar astride his Rabbit. It was his most useful tool, and, save for a dent on the rear fender where he had kicked it one day in an angry outburst, it was unblemished. He no longer remembered what he had been angry about the day he kicked it, but it didn't really matter as he was so often angry. Mostly, though, he tended to his bicycle carefully and kept it in superb condition. He kept the chain oiled and tightened, and he replaced it whenever he spotted flecks of rust in the eyelets. He cleaned dirt from around the wheel spokes regularly. He replaced the brake pads every four months. He always carried inner tubes and a pump, and if he noticed a slow leak he had no qualms about stopping wherever he was, even if it was on the side of a busy highway, and patching the tire straightaway.

The chimney sweep traveled on it six months out of the year—beginning each spring, when people opened their windows and cleaned out the winter. He was unaware that something in its manufacturing had made it unlucky. He was not the type to believe that anyway.

When the chimney sweep crested the hill outside of Zivatar and looked below, he was startled by the size of the village spread out in front of him. He looked for some kind of road sign. He looked at his maps. There was nothing to tell him where he was. He looked again at the village. It was no small affair, a hamlet of close to five thousand souls. That men chose to take root so deep in the prairie always surprised him. Why not head for big cities and warmer climes? The chimney sweep decided it was laziness. The masses were lazy and comfortable. All he could do was service them where they were.

The chimney sweep headed toward the centrum in the distance, toward the church with its onion domes. He rode past the potter's workshop and past Ibolya's tavern. He saw the sign, made note of the strange-looking tavern, fully intending to return to it, but for the moment he was intent on reaching the centrum, which he gauged as being about two kilometers further. He looked at the tops of chimneys as he headed toward it. They were black with soot. He shook his head. A chimney sweep had not passed through here for several years, at least.

"A gold mine," he whispered, "I could make a fortune here." And for the first time in months his face cracked into a smile.

Children and their small dogs took note of the stranger and began following him. It was the same story in every village throughout the countryside. Children would see him, scream, and then come running out of their forts or empty lots to greet him. He always thought of the old chimney sweep who had trained him and of what the man had told him early on: "People, not all of them, but most of them, enough to make it annoying, believe that touching us, or getting us to touch them, means good luck is guaranteed to come their way. In some of the more remote villages even gazing upon us is considered a good omen, and if they can follow up the gaze by looking at a broken pane of glass then they feel like they are doubly blessed."

"Is it true?" he had asked.

"It is true for everyone but a chimney sweep. For us it's a load of pig shit. Still, it's best to give the people what they want. They'll pay you handsomely for a smile and a pat on the back. You should smile more. Try to lighten up."

For his part, the chimney sweep didn't pay much attention to that bit of advice. In fact, he wasn't above spitting at children or kicking dogs to keep them at bay. He considered it an obligation, really. What with them running so wildly and indefatigably through the streets, if he didn't spit at them, or kick them for their own good, they could be run over by a milk truck. And how sad would that be? It would be terribly sad, really.

"Damn mutts," he grumbled as he looked at a young child.

The child waved at him. The chimney sweep smirked back and looked instead at the brick cottages that had been standing for a century and a half. They had been updated over time, mostly with stucco cinder-block attachments connected to the old brick of the main cottages. The roads in the village were devoid of too many cars and they were cobbled. Had he been a romantic man he might have enjoyed this quaintness, but he wasn't. Cobblestone streets would wreak havoc on his wheels. Cobblestone streets would jar his head and rattle his teeth. The day would end in a headache for certain.

"Primitives," he mumbled to himself, trying not to shake too much and bend his rims. "Might as well be apes. Probably inbred."

He was pleased that he had spotted the smoke, though. He always headed toward smoke, and he instantly recognized the blue wisps curling into the sky as hearth smoke.

He wondered if the people in this village would be easy to fleece or not. He assumed they would, but as a test, the chimney sweep stopped and walked up to a cottage at random. The shutters were freshly painted, as were the cement stairs that led to the door. He stood outside the gate and rapped against it until dogs inside the house began to bark. A woman opened her door and looked down at him. It took her a moment to recognize his uniform, but once she spotted the leather blazer and his moustache she screamed and smiled at him. She called to someone behind her.

"Béla, come quickly, a chimney sweep!"

She shooed the dogs away and ran down her steps. She opened the wooden gate and pulled him in. The chimney sweep loved these isolated country women. They were bored and shut in. It didn't take much effort on his part to talk them into anything. When she approached him he didn't smile, but he looked at her dead-on with lascivious eyes. He nodded at her and let her pet his shoulder.

"Good day! Does your chimney need cleaning, miss?" he asked, knowing full well that it did.

"Yes," she said. "Of course it does. It's been ages."

"Well, my fee is five thousand forints," the chimney sweep answered. He was gauging her reaction, but she didn't blink. She nodded and straightened her dress. She was primping.

"Of course, of course," she said, fondling the lapel on his blazer. "As much as you want."

The chimney sweep wasn't shocked too often, and he hadn't planned on beginning work so soon, but since she had accepted this exorbitant price, he felt he should get to work quickly before she changed her mind. He unfastened an array of bristles and brushes from his bicycle and carried them in one hand, while in the other he held a telescopic pole. He followed her inside and approached her hearth. He attached a thick brush to the pole, stepped into her hearth and into the chimney, extended the pole, and began to scrub. While he worked, he couldn't believe that she would actually pay him once he was through. However, when he was done, she walked up to him, put her arms around him in a great loving hug—which he returned—and handed him two crisp five-thousand-forint notes.

"Take this," she said, looking in his eyes. "A little extra. I insist."

The chimney sweep took the money and put it in his satchel. He tipped his hat to her, and despite himself, instead of the slight mischievous grin he usually gave country wives, he smiled broadly back. She walked him to the gate, leaning on his shoulder, and then to a neighbor's house. Her silent husband patted him on the back as he left. The chimney sweep had noticed that the man's eyes were flickering in anger, but the husband didn't flinch or say a word when the chimney sweep walked out of his home ten thousand forints the richer and with the man's wife draped on his shoulder. The chimney sweep felt those flickering eyes burning into his back, though. Like two embers thrown down his shirt. He shrugged it off. *Poor bastard*, he thought.

"Éva," the woman escorting him called out. "Come out. A chimney sweep is here."

Another woman looked through a window and waved. She hurried out of the house and cooed at him. The women chatted excitedly for a moment and he was handed off. They bade farewell to one another and then the new woman led him into her home. When they were inside, as the woman rubbed his shoulders, the chimney sweep looked her in the eye.

"My fee is ten thousand forints." He said it, but he didn't mean it, and he was ready to bolt, fully expecting that she would scream and call the police. But the woman named Eva only smiled at him. She shook her head.

"Hmmm," she said, still rubbing his shoulders. "That's a bit much. Let me see what my husband has in his safe."

She squeezed him, let go, and disappeared from the room, though not before handing him a small tumbler of brandy and pointing to the hearth.

By the time he was finished with this second hearth, he had been in Zivatar half a day and he was besotted and sweaty. When he wiped the grime from around his eyes, he was startled to see the woman hovering next to him and holding a fresh, moistened towel in her hand. He took the towel from her.

"I'm done," he said. "Do you have my fee?"

"Yes," she answered. "Here it is."

Two more five-thousand-forint notes. They were as crisp as autumn leaves, as pink as a fish's belly. Again, the chimney sweep forgot about his grin and was beaming now. When she gave him one final hug, he pressed against her and lingered. In four hours he had made twenty thousand forints. Three days' wages in any other village.

"Tell me," he said, still holding on to her. "When was the last time a chimney sweep came through here? Isn't there one living in the village, or nearby?"

The woman shook her head, remembered herself, and pulled away.

"Wouldn't that be nice? A chimney sweep in the village." She was fidgeting now. Straightening her hair and dress. She couldn't look at him. How he loved these country women! "The last one came through three years ago. Chimney sweeps just pass us by. I guess they figure we're poor and not worth the trouble."

This led the chimney sweep to his next question. "I thought I saw a train station."

The woman nodded. She handed him another brandy and poured a second glass for herself. Expensive plum brandy this time.

"Yes, that's right, but we don't have the train yet. Soon. It's the mayor's pet project. They're almost done, in fact. It won't be a big one. A lot of the younger men in the village are working on it. It'll be a major employer. The mayor says that we're going to get one of those little rail cars, you know, those little bitty trains. Just the one car. A little intercity. An inter-bitty." She giggled here and looked at her glass. She poured more brandy and continued. "Then we'll really be connected to the rest of the country. We won't be so hard for the investors to reach."

"What investors?" the chimney sweep asked.

"Germans, I guess, or maybe the British, or maybe even Americans. Wouldn't that be something? The mayor's been showing Asians around the past few months. He's expecting more."

The chimney sweep scoffed.

"What would they want here?"

The woman shrugged. "You'd have to ask the mayor. He says we have good soil and the perfect workforce for a factory."

"What kind of factory?"

"You'd have to ask the mayor."

"And what do people think of the foreigners and the train station?" the chimney sweep laughed.

"I don't know," the woman answered. "It's okay, I guess. It's good for us. We've been left behind for too long. Things will pick up. I'm okay with it, anyway."

"What is the name of this town? Zivatar? I saw a sign on the tavern, but nothing anywhere else."

She looked at him a moment. "My, you really are lost. Yes, that's right. This is Zivatar. Haven't you ever heard of it?"

He shook his head.

She looked disappointed, but she shrugged and smiled.

"See? The mayor's right. That's why we need the train. Charming chimney sweeps like you could come whenever they wanted. You could walk right up to those nasty little women at rail stations around the country and buy a round-trip ticket to Zivatar, one of the only villages in this country to have never been sacked. We're one of the only towns in Hungary never to have fallen under foreign influence. The village has always been like this, exactly like this. What do you think of our cobblestones? You should really go and see the centrum while you're here. Market Square has some wonderful craft stores. Everything is handmade. The church is nine hundred years old. You saw it on the main road, yes? It's also one of the oldest in the country. The bells had to be repaired in the fifties I think, but other than that, it's all the original masonry. Even the wooden floors have petrified with age."

The chimney sweep frowned and began to gather his things.

"Whatever," he said.

"When the Turks attacked, they marched right past us, knowing we were here but thinking we weren't worth the trouble. They sent a few men and the domes were erected on the church. You can read about that there," the woman continued, not listening to him. "The Austrians didn't bother us either. I doubt if the Hapsburgs ever heard of us. The Germans heard of us, but like the Turks, they never came looking. Even British tanks rolled by. My parents stood on the crest of the hill outside of town and watched them on the horizon. They never came any closer than the horizon. Can you believe it? Not even the Russians cared enough to visit. For three days the tanks came in from Russia. The tanks came for three days, most of them heading for Budapest. Did they ever stop here? No. I was a toddler then. The whole village went out and watched them lumber past. They sent the party, though. Party officials came. They were Hungarians. But it just never worked out. It never took. Most of the officials, after realizing that their superiors had forgotten them as soon as they reached here, just married and settled down. They became part of the village. Looking at it, I suppose we should be thankful that we're just too much trouble to reach."

The chimney sweep shook his head in disbelief.

"I arrived here on a bicycle."

The woman laughed and stroked his shoulders. She was good and drunk. She grabbed his collar.

"Yes, that's right! You certainly did. You must have really wanted to come," she said.

The chimney sweep stepped away from the woman, who was now beginning to paw him with gusto.

"Wait. How did the church bells break? A bomb? Surely the bombardiers must have seen the village from the sky. Was it the Americans? Was it the British? They would have bombed any population center they saw."

The woman laughed and stroked his hair.

"My, my, but what a wild imagination you have. No, we've never been bombed. We're just lucky. Maybe there was a cloud that day. Who knows? No, an angry girl climbed up the belfry and set fire to the ropes that held the bells in place."

"How's that?" the chimney sweep asked. "During the middle of a war?"

"But I told you, there was no war here. No wars. No revolutions. No counterrevolutions. Just us. The way it's always been. Uneventful. Maybe after the station is finished things will pick up. We could use a little picking up."

The chimney sweep shook his head. He thought about the twenty thousand forints in his pocket. He certainly wasn't upset that he had left the main road and stumbled onto this place. He gathered the rest of his belongings and thanked the woman for the drinks.

"That tavern on the edge of town, is there lodging there?" he asked.

"I suppose Ibolya could arrange something for you," she replied, and her voice was clipped now. He had rebuffed all her advances. "She's a bit wild, though, and her tavern isn't really a place for gentlemen."

"Ha," the chimney sweep laughed, and then he bade the woman good-bye, turned, and walked out. She followed him to her gate and tugged on his jacket, but he broke free, and she could only wave as he pedaled away, back toward the crest of the hill, toward the main road. He didn't look at her again.

Something had crossed the chimney sweep's mind as he left. In fact, he was thinking about what it would mean if he were to stay for a while. He was getting older and knew he should be thinking about his retirement. The new system had left him almost completely on his own. He knew he shouldn't expect any kind of retirement worth a damn from the state. In fact, with inflation in the high digits, he knew his money could lose value on a walk to the market. Capitalism was killing him. Maybe he could settle down here and find a simple country woman, he thought. Maybe that was the answer: a woman of means in a cheap town. An easygoing spinster who wouldn't care if he caroused, who would be glad to have him around. The villagers might appreciate him staying as well, and if he were to stay, if he were to go from cottage to cottage, repairing and cleaning out chimneys and hearths, as the only chimney sweep, he might even make a handsome fortune. It would be a comfortable retirement, at least. And all he needed to fulfill the dream was a woman of means.

The chimney sweep scratched his head and sneered. It was too easy. A perfect ending for him. Like falling off a cliff and landing in a tub of butter. He'd begin hunting for that special country maiden at once.

"Zivatar." He looked overhead. "No clouds in the sky today."

He arrived at Ibolya's tavern and rested his bicycle against a tree. Then he skulked into the bar, not wanting to speak with anyone, not wanting to have to explain himself, and not wanting to be touched. He found a table in a corner that looked like it had been fashioned out of an old door. He sat on a small barrel that served as a stool. The barrel was cushioned, but the cushion was tattered. He picked at the stuffing and waited for a waitress. When he realized that one would never come, he got up, walked over to the bar, and ordered several drinks from the bartender. He hoped the bartender wouldn't say anything, and she didn't; she didn't look at him. She was busy with her other patrons, moderating a discussion that only locals would find interesting. The peasants seemed to be in a tizzy of some sort. The chimney sweep was only half listening, but he gathered that there was a commotion in the village. A love scandal. They seemed to be cursing someone. The chimney sweep noted that the bartender was the loudest.

He carried three bottles of beer back to his table himself. He drank the first two quickly and then nursed the third. He could tell that most of the men in the pub were farmers, though why they weren't working their fields he couldn't say. He remembered that the winter had been especially cold. Most of the spring so far had been dry. The rivers were low; the canals were low. Irrigation was surely a problem. Sunflowers—the chimney sweep figured it must have been sunflowers—needed moist soil. They sucked nutrients right out of the earth. He knew the story. He'd heard it a million times, in fact. Whenever they rubbed his shoulders and begged. The poor peasants had probably hocked everything to buy extra seeds, hoping to press some of their harvest into oil, sell some to the food companies, or hold on to the remainder for next year's planting.

Of course, because of the warm weather, the sunflowers would dry up. The bank, or loan shark, or whoever they borrowed the money from would hound them, throw them off of their farms, beat them with sticks, or auction off their land. It was the same story in every other remote village in the country, the chimney sweep thought. Little country farmers were losing their shirts to bigger operations. He just couldn't understand why people never learned.

He looked at a large, broken-backed man sitting at the table next to his, saw the dirt under his fingernails—the sign of a man scraping a few measly coins from the mud. In a moment that was rare to the chimney sweep, probably because of the money in his pocket, probably because he figured that these people might soon be his neighbors, he handed his beer bottle to the man.

"Your fields all dried up, are they?" the chimney sweep asked, trying to sound sympathetic.

The redhaired man named Ferenc looked up, his eyes watery, his nose swollen and pink. He took the beer and took a long swig. He wiped his mouth with the back of his hand. He shook his head.

"Thanks. I was thirsty."

"Don't feel bad, friend," the chimney sweep said. "Things will turn out for the best. Sell out and move on. That's my advice. I knew a peasant who lost everything, went to Székesfehérvár and met a rich German. He's doing well now, bottling soft drinks. Making a killing on orange soda. Things can only get better."

The man looked at him and shook his head.

"I'm sorry. What are you talking about?"

The chimney sweep was startled. He looked at the man again with raised eyebrows.

"Your fields. Isn't that your trouble?"

"My fields!" The man shouted it so that everyone in the pub stopped what they were doing and looked at them. "What's the matter with my fields? I just checked them a few days ago. Did you see something?"

The chimney sweep shrugged.

"I thought maybe with the lack of rain that your crops were in trouble."

The man shook his head.

"What are you talking about? I paid a lot of money for a new drip irrigation system. My fields are fine. I'm expecting a bumper crop. I've even worked it out with the mayor to get most of the produce sent off to Austria."

"Sunflower seeds?"

The man shook his head. "Beets."

"Beets?"

"I'm going to do the best I have in years. Sugar beets."

The chimney sweep reached over the table and snatched his beer back. "Give me that," he barked.

The peasant shouted and jumped up. His chair was already hoisted in his hands.

"No fighting in my pub, Ferenc," Ibolya said. "I'll throw you out."

She gave the command while she poured a drink. Her back was turned to them. The farmers looked at the chimney sweep. Some recognized him by his outfit right away. It took Ferenc a moment, but finally he recognized the chimney sweep as well and put the chair down. He walked away, but not before patting the chimney sweep on the shoulder and begging his pardon. He walked to the other side of the bar and sat down at a table with three rough-looking men. From time to time the men looked over at the chimney sweep. The chimney sweep, tired from a day of riding and cleaning, and wanting to get an early start in the morning, finished his beer as

125

quickly as he could and left. He didn't bother asking the bartender for a place to sleep. Instead, he found a spot further up the hill, at the potter's workshop. He walked over to the workshop and stuck his head in. The potter and his apprentice were working at their tables.

"Hello," the chimney sweep said as he entered. "I was wondering if you'd mind me sleeping out front there. I just rode in and thought I might sleep under the poplars."

The potter and his apprentice looked at him, recognized his outfit, and invited him in.

"Don't be ridiculous," the potter said. "You can sleep here. There's plenty of room."

"Thank you, no," said the chimney sweep. "It's warm out and I have bedding. I'll be fine outside. I just wanted to let you know. Perhaps I'll start a campfire. I wouldn't want you calling the police."

"Feel free. Feel free," said the potter.

The chimney sweep nodded and left.

The potter was smiling.

"That's a good sign," he said to his assistant. "An afternoon miracle. My boy, I think our luck is about to change."

The chimney sweep hid his bicycle underneath some brush by the side of the road and rested against a tree. He lit a campfire and spent the rest of the day and night dozing there. He was dreaming of his new life, of his country woman, of his pocketful of money.

Twelve

The next morning a riot of small children ran through the streets. As many dogs followed them and the ruckus was enough to pique the interest of the nesting herons that looked down lazily from their streetlamps with tilted heads. Diversions were rare for the young villagers, rarer even for the herons, and the chimney sweep's arrival was a huge diversion for them all. The birds cawed and beat the air with their wings, applauding an unfolding spectacle.

Earlier, the children had arrived at the chimney sweep's tree and surrounded him while he slept. They waited a good five minutes for him to wake up. They were patient for children. They caught their breath and picked their noses. They squatted around the sleeping man.

The chimney sweep's campfire had long gone out and the coals were cold. The children couldn't understand how he remained so still wrapped in that coarse blanket, a blanket that in their homes would have been a plaything for the dogs. But the chimney sweep was sleeping soundly in the cool morning. His breath was steady and deep. He didn't fidget or make faces. He slept with the audacity of the innocent. The children looked him over even more closely. He had a narrow face with black stubble growing from his cheeks. His forehead was large with recessed wrinkles. In the hollow of his left cheek was a scar, an indentation really, where an angry husband had belted him for pawing his wife. The chimney sweep was only as tall as a fourteen-year-old, and this emboldened them. Concluding that he was taking too long to rise for their liking, the children acted.

"Poke him with a stick."

"I can't find a good one."

"How about that one?"

"Can't you find anything bigger?"

"Look! Just use your fingers. Like this. Like this."

"That's disgusting. Look at all that hair. His nose probably has germs in it."

"He's dirty."

"He smells funny too."

They continued this prodding until the chimney sweep opened his eyes. He looked around, panicked for a moment, and then sat up and grimaced at them. He swatted at them. His neck was strained. His back ached. His eyes were crusted. He wanted a cup of coffee.

The children were clean and towheaded. Their own eyes were clear and their skin ruddy. Anyone would have commented on their chubby cheeks or bow-shaped mouths and would have instinctively sought to protect them from the world's vagaries. Nobody could have looked upon that gaggle of children without feeling hope for their country and collective future. Not a runny nose or wet bottom was among them.

"You fucking monsters! You're lucky I don't murder you. Don't you know you're supposed to let grown-ups sleep in peace? Get lost." He picked at his eyes, then inspected them. He spat at their feet.

"Hey! You can't talk like that. We're children," the eldest boy answered him.

"You're a bunch of filthy monkeys."

"Are we going to have luck now?" a little girl interrupted the argument to ask, and she was the cutest and most towheaded of the lot, the kind of little girl who could sell detergent to Scandinavians.

"Fuck no. Fuck off."

"But my papa broke his arm working on the station and hasn't worked a day all month. Now he's angry because Mama makes him sleep on the kitchen floor next to the doggie," she answered.

The chimney sweep laughed. "And what does your papa do about it?"

"He says he's gonna give her a punch in the face."

"Ha! Ha! Which house do you live in? Maybe I do have some luck for you. Maybe I'll clean your darling mama's chimney first. I have a pocketful of money I'm sure she'll take a shine to."

"I live in the cottage with the broken fence."

The chimney sweep shook his head and looked to a little boy.

"And what about your sweet mama?" the chimney sweep asked.

"His mother's a whore," the eldest boy answered.

"She is not! My mother's not a whore! Take it back."

"She is. Everybody knows it. My mother says it all the time."

The chimney sweep looked hopeful.

"Do you have a papa?" the chimney sweep asked, and put his hand on the boy's shoulder.

"No," the boy said.

"Is it your mother's house?" the chimney sweep asked, ever more hopefully, and put his other hand on the boy's other shoulder. He was ready to adopt.

The eldest boy laughed. "Ha! They let a room in a shack."

The chimney sweep pulled his hands away.

"Well your mother eats too much."

The conversation went on like this for a few minutes before the chimney sweep stood up and dusted the seat of his pants.

"Now listen to me, you little fucking turds. If you don't get away from me right this instant, I'm going to kick you. Beat it."

He pushed them aside and got on his bicycle to ride away. He didn't even bother to pack. The children surrounded him and ran beside him shouting as he began to pedal. The further along they traveled, the more other children came out and joined them. They mobbed him.

"This is hopeless," he said to them. "Why don't you be nice little children and go home now? I'll be at all your homes soon enough. Go on. Go on home."

"Hey!" one girl shouted at him. "My mother wants you to come to our cottage. Will you? Will you stop at my house first?"

"Fuck off. He can't. He'll be coming to my house first. He told me so under the tree. Right, chimney sweep? My mother baked biscuits and made crepes for him. Isn't that right? Tell them you're coming to my house first."

The chimney sweep sighed. Hoping to tire them out, he traversed the breadth of the village, starting from his tree, and then riding past the pub, through the centrum, onto the other side, and back again. He didn't answer them, didn't speak to them for the rest of the time on his bicycle. But the children were full of energy and ready to run to the continent's edge if they had to. They had no problem keeping at his side.

Some of them were probably too young to know what a chimney sweep was anyway. He figured, in the end, that it must have been the work of the wives. Yesterday's women must have been on their phones with half the village throughout the night.

Now the children were bounding alongside his bicycle, screaming joyfully, and the chimney sweep was having a harder time stifling his anger. He slyly kicked at the littlest ones, hoping that when they fell they would trip the others. With his front tire, he caught the heels of the bigger children in front of him and sent them sprawling, knocking down two or three others at a time. The children thought this a wonderful activity, but no sooner did he knock three down than five others took their places.

"Oh! Me next. Please. Please. Me next."

Meanwhile, the adults who heard the commotion came out into the street. As soon as they saw him they began clapping in unison.

"A damned parade," the chimney sweep said to a small dog caught under his wheel. "This is a first."

What he knew was that it had been three years since luck's last visit. Even the mayor—never one to miss an opportunity to show that he was a man of the people—left his official business and stepped out onto Market Street to wave and whistle when the chimney sweep rode past. The barber, the teachers, the young and old, they all stopped what they were doing and came out to see him, if only for a moment. They called out to him. They begged for just a glance in their direction.

"Look this way, chimney sweep. Over here. Over here."

The chimney sweep looked about. Women who had lined themselves up along the curb were batting their eyelashes and waving at him. He sized them up and put them into categories. He dismissed most of them outright. *Too desperate*, he thought to himself. He wanted tranquility.

"You're fanatics," he shouted at them, but they couldn't hear him over the screaming children. They laughed and nodded. They waved their hands and clapped. Disgusted, he turned his bicycle around and headed back toward the hill, back toward the pub. He pedaled hard, almost running over another unlucky mutt. He raced as fast as he could up the hill. His heart was pounding, but he managed to get away from the children, and when he made it to the pub, he hid his bicycle behind it and sneaked inside. He sat at the same corner table away from the entrance. It might have been early in the morning, but there were men all around. They nodded at him.

"To hell with that. I'll start tomorrow," the chimney sweep announced.

Ibolya was at her bar wiping away a pool of spilled beer. She'd heard about the visitor already. The potter's apprentice had told her. She'd expected he'd stop in for a drink, so she had even dressed for him. She wore her most flattering skirt. It was too short for most women her age, but most women lacked her confidence. Ibolya knew she looked great. She had even shaved.

She looked up at the small man summoning her from the corner. She nodded and approached him. He looked strange. He was petite. Not quite a dwarf, but petite. Typical for a chimney sweep. He drank from a half-empty pint of beer that he had found on the way in, and it took him both hands to hold it. He was wearing the requisite black leather blazer and his fingers were dirty from years of coal dust. Ibolya also noticed that he was staring at her breasts, but unlike her regulars he wasn't shy about letting her know it. She felt a buzz in her head and straightened her back. *Go ahead*, she thought. *Get a good look. Take it all in.* She stood as tall as she could in the sunlight that poured in through the gaping hole in the wall. He was sitting at Ferenc's table and she knew just where to step to use that morning light to its greatest effect. She would show him a thing or two.

"Hello," Ibolya said cheerfully as she petted the chimney sweep on the shoulder. She thought she saw a flash of anger on his face, but surely she was mistaken. She was certain that she was radiant.

"Another beer," the chimney sweep said gruffly. "Make it two. Make it snappy. Wait! I'm sorry. I mean, hello. How are you?"

Ibolya was taken aback. She almost felt deflated. This was certainly no ordinary chimney sweep. Most were only too happy to let a woman touch them, caress them . . . she had even known one who insisted that every woman who wanted to touch him sit on his lap to do so. She had even known women who agreed to it.

The chimney sweep shook his head. "A beer," he said again, louder.

Ibolya turned, taking care not to step out of the light that was on her legs, and went to get him a beer. She chuckled to herself as she brought it to him. She didn't care about the light this time. A chimney sweep with this disposition would be good entertainment indeed. If she could keep him in the bar long enough, somehow get the word out, business might pick up for the week.

She handed the beer to him, sat, and perked her chest out.

"Are you passing through on work?" she asked. "The chimneys here are in bad shape. I'm surprised there hasn't been a fire yet."

The chimney sweep nodded and eyed Ibolya's décolletage while he took a slurp of beer.

"You know, you could at least pretend not to look," she said. "You could behave decently."

"Ha!" the chimney sweep scoffed. "That's rich! Why would you want me to do that? You're presenting. I'm looking."

Ibolya shook her head.

"Perhaps. But I'm not a piece of meat."

"Married?"

Ibolya shifted. The chimney sweep was dangerous.

"No thanks. I've been in that shop. I'm not buying. You'll be working the village for a wife then? Thinking of settling down?"

Again, the chimney sweep nodded. Again, he looked straight at her. His eyes were red, and the skin underneath them drooped.

"I've already made twenty thousand forints. I arrived yesterday. I'm taking the day off." He motioned behind him. "Besides, too many damn children. They practically chased me in here."

Ibolya laughed. She was thinking of the money. She almost reconsidered the proposal. Almost.

"And the dogs," he continued. He was calming down now. He could even manage to give her his special grin. Ibolya didn't blink and responded with her own special grin. It was a stalemate. They shrugged and then laughed like old friends.

"Isn't there a vet in this village?" he asked. "It really is criminal the way the dogs run about. They're feral. Rabid, I'd say. What this village really needs is a dogcatcher."

Ibolya laughed and suddenly thought to touch him again. He allowed her. There was no subtle flinch. He didn't pull away too soon. She felt comforted.

"But the children are the worst. I really couldn't bear them. Frankly, miss, I'm just tired of being touched. Oh, no! Not you. Not now. I'd never mind a handsome woman like you touching me. I mean them. I'm tired of the begging. It is the part of the job that I always liked the least. The begging. It just seems like there's hopelessness in it. And I don't know if it's my age, but it just seems to have gotten worse these last five years. Everyone wants a winning lottery ticket. That's all I ever hear anymore. I swear, if I could, the only touches I'd give any of them would be with my foot on their backsides. I think it'd do them some good."

Ibolya couldn't stop laughing with this man. "You're the most interesting chimney sweep I've ever met. Why don't you find a new job, if you hate this one so much? Why not try something new?"

The chimney sweep shrugged but looked at Ibolya earnestly. "Funny you should mention that," he said. "Like you said, I am interested in settling down. Retiring, as it were. This seems like a nice enough place. Why, I could have a monopoly here, you know. Live my days out comfortably. No, I don't want any job but this one."

Ibolya shook her head.

"It's a tempting offer," she said. "We'd make a lot of money together. But my mind is set on someone else. I'm old enough now that I want a little romance."

The chimney sweep shrugged.

"And yet you're dressed like that?"

"It sells beer."

"Beer sells itself. You're an exhibitionist is what you are."

Ibolya considered this. She hadn't thought of it. She couldn't think of anything wrong with it either.

"Maybe," she said.

The chimney sweep shrugged and took a long draught.

"No one really appreciates us sweeps anymore," he said when he put the bottle down. "Only out here in the countryside. Banished to the villages. Can you imagine my job in a city? In Budapest? People there heat their flats with gas. Technicians come out in trucks with computers and electronic equipment. They are called heating and air specialists now. I'm a relic. A novelty. Useful only to the hopes of desperate country women and children. Things change, I guess. Wouldn't it be nice if they didn't? I think it'd be nice." The chimney sweep drank again. "You watch. Gazprom will rule the world. Hrmph. I hope they all die from carbon monoxide poisoning."

"Carbon monoxide?" Ibolya said.

The chimney sweep nodded and took a long drink of beer. Ibolya had an idea.

"Where are you staying?" she asked. "Stay with me. You can try again tomorrow. There is someone in our village I think you should meet. It sounds to me like all you need is the right woman. I know the perfect one. A spinster, mean as they come. She looks like a bear, but I have a feeling you'll have her eating out of your hand in no time. You'll also be doing me a huge favor."

"Yeah, I'd like that. I'm sleeping up on the hill under the poplar there. I'll get my stuff."

He looked out the window and spotted some children loitering out front. He shook his head.

"Later," he said. "Let me buy another beer."

Thirteen

If the potter thought it would be easy to continue avoiding either woman, he was wrong. He saw them both all too often. It was a small village, after all. There wasn't enough space for anyone to avoid anybody else. Sadly, there was no getting away from things. Everything had to be faced, and the happiest of citizens were those who faced their turmoils right away.

Some citizens, the younger generation especially, complained over this lack of privacy and the lack of opportunity. The notion of keeping their mouths shut and their hands to themselves didn't rest well. The young wanted to screw and talk about it. They wanted to be young. They didn't want to have to live with bumping into their indiscretions every day for the rest of their lives. So, quite often, those people of the younger generation left the village to live in bigger cities, and when they felt that even the country was too small for them, they left for abroad. Nothing was stopping them anymore; neither politics nor nationalism could hold them back. They fanned out across Europe. Fanned out across the world. They embraced the anonymity of globalism.

For the older generation, maybe they had felt the same way once, but they had never felt that tug to leave as strongly as their children. They were prisoners of history; certainly that was the biggest part of it. Mostly, however—and they understood this in their bones—they knew that to a certain extent, towns and villages with one thousand years of history can't maintain their longevity if everybody leaves.

Also, most of the elderly, having lived through the bloody dramas of the twentieth century, were only too happy to forget that a world existed beyond the tips of their noses. And if such a world did exist, it was best kept at arm's length. Who needed the troubles? A family could stay in a small village and raise its children in security. Zivatar was that kind of place. Isn't that the kind of place where their children would end up when they began raising their own families? Of course it was. Why bother leaving? While there might not have been enough irresponsible diversions for the young to partake of, there was more than enough work for everyone to do, and so what if the same souls walked by every day. That's what a community is: the same boring people telling the same boring stories. If a man was going to be happy or successful, then he had to learn early on to either face things as they came or to not care about them altogether.

Valeria's last words still rang in the potter's head. He thought of the sour feeling in his stomach when she had slammed her door in his face. Despite that clench in his gut that he walked around with, he still could not face his troubles. He could not act. He had not chosen. And he remained unsuccessful in his attempts at avoiding either woman.

Ibolya he couldn't help but see. Proximity had placed her on the same stretch of road, in the same vicinity. If he left for anything, he had to pass the hole in her tavern's wall, and if he passed the hole in the wall, he had to say hello.

"Yes, yes. So lovely to see you." He hurried past, waving and nearly crashing his bicycle. "I have to rush, though. I'm off to visit the mayor. Yes, yes. I'll visit you soon. You look very lovely today. Very lovely indeed."

He wanted to kick himself for saying those things. He had begun to agree with his apprentice that he was not helping his situation with flirtatious banter. He wondered if he really was merely keeping both women warm. Stringing them along until he could make a decision.

And if he fared poorly with Ibolya, he fared even worse with Valeria. They bumped into one another very soon after his last visit to her cottage. It was in the belly of the same market where they had first met. Valeria had gone back to her work inspecting stalls and was haranguing market vendors with a vengeance. If she appeared to have softened in the days immediately following her involvement with the potter, now she was harder than ever. Emotions were not necessarily spilling out of her, but alone at home she had begun to grow a little stir-crazy. The prospect of romance late in life had never occurred to her before the potter, but now it was all she could think about. Secretly, or not so secretly, Valeria really wanted a man to call on her. At first she really wanted the potter to call on her, but after a time, she started looking at other men in the village and she noticed that most of them were single again, cuckolded by death. She wondered if they were as lonely as she was. Valeria's involvement with the potter had changed her sufficiently to where she wondered why she had chosen to be so pugnacious, why she had never been just a tad more yielding. Not a doormat—certainly she could maintain her principles and values—but yielding. Softer and more approachable. Valeria thought about it, and the thought of growing old with someone beside her instead of alongside the few tired animals who were really her only friends seemed to make a certain kind of sense to her.

So Valeria did something different. She tried.

She started going on walks around her neighborhood. She started visiting the centrum and allowing herself the enjoyment of coffee and a tasty pastry. What did it matter? Why hadn't she done it before? She even smiled at people. Of course they never smiled back. Most figured she had gone crazy and walked hurriedly past her, but she smiled nonetheless.

I'm not getting any younger, she thought to herself, and smiled at an elderly man walking down the street. It was Mr. Toth, a retired archivist of church documents. Valeria imagined how nice it might be to have someone like that to converse with. Someone with a little culture. As he approached her, she smiled dumbly at him and even stopped walking. She thought she might ask him if he had ever discovered anything interesting in the old church records. She stood and smiled at him and let her body language convey interest. *Like when I was young*, she thought. She remembered how quickly young men would stop and talk. How it took very little effort on her part. Valeria perked up at the memory, but it did not work this time. Mr. Toth looked horrified. He crossed to the other side of the street. He sped up and kept looking back. She hadn't even had the chance to say hello.

It panged her, and she thought about the life she'd lived. The long, uneventful life she'd had. The quiet, long, and uneventful life she'd lived for sixty-eight years. It was a wonder she didn't break down and cry in her pastry later on that day.

"Well, no more of that," she said.

She resolved to chat with everyone she could. At first she was awkward and the conversations were stilted. She went to one of those new clothing boutiques and looked through a rack of new dresses. When she spotted a group of young women she grabbed a sweater and draped it across her chest. She approached them like that.

"Does this look too young for me?" she asked. "Do you think I could get away with wearing this?"

The girls looked at her and then at each other and shrugged. They left the shop very quickly afterward. Valeria sighed and went home. There were always chores to keep her busy. She hated to admit it, but even if the potter were to say he was done with her, Valeria would never be the same again. She felt like steam rising from the hot earth after an evening shower.

What she felt like, what she was, was a blocked teapot. Hence her hastened return to the market.

In her defense, the market had never been cleaner and the quality of goods had never been higher. The mayor even noticed, and when a new contingent of Asian businessmen came to visit—the fourth visit in six weeks—he brought them to the market on a tour. They walked around squeezing fruits and nodding their approval. They even marveled at the cleanliness of the ground. Everything had been swept and mopped. The businessmen sidled up to an attractive vendor. They all smiled at her. Within a minute, the mayor had arranged for her to begin selling starfruit and coconut milk.

"Don't know what they are or how to eat them, but if that cow over there can sell Costa Rican coffee, I'll sell your coconut milk as creamer."

The mayor was pleased. The Asians were pleased. Everyone was pleased. The mayor spotted Valeria and pulled the men to see her.

"Valeria, hello. I thought you might want to meet our guests."

Valeria looked at the mayor severely. Her opinion of him had not changed in any way, but she let the foreigners shake her hand. When they started speaking and gesticulating at the stalls, she waved them away.

"I don't understand what you're saying. Don't bother."

"I told them what a good job you do for us," the mayor joked. "I think we should start paying you."

"Bah," Valeria said, and walked away.

The mayor, embarrassed that she would walk away before they did, called out to her.

"The potter is making a fine statue for the front of the station, Valeria. You should see the models he has made. The figurines look just like you. It's astounding. They are true to life. You have inspired him. My wife kids him that you have become his muse."

Valeria stopped. She turned around and walked back. She wanted to hear more.

"We have to run now, though. No time to talk." The mayor turned and walked away, his guests beside him. "Thanks for a job well done, Valeria. I'm going to look into you receiving some kind of recompense."

They left Valeria wondering about the statue.

The curiosity gnawed at her. It followed her around the market for a few days and would not let up. She stopped often to consider the mayor's words. A muse. She put her hand to her throat, caught herself and let it drop to her side. *He must want a companion also*, she thought. She tugged her keys. She thrilled at the thought of it. She felt special, powerful even. Then she saw the potter. She looked up from one of her reveries to see him standing in the very same spot where she had noticed him the first time. He was buying another bag of mushrooms, snapping the heads off with those strong tapering fingers of his. The wind escaped her in a breathy sigh. She walked to him. She was ready to forgive him. She smiled. He spotted her and smiled back.

"Hello, my dear. How are you?" he said, and reached his hand out to touch her.

"I'm well," she said in a low voice. She reached out and touched him back. They pecked each other on the cheeks and smiled nervously. Business stopped in their aisle and the aisles adjacent to theirs. Vendors and customers hushed and pointed. Valeria and the potter smiled nervously.

"Get her out of here, potter," a voice called out. "She's driving us crazy."

There was a laugh.

"Look out. Ibolya's going to get you," someone else shouted.

Valeria ignored them. The potter looked sheepish.

"I spoke with the mayor," she said. "He says your statue is coming along nicely."

The potter fidgeted. He cleared his throat. He looked around as though he hoped the mayor might appear.

"Is the mayor here? Wonderful! I must speak with him at once. I can't talk now, my dear. I'll bring the vases to you soon, though. It's so good to see you. You look lovely. Lovely, indeed."

He walked away. He left his bag of mushrooms. He left her standing there. She was fuming. The women around her snickered.

"You should wash your face," one of them said, shaking a bottle of cream in her hand. "You can't keep a man without a clean face. I promise. Why not try it? It's never too late. He's still interested. I can tell."

Valeria shrugged and bought the cold cream. She left the market early and returned to her cottage. A sigh of relief followed her out of the market.

The potter's latest piece *was* a figurine of a woman, a miniature of what he intended for the station. He had taken the model to the mayor's home and presented it as a gift to the mayor's wife. The pair welcomed him in. They were entertaining the Asian businessmen and had invited him as an honored guest.

They introduced him as a local folk artist. The potter didn't quite know how to act, so he took on an air of sophistication, or of what he thought was sophistication. He stroked his moustache. He nodded and smiled. The mayor's wife cooed over him and showed their guests her collection of his work. The businessmen oohed and aahed. They spoke and nodded. They all agreed to visit his workshop the next day, and then when they did, as the mayor's wife had promised, she insisted that they take something for their wives and paramours back in Korea. The six Koreans bought stacks of plates and every small ceramic figurine he had. It was nothing short of a windfall. When the potter's apprentice came in and saw the smiling potter and the empty shelves, before he could say anything the potter was embracing him.

"It was that chimney sweep what brought us this luck," he told his apprentice. "The mayor's wife advised me to double my price for those businessmen. We've made five months' worth of sales! This has been the most successful day of my career."

The potter was happier than his apprentice could have imagined, and it had to do with more than good sales. He was also glad to have presented the mayor's wife with his final figurine, the figurine that would be the statue in front of the station. He was glad because in every new figurine he had made, he had perfected different things. In that last model, he had finally figured out how to represent fabric in clay. He had created a perfectly pleated skirt and the crease of a blouse. He had learned how to add depth. He had really moved beyond throwing clay. He was, in fact, sculpting, and using the tools he had always used. Like Prometheus, his forms carried a spark of life in them, and this was something entirely new to him. He was imprinting himself into his work. He was imprinting his feelings and experiences into everything he touched. His fingers moved around the clay. He formed and defined the lumps into meaning. He wasn't a village potter anymore. He was an artist. In the mayor's wife and soon the entire town, he would even have an audience.

The figurine was that of a woman. A country woman. He had painted it. The figure was standing in the wind. Her dress pressed against her legs like gauze and fluttered behind her. Her blouse tugged at her bosom. She wore a kerchief over her head, and even that looked like it was flapping away, trying to lift off. She was carrying a milk container and a bicycle rested at her feet. If an inanimate object could be filled with longing, this figurine of a lone woman elicited that feeling of longing and desire. Indeed, it would make a perfect statue for a train station. It was the look of a lover waiting upon the return of her beloved.

"How romantic," the mayor's wife cooed, and kissed his cheek. "You're so romantic."

"I beg your pardon, miss?" the potter asked.

The mayor's wife looked to her husband.

"Why can't you be more like this?" she said. She explained the figurine to the Koreans. "It's to be a statue of his lady friend. A nice woman here in the village. The one who works in the market."

The men nodded and pointed. "Your girlfriend?" one of the businessmen said.

The potter shook his head to protest, but then he saw the figurine and the blood left his face. The same potato shape. The same knotty legs. He hadn't noticed it or seen it until it was pointed out.

"I told you," the mayor's wife said to the mayor. "She is his muse."

The mayor was chewing a cigar, but he stopped and regarded the piece. He held it in his hand and examined it. He made an appreciative grunt and patted the potter on his shoulder.

"Good stuff, potter. This will look great. Maybe we'll make it a fountain. Water can pour out of that container there. I like it much better than a soldier or a poet. The country is full of statues like that. But a simple country woman. I like it. It's different. It's quaint. Shows we have values. Maybe we could put it in the city's brochure and lure visitors in. Or maybe we could use it as a center-piece for a festival of some kind. A flower festival or something.

145

A mayor friend of mine did something similar in his town. He says tourism's up twenty percent in August alone, and he doesn't even have a fountain!"

The potter fidgeted.

"A fountain is a wonderful idea," the mayor's wife said, ignoring her husband. She winked at the potter. "With or without a festival. Valeria will be so proud of you. What started out as a figurine became a sculpture and is now finally a fountain!"

"Yeah, potter. Congratulations," the mayor said.

There was something hollow about how he said it that caused his wife to frown and put a friendly hand on the potter's shoulder.

"Don't mind him," she said. "It's still your train station, dear. It's still your flower festival."

"I think a flower festival is exactly what we need during the summer. We can say it's the oldest in the country. Who'll know the difference? Maybe we'll get a couple of folk dancers to twirl around. Maybe we can sell out the hotel."

The mayor explained everything to the Korean businessmen. They nodded and smiled.

"We have many festivals in our country," one of them said, and smiled at the potter. "They are happy occasions."

The potter smiled back and nodded. He tried to take the piece away from the mayor.

"Maybe it's not right," he said. "Maybe I need to work on it some more."

The mayor handed him a cigar.

"Don't be silly, potter. It's only a statue, and it's going to look great in front of my station. You're done. I'll call the foundry in the morning. We'll start making a cast right away, to your specifications, of course. Good work, old-timer."

The Koreans nodded their approval.

"It is great work of art," one of them said. "As gift, we will send peonies to place at her feet for new festival. A gift to your village from ours. A gift to our new friends."

The mayor bowed.

The mayor's wife put her hand to her cheek.

"I'm afraid I must go now," the potter said.

His usefulness over, the mayor escorted him to the door and shook his hand firmly.

"Congratulations, potter," he said, and winked. Then he whispered, "I can see that we're cut from the same cloth. I can respect that. You and me will live as long as that building is standing. You should go and let your women know. Show them that a man who's not afraid to get a little blood on his dick can accomplish anything. This town should stay in the Middle Ages because a Dutch environmentalist wants a bird to lay an egg? No, no, no. This is a new day, potter. It's a new day and a new era, and just like you, I'm changing my part of the world. This is the West now, or it will be very soon. Hop on board or get out of the way, because we're not slowing down. Never again. That's my motto."

The potter shrugged. He was unsure of what to make of all this, but he was disturbed that the mayor saw him as a kindred spirit. "You think I'm changing my part of the world?"

"Aren't you?"

The potter shrugged again. "I'm an old man. I'm not sure I am who you think I am."

"Don't be ridiculous. Of course you are. If you weren't, then you'd be happy making plates and nothing more. That's not enough for you, though, is it? This town will be better off because of you. You mark my words. In fact, it needs more men like you. Men who aren't afraid to admit they're ambitious, who aren't afraid of progress. Men who know what they want and how to go after it —whether it's train stations, hotels, fountains, or women. The point is that this country needs men who aren't afraid to grab, potter. That's the only way other men know to take you seriously and treat you with respect. Absolutely."

The potter was silent. He felt convinced that he wasn't that type of man. He nodded at the mayor and the two shook hands again. He left.

"Have a good night," the mayor called after him. "You old scoundrel."

Fourteen

Ibolya helped the chimney sweep prepare for his day. She made him coffee and even brought him toast. She wanted him to feel strong enough to carry out her plans. The chimney sweep would be her salvation. She felt that her problems with the mayor and Valeria would be taken care of in a single stroke.

It took three cups of coffee to get him started, but once he was ready, he smirked once, nodded at her, and then left the tavern toward the centrum again. This time when the children approached —not one bit warily—the chimney sweep gritted his teeth and allowed them to pet him. It was uncanny how quickly they surrounded him, a knee-high ambush of sorts, and better coordinated than any military unit. The children were that thorough. In fact, it was more like they were escorting him, more like he was their prisoner than anything else. When he reached the centrum, the mayor stepped out of his building and beckoned to him—or was it to the children? Either way, he was soon parked in front of city hall.

"Good day, chimney sweep," the mayor said. "I'm glad to see that you have returned. We were worried that we'd lost you."

"No, no, I was just getting the lay of the land," the chimney sweep answered.

"Well, as mayor, I'd be honored if you would work on my chimney first. If you don't mind, of course."

"I don't care whose I clean first," the chimney sweep said. "It's all the same price."

The mayor laughed. "Certainly, certainly. I like a man who gets to the point."

"Ten thousand forints."

The mayor balked.

"How much?"

"Ten thousand. I have a special technique, use some special solutions."

"What kind of solutions?"

"German. The stuff I have cuts through grime and ash much quicker than the old socialist stuff we used to use. It's better for the environment too."

The mayor looked at him skeptically.

"Well, while that may be true, chimney sweep, ten thousand forints is a lot of money. Are you sure it's not a little steep?"

The chimney sweep shook his head.

"It's a new day, mayor. Only the finest German engineering could have come up with this cleanser. Strong enough for industry but safe in the home. If she were still alive I would use it in my own dear nana's chimney."

The chimney sweep had spent the night practicing his lines with Ibolya. She had told him exactly what to say.

The mayor nodded his head. It was clear that he liked what he was hearing.

"Well," the mayor said, "you know your business, and the village of Zivatar is a forward-looking one. If ten thousand is what it costs, ten thousand is what I'll pay."

"Very good, mayor. Lead the way."

"Oh, I prefer to drive us. My car is just right here."

The chimney sweep followed the mayor to his car. There was no rack on it.

"What about my bicycle?"

"Don't worry," the mayor said. "We'll put it in the trunk. Tell me, have you ever ridden in a Mercedes?"

The chimney sweep shook his head.

"Oh, well, you're in for a treat. Nothing like those old Trabants. This is state-of-the-art. Just like that solution of yours. What did you say earlier? German engineering? That was funny. I liked that. Well this is the same, but better. Go ahead, get in."

The chimney sweep opened the door and sat in the mayor's car. It was nicer than his mother's rest home.

"Do we have far to go?" the chimney sweep asked, looking around him.

"No, not at all. About half a kilometer. I just prefer to drive. I don't like weather."

Children and women followed the car as it pulled off but were soon left in a cloud of diesel. The village's men didn't move, however. They stood in front of city hall muttering under their breaths.

"Ten thousand forints, my ass," one man said. "I can't believe he's going to pay that twerp so much money."

"German solution, can you believe it?"

"What cheek."

"Sometimes the mayor is an idiot."

"A real fathead."

"A show-off."

"He's not cleaning my chimney, the little thief."

"I don't know. My wife isn't going to let him leave without cleaning ours. I can hear the whining already. That's going to break me for the rest of the month."

The mayor called his wife from a cell phone to let her know

they were coming. When he hung up, he handed it to the chimney sweep.

"Have you seen one of these yet? They'll be all the rage pretty soon. You won't have to wait for months for the phone company anymore. You'll be able to walk into a shop and walk out with one of these in a matter of minutes. I'm going to get them to put up a second tower soon."

The chimney sweep looked at the phone and shrugged.

"It looks like army issue."

"This? No. It's made for the public. They'll get smaller."

"Who would call me?"

The mayor laughed. "Customers. Why, you could get yourself a van, paint your phone number on the side, and people would call you when they wanted your service."

The chimney sweep looked closely at the mayor to see if he was joking.

"Why in the hell would I want anybody to do that?" he shrieked.

"Well, to make money. I thought you were a forward-thinking man!"

"I get along as it is. Besides, people would be calling me at all hours. I'd never get any rest. No, mayor. Business is fine just the way it is."

"Come, come. You're already using Western products to clean your chimneys. Why not use Western management techniques? Much more efficient. You could get more work in every day."

"Why would I want more work?"

"To maximize your profits. You could easily add three more customers in a day. I'm sure of it. If you were efficient."

The chimney sweep laughed.

"You talk like a capitalist."

"Well that's what I am. A capitalist. And if you're in business for yourself that's what you should be too."

"Bah," said the chimney sweep. "Not me. I'm fine the way I am. In fact, I miss the old days. I knew what was what. I knew what to expect. Things were safer for all of us. I'm afraid of getting old now, you know. I'm afraid of it. Who can afford it? The old days were good for us. The state took care of us well enough. Socialism worked."

"What's this?" the mayor said, shaking his head. "Listen, I understand where you're coming from. I was in the party myself. Maybe things seem harder, but you're free to make money now. As much as you can. You're free to do that. Nothing's stopping you. I know it's especially hard on you old-timers. I understand that. But try to think of the future. Think of your suffering as patriotism, as your patriotic duty to the country. I was just telling this to another man of your generation. Really. The country needs men who are willing to grab what they want."

The chimney sweep tried not to laugh. It was the same story in nearly every village in the countryside. Modern men were pulling their villages kicking and screaming into the capitalist world, and they didn't give a damn how many old ladies were left begging in front of the markets. It didn't matter one bit to these men that a generation of people—his generation—was left to fend for themselves in a world that didn't value them and that they didn't understand. The chimney sweep was thankful he was on this mission for Ibolya. Just once, he had always thought, just once he would have liked to be the agent of one of these powerful men's suffering. Just once, he thought to himself, he would like to eat a rich man for dinner and then shit him out while reading the paper. What a switch that would be.

"I hear you are almost finished with a train station?" he asked.

"You heard that?" the mayor answered proudly. "Wonderful. Yes, just one car for starters. We're calling it the Inter-Bitty. Cute, huh? Ride the little bitty Inter-Bitty! You watch. It's going to change this town forever. Maybe you could ride your bicycle around it and let us take pictures." The mayor winked at him. "For luck. It'd be a great photo opportunity. We're going to have a flower festival."

The mayor's home, a newly constructed stucco ranch, was not too far from Valeria's cottage. The house was landscaped and decorated in the American style. There were box shrubs along a sidewalk, a low picket fence, and potted ornamental trees that needed to be brought in during the winter. There was also a lawn, the only lawn in the village. It had been fertilized, was freshly cut, and resting atop it was a brick path cutting it in half from the gate to the front door.

At the door of this house was a young woman. The mayor's wife was waiting with a silver platter of cookies and gin and tonics. When the chimney sweep saw her in her short skirt, with her thin strand of pearls and her blouse unbuttoned to her sternum, he immediately bounded up the brick path, leaving the mayor behind, and began pawing the young woman's hips.

"For luck, my dear," he insisted. "For luck."

"Oh!" She blushed, patting him on his shoulders. "Well, it must be my lucky day."

The chimney sweep moved his hands from her hips to her shoulders. He squeezed them.

"I'd say it's your lucky year! Or mine. But you're the spitting image of my poor dead fiancée! She used to sit on my lap and let me comb her hair. God, how I loved her."

The mayor's wife laughed nervously. The mayor grabbed a drink. The chimney sweep reached for a cookie. He entered their house, sat down, and was offered a tumbler. He drank from it, and the mayor's wife sat beside him. He rested his hand on her naked knee for good measure. A few moments of awkward silence passed between them, and then the mayor motioned to the chimney.

"Well, the chimney is right over there. But I guess you can see that. Let's see this German solution of yours, though, shall we?"

"You're going to watch me work?" The chimney sweep looked pained. He looked at the mayor's wife and shook his head.

The mayor's wife looked at the mayor and shook her head.

"It's bad luck," the chimney sweep whispered to her.

"It's bad luck," she said to the mayor. "Go back to the office and let him work."

The mayor hesitated.

The chimney sweep had risen and walked over to the chimney. He was inspecting it.

The mayor looked at the chimney sweep. He had his head in the hearth and was looking up the flue. He sneezed.

"You've got a messy one here," he said.

The mayor nodded and pecked his wife on the cheek.

"Very well," he said. "Here's some money. Call me when he's finished. I hope it's not too messy for you."

The chimney sweep muttered something in return. He pulled out a spray bottle Ibolya had given him. He had prepared a solution of soapy water and vinegar at Ibolya's tavern. He climbed out of the hearth and shook it. He shook it for the mayor to see.

"Here she is," he said. "German ingenuity. Cuts through gunk in a flash. I'll just spray a little and let it set."

He sprayed the soapy water up into the flue.

The mayor hurried to the door.

"Thanks again, chimney sweep," he called out. "I hope you enjoy your visit to our town. Think about what I said. More forints in your pocket."

"Thank you. I think I will."

After the mayor left, the chimney sweep finished the job rather quickly. The flue wasn't dirty at all. The mayor used gas. There

155

were tanks outside the house. The couple only burned wood when they were feeling romantic.

"Bastards," he muttered.

The mayor's wife hovered beside him while he collected his things.

"Tell me," he asked. "That pub on the outskirts, do you visit it often?"

"That eyesore!" she answered. "Only sometimes. We buy drinks there when we return from our trips abroad."

"Funny," he answered. "That woman there said you were the loveliest girl in the village and that it was a terrible shame your husband was such a scoundrel."

The young woman smiled at him but knitted her eyebrows.

"I don't like to get involved in things like this, but she said you were very kind and she asked me to mention to you that you should pay your husband a visit in his office next Tuesday. Early in the day. Eleven A.M., if you can."

"She did? Why would she say that? Who does she think she is?"

The chimney sweep shrugged. "I don't know, miss. She just said that you should do it, that she would come and tell you herself, but she knows how the mayor would feel about the two of you talking together. It's none of my business. I'm just delivering the message."

The young woman nodded. She bit her lip.

"Of course, of course."

"She said to tell you that you can talk to her whenever you need to. She said to tell you that she knows about the trials of married life. The unrewarded sacrifices. She said that she knows how hard it is to have to deal with the other woman. I think that's what she said. I can't remember now. Next Tuesday, your husband's office, only don't tell him. Heavens no. Surprise him."

"What? What are you talking about?"

156

The chimney sweep shrugged. "I don't know, miss. I just arrived here, and the woman in the bar—she's nice enough, miss—the woman in the bar said that if I should meet you today, I should just give you that message and beg you not to mention it to the mayor."

He put his arm on her hip again and kissed her cheek. She wasn't paying attention to him and didn't push him off. She was lost in thought. "Ah," he sighed. "But you're the spitting image of my poor dead fiancée. If luck is mine to give, miss, I give you all the luck I can muster. May you have a long life full of happiness and cheer, and not a life like my poor dead fiancée. The most beautiful girl I'd ever known. Oh, how she smiled when I brought her oranges!"

The young woman looked at him.

"I like oranges."

The chimney sweep put his other hand on her hip and shook his head. He pulled her closer.

"No! That's just too much. Stop, stop." He sobbed. "You mustn't speak. You mustn't tempt me. I'm no priest. I'm a terrible man."

The mayor's wife pulled him to her breast. "Oh! You mustn't do that. There, there, she's in a better place. Believe me."

He stared down her open blouse. He sniffled. *What a woman*, he thought. He pulled away.

"You're right, and now I must go." He motioned his head at the commotion outside. "Don't forget about your appointment, though. Everything will be much clearer."

Women were clamoring outside the mayor's home. They had lined up there to take turns with the chimney sweep. He left the bewildered mayor's wife where she was and stepped out the door unaccompanied, invincible. People in the crowd surrounded him, pawed him, caressed the lapels of his leather blazer, and begged him to follow them home next. He pushed them aside angrily, stepped over the ones who had fallen to the ground, and walked into the very next house on the lane. He intended to work his way down the road, from street to street.

In every home women begged him to sit down and make himself comfortable. They brought him warm biscuits and sweets they had only moments before pulled from their ovens. The chimney sweep ate as much as he could, and when he'd had his fill, he took handfuls of food—crepes, biscuits—and crammed them into his bag. Dim-witted husbands allowed this, knowing that they were being eaten out of their homes but hoping just the same that the small sacrifice would prove to their wives that they were good sports. These men suffered quietly but remembered every last detail of the abrupt and smelly little man drinking their liquor. They fantasized about throwing him against walls and through panes of glass.

In the chimney sweep's defense, the women were proud of their biscuits, and they insisted he try them. Each claimed that she had a special family recipe, different from any other, and that he would never find another biscuit like it in the entire country. They were as individual as snowflakes.

"Bah," he said with a wink. "I've heard the same said by too many women, too many times before." Still, he drank the shots of brandy they had poured and tossed the biscuits into his mouth before grimacing and saying, "I've had better."

Then began his complaints. The biscuits were either too salty or too sweet. They may have been fresh, but they tasted moldy, and he would gag purposely until they poured him another drink to wash it down with. If the biscuits had cheese baked on top of them, then he would exclaim it was rancid.

"Are you trying to poison me? This isn't fit for a sow!"

The women grinned diffidently and caressed his shoulders as he railed against them. They didn't mind the soot on their sofas or even the insults. Wiser women in the crowd outside reasoned, "Good fortune so rarely comes walking in your door, who cares if it's wearing dirty shoes?"

After each repast, the chimney sweep created a din on his way to their hearths. Purposely he'd let his extended chimney brush knock over vases or paintings. He'd lost count of the number of urns he'd caused to shatter against the floor. All the while, husbands and wives humored him as he maliciously destroyed their property.

"Idiots," he'd swear to himself.

Once in the chimney, he would kick and cough as loudly as he was able. He'd curse, whistle, break wind—do anything he could to show his contempt. The wives couldn't get enough. They were beside themselves. Husbands also would laugh good-naturedly and break wind in approval. Houses became soot-laden methane traps. Slivers of unswept glass threatened bare feet.

He made a fortune. Ten thousand forints from each home, and he was carried from one house to the next. He was celebrated like a Caesar, passed around the village like communion. But the more the villagers rushed to greet him and the higher in esteem they held him, the more violent he became. In one home he blatantly broke a window, only to have the owners burst into tears of joy—for not only had they touched him, but they had also seen him and a broken pane of glass, good luck for years to come, no doubt. They were only too happy to slip him extra forints for his trouble.

And all Ibolya had really said to him the evening before was, "The key to this village is to treat all of its sons and daughters with contempt. I promise that they will love you for it."

The chimney sweep was lining his pockets with their love.

Fifteen

It was at the moment when the chimney sweep broke a ceramic vase when Valeria caught her first look at him. She thought she heard a crash of glass and rushed outside to make sure it was not something of hers. She immediately noticed his scowl. She saw the furrowed lines on his forehead, so much like her own, and the twisted mouth frozen in a grimace somewhere between anger and pain. The disgust for the villagers he wore on his face was palpable. The smell of him wafted over to her. She breathed it in greedily.

Valeria had been feeling restless. She had stayed in or around her home for the last couple of days. She was confused, still reeling from what the mayor had told her but furious over the way the potter had left her standing in front of the mushroom vendors. She could choke him for that. It was mortifying. She had stopped her morning trips to the market altogether. Partly because she was waiting for an apology from the potter, and she thought that if she went to the market she might miss him if he came by her home. Partly, also, because even on the walks through the village she had kept at, women in the salons were trying to sell her bath products she really had no use for. Valeria hadn't reached the point where she felt compelled to protect her looks the way other women in the village might have.

She had broken down at the market and bought the cold cream, but she still hadn't used it. She decided that she had only purchased the item to save face from being left standing alone.

"It's just cold cream, Valeria." The women shook their heads at her. "It will clean your face. The potter might like you better with a clean face. We hear he hasn't come around in a while."

"I clean my face every morning with soap," Valeria snapped. "Or haven't you heard that?"

"No, we hadn't," the women responded dryly. "This cleans deeper, though. It might help those large pores on your nose. Try it."

"Is that what it did for you?" Valeria responded. "Couldn't I just scrub my face?"

"Valeria, you're hopeless."

Valeria generally had no use for perfumes or sweet-smelling soaps; her face was severe from toil. She was proud of it. She didn't own tweezers or a razor. It was all proof of her character, she thought. Why diminish character with a dab of lipstick or a swipe of rouge?

Makeup was a weakness, in Valeria's mind, and she disdained weakness. In fact, it was a thing she could say she truly despised: vanity. Will, on the other hand, was what mattered most. Will and the steely nerve to survive. To persevere. Valeria willed her life; she willed her survival. For sixty-eight years she had willed herself an existence and had not once hoped for luck or circumstance. Certainly not since she had been a young girl.

Valeria's first love had been her grandfather. She spent as much of the day as she could chasing after his heels, batting her eyelashes at him until he picked her up, and hiding his pipe tobacco until he tickled her into giving it back.

"Will you marry me?" she asked him.

"Darling, I won't live that long," the old man laughed. "Besides, I'm your grandfather. You'll find a husband soon enough."

Valeria hugged her grandfather's neck. She decided that she wanted a man with a moustache and a barrel chest.

When Valeria was two, her father had died of a heart attack beside a haystack. He was pitching hay for the sheep. Valeria didn't have much use for the women of the household. Her mother had also died, of consumption, and all Valeria really remembered of her early childhood was a sick woman she wasn't allowed to be near. That was her grandmother's rule. Valeria hated her grandmother. She never understood why her grandfather would seem so happy about going to sleep with her. Valeria thought her grandmother was ugly. She had a big red nose. She always wore black. A black kerchief was always wrapped around the woman's head. Her grandmother never smiled, never sang, never whistled. She never really said anything to Valeria, unless it was a harsh command. No, Valeria did not like her grandmother, and she was insanely jealous that her grandfather did. In fact, when Valeria found the old woman hanging by her neck in the pantry she waited a whole five minutes before she ran for help.

Her grandmother's face was blue-black. A purple tongue hung heavily from her mouth. Blood seeped at the corners. Her eyes were glassy. Valeria was reminded of a dead sheep she had seen. She was seven. After the five minutes had passed, she ran into the field looking for her grandfather. She found him feeding salt to the sheep.

"Nagy is dead."

Her grandfather looked at her.

"What's that?"

"Nagy is dead. She's hanging in the pantry."

Her grandfather, a normally boisterous man, cried for a week. Valeria hated her grandmother even more after that. She tried to console her grandfather. She put her arms around him and kissed his neck.

"It's all right, Grandfather. I still love you. You can sleep with me if you want."

The year was 1939. Her grandfather would die ten years later. Valeria was alone after that. She had to be strong to survive.

In fairness to the villagers, being consumed by will had made Valeria caustic and dour, even toward strangers like the mailman, who, when he came on his weekly visit, after riding his bicycle for kilometers, she refused a drink of water—going so far as to snipe at him on a hot summer day when he begged for something to quench his thirst.

"Hard living gives life flavor. You should embrace your suffering."

And she meant it.

An appreciation for hard work and attention to details were what had determined the success of her garden. They were what made her garden the best looking and most bountiful in the village. They were what made her pigs the plumpest. Weeds didn't pull themselves. Luck and circumstances have nothing to do with success. So when the village children screamed, "Look, a chimney sweep!" at her from the other side of the fence and pointed at the short man who was mobbed and unable to move, Valeria's initial response to the children was, "My chimney is just fine. I cleaned it out myself with a rag tied to the end of a broomstick."

"But he's lucky," the children squealed.

"Pig shit," she muttered to herself. If the chimney sweep brought feast or famine, it was all the same to her. She would survive.

But there was something about this particular man. There was something in the way the chimney sweep shoved those same children aside when they dove in front of him that made Valeria tug her keys. She suddenly found herself skipping into her foyer, where she looked herself over in a small mirror on the wall. There was something fiery in the small man that the potter seemed to lack. There was a will there. A purpose.

"I wonder what that potter is waiting for?" Valeria asked herself, thinking of his white moustache. "We're not getting any younger."

Then she shrugged him out of her mind. She wrote the potter off, right there in her foyer. *His loss*, she thought to herself. She was a live wire. Alive and wanting to feel things while she was still able. She straightened her housedress, brushed wisps of silver hair out of her eyes, and pinched the cheeks on her plumpish face before returning to her front door. She opened it and stepped outside. She saw the desperate need for escape on the chimney sweep's face now. He'd been surrounded and couldn't break free, though he was valiantly trying. Valeria shouted out in her harshest voice, the one she often used on the children and the cow, "Chimney sweep!"

The crowd that was smothering him parted at the gruffness of her voice. The chimney sweep, seeing his chance, darted to her gate. A mangy dog bounced wildly in front of him, and he kicked. It yelped, and Valeria's heart raced. She opened the gate for him while shooing away the children nipping at his legs.

He snickered at the sadness that clouded their young faces and was tempted to spit. He looked at Valeria instead. She was pasty, old, and severe, but she had the reddest cheeks he had ever seen. They were beet red, blood red—a red as deep and terrifying as lights at a train crossing on a frozen night. He was awestruck.

Here, in this miserable village, in the middle of nowhere, was the angriest and most beautiful woman he had ever seen. This was the woman Ibolya had told him about the night before—"The spinster. The old maid. The priggish fuddy-duddy." He recognized her right away. She was in front of him, a train wreck waiting to happen—a spiteful, willful locomotive intent on crushing any cherub in its path. Here was a woman he could want. Here was everything he was not, and as an added bonus, here at last was his woman of means. He took in her yard and home. Then he looked into Valeria's stern face and was pulled into its sway. He was excited to have found her. He had the presence of mind to grin, though. He grinned for all he was worth.

"I have work for you." She bit her words. "And if you break my window, you'll pay for it, or I'll call the police."

They entered her house. The villagers pleaded with him not to go inside. "She's a mean old woman!" they cried. "She doesn't believe in you." But the couple quickly disappeared. Once inside, the chimney sweep stood, grinning, waiting for his drinks and morsels.

"Well?" she questioned. "What are you standing around with that stupid smile on your face for? I have no food for you, you scoundrel! I'm sure you've eaten enough today, and how you're still standing after a liter of brandy I don't know, but I'm sure it means you're no good! The chimney is over there. And careful where you step."

He regarded her for a moment, stared into her eyes. She still hadn't pet him. She hadn't brushed against him. Their fingers hadn't even touched. She was wholly unresponsive to his smile. She returned his regard with an icy and unblinking composure. He smiled broader then and nodded at her. He tiptoed to her fireplace and did the best job he had ever done in his life. Quieter than a beetle, he scrubbed the walls of her chimney without so much as a sneeze. It was an easy job. The hearth was already clean. He knew that Ibolya's guidance would be right in this matter.

"Her bluster is bluff," she had said. "Do the most thorough job you can and stay the course. You'll see. You'll find yourself signing your name to her bloomers in no time. You want to settle down? You want a wife? This woman has wife written all over her. She's dying for it. Hera incarnate, she is. I guarantee you'll practically be married that night."

The villagers outside listened for the breaking of glass or banging of walls, but they were disappointed to hear nothing. Minutes became hours, and the sun began to set, yet no one moved. They didn't know whether to break the door down or run for the police. When the sun finally disappeared, the crowd outside Valeria's home disbanded.

"I thought she was crazy over the potter," one woman said to her friends as they walked away.

"I think she's just crazy."

"Well, someone should tell the potter."

"The poor man."

"Well, I guess Ibolya's won him."

"What do you think she's doing with the chimney sweep?"

"What do you think she's doing?"

"It's hard to imagine."

"Still, she must know a trick or two. He's been in there over three hours."

"Do old ladies work the same as young ones?"

They did not realize that hours were nothing now that the pair had met. What is an hour? Seven days would pass, 168 hours, and the villagers would not see the pair emerge from Valeria's home, nor even a shadow in her window. They would not see a single lace curtain move.

A group of concerned women did go to the potter's workshop. His door was closed as well—and locked. He wasn't letting anyone in. Not even his own apprentice.

"I'm busy," he shouted angrily when the women rapped against his windows.

"But—"

"I said I'm busy."

Furthermore, for the record, it had become quite an unlucky period in the village. An early hot spell from the south had stalled over the fields, and most everyone's crops became infested with caterpillars. At the school, a lice epidemic broke out, causing children of the hamlet to scratch at their scalps and pick nits out of each other's hair. For seven long and muggy days there was nothing but the sound of caterpillars devouring crops and people scratching their heads. The following Tuesday, the mayor's wife caught her husband in an amorous embrace with her favorite hairdresser. She threw a hair clip at them and told him he would have to move into the newly constructed hotel in the centrum.

Finally, after a week had passed, with votives in hand, the villagers held a vigil outside Valeria's door and begged the chimney sweep to leave. They began to shout and throw chestnuts against the walls of her home. Still, there was nothing but silence. Some of the more daring villagers opened the gate and put their ears to Valeria's door. They claimed that they could hear her moaning.

"Like a bear waking up at springtime!"

Three more days passed before they saw a sign of life. Ten days! On the tenth day, the heat finally broke. That evening, with shouting and cursing from the crowd, the light under Valeria's portico turned on. For the first time in ten days, the villagers' shaven heads felt cool under the starry sky. Someone heard stirring within the house, and the crowd outside Valeria's window became silent, breathless.

The door opened, and light from inside burst into the night. Valeria emerged. She floated in front of them. Her silver hair was loose and flowing down her back, her blouse was falling off her shoulders, and her brassiere was clearly visible. Her flaccid, pink breasts were bruised and on fire; she had what appeared to be bite marks on her shoulders. Most shocking of all, however, was the faint smile dancing upon her lips and the dreamy, satisfied look in her eyes.

Eyes usually as cold as granite shone and twinkled. She waved at the crowd. Those who were able waved back. They stood, silent, waving quietly to one another like the deaf. Even the dogs stood motionless, heads tilted, tails still.

Then the chimney sweep appeared. His bare chest glistened with sweat; his belly sagged over his pants. His feet were dirty and bare. He was a head shorter than she was. He had one hand holding on to his suspenders and the other running through his hair. He smiled and nodded. The men nodded in return.

Valeria went inside and brought out his shirt. The chimney sweep casually put it on and buttoned it up right in front of the villagers, as if it were the most natural thing in the world. When he was fully dressed, he pulled Valeria by her wrist, put an arm around her waist, patted her on her ample backside, and kissed her on the mouth. Then he released her, and they looked up at the stars. The crowd looked up as well and whispered to one another.

"What are we looking for?"

"Probably his spaceship."

The chimney sweep pointed up toward the sky with his arm around her waist.

"You see those there?" he asked.

Valeria nodded. It was Taurus, the bull.

"That's Cassiopeia. Do you know that story?"

Valeria shook her head.

"Cassiopeia was kind of like a milkmaid to the gods. She wasn't a god herself. She was a nymph or something like it. The point is she wasn't immortal. Anyway, she was the woman who brought them their ambrosia. She was also Apollo's lover." Valeria looked at him. She knew he was lying, but she didn't quite know what to say. *At least someone is trying*, she thought to herself. The potter would never say things like this for her benefit. Valeria wrestled with how she felt.

"She was Apollo's lover and she wanted to be with him. The gods had warned her about drinking the ambrosia. It would kill her if she tried. But to be with the one she loved, she drank a whole urn. Ambrosia is the stuff that made them immortal. Did you know that?"

Valeria nodded.

"So of course she died. And here's where it becomes beautiful. Apollo is heart stricken. He refuses to do his godly duties. I don't remember what those were, but it was bad that he wasn't doing them. Earth was in peril. So Zeus commanded him to do his godly duties and he tells Zeus to stuff it. Can you believe that? He's this distraught. Finally, and I guess it's because Zeus can't do the job himself, Zeus asks him what he wants, and Apollo tells him that he wants his Cassiopeia back. He wants her back. He can't stomach the thought of Hades pawing her, you know? So Zeus agrees and they take Cassiopeia and put her up there. Right where you're staring right now. He puts her up there where Apollo and everyone else on the planet can see her."

The chimney sweep stopped speaking and regarded the heavens. People in the crowd stared at one another and shook their heads. Valeria looked up.

"My dear, you're even lovelier than that," he said.

The more he spoke, Valeria noticed, the more pleased he seemed with himself. Why he should feel pleased with himself, she couldn't tell. He was being asinine. She immediately regretted having even spoken to him. She couldn't tell if he was making this show for her or for her neighbors. She shook her head and escorted him to her gate.

"Yes, yes," she said. "That's sweet poetry. I'm afraid you'll have to go just now."

She all but pushed him out. The chimney sweep made his way to his bicycle and the crowd parted for him. No one followed as he pedaled away, but they all watched him go. When he had faded into the night, they looked back to Valeria. Her face had once again transformed itself. It had returned to the look of severity they were accustomed to.

"What are you looking at?" she shouted. "Do you think I can be trapped like a schoolgirl by the first stray that comes to my door? Go away. I'm a grown woman."

Sixteen

Only Ibolya had enjoyed the last ten days. They had been good for business. She had even finally convinced young Zsofi to help her in the mornings. Misfortune always filled the bar, and since the chimney sweep had officially arrived, her tavern was buzzing with drunks. Always the entrepreneur, Ibolya held a contest and gave an evening's tab to the man who had suffered the most over the last week and a half. Everyone agreed that the mayor had won hands down, although the redheaded man named Ferenc came in a close second. It was hard to say what the deciding factor was, but most agreed that the mayor's fall was much more spectacular, and therefore no one complained when his name was announced.

But Ferenc's troubles had arrived first. He came in blubbering very early during the period of bad luck. It turned out that the new irrigation system he'd purchased—with the mayor's help, he reminded them—was damaged goods. The system's timer had a loose wire, and instead of a direct connection to its contact on the motherboard, electricity was passing from the wire to the contact in a small arc. That worked fine for a while, but in the surprise heat wave, when the rising thermostat triggered the spray of water, a more stable connection was required. The electrical arc made the system work harder and eventually the system's motherboard fried itself under the strain. In simpler terms: The water couldn't turn off, except manually. Ferenc had been spending so much time in the pub looking at Ibolya, he knew nothing about it. The water had been running for five days before he turned it off. Ferenc drowned his entire crop of sugar beets. Two hectares' worth. In fact, when he met the chimney sweep on that first day, the sprinklers were already broken—though he didn't realize it. The beets were rotting in the overly saturated earth and standing water.

When he finally did check on his fields again, the stench of the decaying plant matter nearly overcame him. He spent two days trying to save his crops. He ran the breadth of the rows pulling beets out of the ground. He built several canals, hoping to drain the field. The beets that he pulled slipped out of the earth with a long slurping sound. It was hopeless. They were soft, soft enough that he was able to squeeze them to a pulp in his hands. He raked the ground with his fingers and threw mud clumps in the air. Then he went home to tell his wife, and she called him an oaf and a son of a bitch and she left with the children and went to her sister's home in another village.

"And don't think I haven't heard about how you carry on over at that slut's bar," she said as she left. "Frankly, I'm glad to be done with you!"

All that money. All that work. Ibolya couldn't help but feel sorry for him. Ferenc was like a pet to her, after all. A big lovable dog. After she'd heard the news, when she spotted him sitting alone with his head in his hands at the corner of the pub, she went over and patted him on the back. She told him that she would cover his tab for two whole hours.

"Because you're special," she said.

"I appreciate that, Ibolya," he said. He grew misty eyed over her noticing him. Had this been any other time he would have been over the moon. "I really do. I appreciate it greatly. But why won't you run away with me? Let's leave here. This village has become messy."

Ibolya shook her head and walked away.

"Don't push it," she said. "Look to the mayor."

Ferenc nodded. When he thought of the mayor's plight, he couldn't help but feel better himself.

The mayor's fall was a spectacle that would be remembered for years to come. That he was patronizing the pub at all was a good omen. He had been sitting at the bar for nearly a week. The Asians were being entertained by the chief inspector and his deputy. He had stopped taking care of himself. The mayor's hair seemed to be growing grayer every day. His eyes were dull. He looked like he had gained five kilos. Without him breathing down everyone's neck, final construction on the train station had all but stalled. The workers weren't being paid. In fact, the only one presently working at the site was the potter, and this confused everyone because what the hell did the potter have to do with the train station? He had finally left his workshop, but he wasn't speaking to anyone. Instead, he was out at the train station with a team of workers from out of town. He looked like a wild man, men said. Someone said the men working with him were metalworkers from a foundry in Budapest. That they had made a cast and were pouring metal. Rumor had it that the potter was paying for all of this himself. Nobody knew anything for certain because everything was under wraps—literally under a yurt, and the men worked inside the yurt, did whatever they were doing alongside the potter and out of sight, and the potter never allowed them to come visit the pub.

The mayor wouldn't tell them anything either. Anytime someone mentioned something about the potter to him or tried to engage him in a conversation about his own troubles, he shrugged them off and his response was always, "That dirty little chimney sweep!

At the very least, I'm going to run him out of town. At the very least."

However, the chimney sweep had disappeared after leaving Valeria's. Ibolya was hiding him in the back where she slept. She had told him to lay low.

"Let everyone stew. I'm making a lot of money. I'll give you twelve percent."

Regarding the mayor's problems, all the men knew was that the mayor had been thrown out of his home for having an affair. And since he had been thrown out, Ibolya's tavern was the only place he could go and sulk with effect. Ever the consummate politician, the mayor wanted to sulk publicly. He wanted to wrench his hair out and howl for all to see. Not entirely because he was sorry, but because he knew it might be politically advantageous to appear humbled. Ibolya instinctively understood this. She knew about the plans to build a new tavern at the new hotel over by the train station. She also knew that the mayor had looked for other places to sulk, but when he sat in the great church's pew, not enough people were there for it to matter or make it worth his while. Ibolya's tavern, it turned out, was the only place where voters could see him.

So for the first few days of his separation, patrons tiptoed around him and whispered to themselves. They did not actually speak with him. They watched and waited. They couldn't remember him ever looking more wretched. Not this man.

"Amazing how low and how quickly a woman can make one sink," they marveled.

A few days later, when it was clear that he was not there to close the tavern, they started buying him drinks. The mayor waved them away and sobbed into his beer. He only stopped once or twice to smile at Zsofi. He felt immediately guilty, however, and sobbed harder.

"That's how I got into trouble in the first place," he muttered. "I'm too nice. I can't say no. I'm a wretch. I've never met a pretty woman I didn't instantly love. She's so young. So pretty. How old are you, dear?"

Zsofi looked at him and smiled but took a wary step back. The mayor was an old man to her. Old enough to be her father. She had only taken the job in hopes of catching the apprentice's eye and making him jealous. He was slow, the potter's apprentice. She was getting tired.

"Twenty-three," she answered.

The mayor let out a moan. He put his hands up in front of him like he was warding off an evil eye. He refused to talk to her again that night.

Ibolya let him sulk, but every day she asked him if he wanted to talk about it. She insisted on filling his glass, even when he protested. He had only paid for a third of his drinks. Ibolya didn't mind, as she was raking in so much money from the others. She figured having the mayor sitting right where he was, where she could keep an eye on him, where he couldn't cause her any real trouble, was a cost of business she didn't mind paying. Ibolya was wise enough to know that she couldn't hold the mayor up forever. She was wise enough to know that change was on the horizon. She would fight it as long as she could, though. She would save as much as she was able. She had to look after herself.

"The only good mayor is a drunk one," she whispered to the others. They snickered and agreed. They bought him more drinks.

"I didn't mean anything by it!" the mayor finally broke down and announced. After a week of prodding and his stony silence, his outburst was like a lightning strike. "She came on to me! She came on to me! I swear it."

Ibolya poured him a shot of brandy and smiled over his head

to the others. The men licked their lips and gathered around. She patted his hand.

"Of course she did, dearie. Who wouldn't? Tell us all about it."

The mayor looked around to make sure all eyes were on him, then sniffled into a handkerchief.

"She has such a big bottom! I would never have considered it if it weren't for her bottom! I was just curious."

Until this point the men in the pub hadn't known who he was caught with. None of their wives would tell them. They only knew that whoever it was, she was bad news. Some kind of taboo. They looked at one another and tried to think of all the large bottoms in town.

"Wait!" one of them finally shouted, his eyes lighting up. "You mean you've been fooling around with that hairdresser over on Forest Street?"

"I have." The mayor nodded. "My wife's favorite hairdresser."

There are few moments in a man's life—especially a politician's—when the esteem of other men is palpable, when his measurements are taken and he's deemed worthy. A cut above, in fact. This was one of those moments. The mayor was basking in his constituents' esteem. It was heady stuff. He couldn't help but puff out his chest. The silent admiration swept over him. "Yes," he said again, "it was her. Twice a week."

He stole a glance at Zsofi.

"Whoah!" one of the men finally said. "She does have a big bottom. Massive. Mayor, you shouldn't be complaining. If anything, that was a conquest. Like climbing Everest. You should feel proud."

"But my wife!"

The others nodded. There was that. That could be more than a handful of trouble. But even so, the mayor's wife was nothing like their own wives. The mayor's wife was thin, tanned, and

176

beautiful. None of them could imagine her raising her voice or lifting a finger, let alone cursing and throwing things.

"Wait. How did she find you out? Who caught you?"

"My wife! She caught us herself. Right in the act."

The men tittered.

"How's that?" Ibolya asked.

The mayor looked up sheepishly. He shrugged. "I don't know. She said she was suspicious, but I think someone told her. I think that chimney sweep told her. That little bastard with his cleaning solutions and that high fee."

Ibolya smiled. Everyone's ears perked up.

"How long had you been seeing the hairdresser?"

"I'd been seeing her for eight weeks. We had a couple of close calls. Sometimes when I visited her I would leave only moments before my wife arrived for her appointment. She has a side door. I'm such a scoundrel."

Ibolya shook her head. She smiled to herself. You could bank on the stupidity of men. What did he think? Didn't the mayor know that *she* was the one who was really in charge? He was like a plaything. Just her fat little plaything. Ibolya considered a future in politics. She decided she would run for mayor in the next election.

Men ordered more beer and gathered around the bar.

"And one for the mayor!"

"Here you go, mayor. Have mine also."

"She was just so . . . so, well, you know," the mayor said.

The men nodded. "Yeah? Yeah? Go on!"

"I couldn't resist."

The men shook their heads. "Who would? Tell us about it."

"Tell us, mayor. What is she like? Is she wild? Did she scream with passion?"

Ibolya clucked at them.

"It was my wife's fault," the mayor said. "She shouldn't have left us alone together. That's how it all began. I went to meet my wife after her appointment. I was going to pick her up. Only she hadn't made it and hadn't told me. When I arrived the hairdresser was furious. She had been sitting there for an hour waiting. What was I to do? I offered her my head instead. I told her I'd pay her a little bit extra for the time lost, you know. I was just trying to be nice."

The men sidled up closer. They sensed details. They sensed sweaty skin and flesh against flesh. They could all smell her—the hairdresser—right there with them. Right at the bar. Hair, sweat, bottom, and all. And the mayor was pulled in also. Now that he had begun, he couldn't stop. He would tell them all of the details.

"First she wet my hair," he began, and the room was still. "Then she combed it with that little black comb. Then she pulled out her scissors. The odd thing was . . ." He paused. His glass was empty. He looked at it.

"What? What was the odd thing? Don't stop." They filled it. "Go on."

"The odd thing was that she was looking at me through the mirror the whole time. She never took her eyes from mine."

The men whistled.

"Then she pulled my head back and pressed it against her bosom." The mayor leered at Zsofi. She blushed.

"You're pigs," she said. "Don't continue, mayor. It puts you in a bad light."

"Go on, mayor. Go on."

"Mayor, if you want another vote in this town, you will finish telling this story," the men said.

The mayor nodded. Zsofi threw her hands up and walked away.

"When she pulled my head against her chest, I could feel her mammaries pressing against me. She was breathing heavily. My head rose and fell with every breath she took. And she was still looking in my eyes! Right into my eyes. She wasn't shy; I can tell you that. Well, you all know I'm a man of action. I knew just what she was thinking, I did. So I kept my head right where it was, stared right back at her, but lifted my arms and reached around her body. I grabbed her bum, squeezed, and pulled her closer. Then she grabbed a handful of my hair, pulled my head further back, and we kissed. And that is exactly how it started."

The men applauded.

"Funny, I've been thinking about switching barbers," one of them said. "Ibolya, do you think I need a haircut?"

"We should all get haircuts!" The men in the room cheered.

"Well where were you when your wife caught you?" Ibolya ignored the men and asked the question.

The mayor looked shamed. He sighed. "In my office. I thought we were safer there. My wife never comes there. She thinks it's boring."

The men laughed aloud and smiled to show their admiration. They patted the mayor on his back.

"You mean the people's office!" Ibolya scolded. "Tsk tsk, mayor."

"I know it. I've broken every vow I held dear," he sobbed into his handkerchief. "I just hope you all will accept my apology and think of my suffering at the next election."

The men consoled him and bought him more beer. Ibolya was happy. Everyone was good and drunk.

"Ah, don't worry about it, mayor. At least we know that something interesting was going on in that office."

Then the men shared stories about their own dalliances to make him feel better. They had to be careful, though, and not let too many names spill out. It was, after all, a small village, and cuckolded husbands were plentiful and present.

"I have to admit something, mayor," one man volunteered. "I think I like you even more now. You'll get my vote."

"See," Ibolya consoled him. "This might just get you reelected after all. Don't worry about your wife, mayor. You're a wealthy man, and she likes to spend your money. She'll come back to you soon enough. You'll pay for it, though. Dearly and through the nose. She just wants you to sweat a little. That's all."

The mayor looked up at her.

"You think so?"

Ibolya nodded.

"Of course she will."

"No, I mean about the election."

"A landslide, mayor. A landslide."

The mayor seemed instantly better after that. He bought a last round for the house and beamed up at Ibolya. His face was puffy. His hair was mussed.

"That young Zsofi." He motioned in the girl's direction. "She's a looker, heh?"

"Now you're being greedy," Ibolya answered. "Besides, she's in love with the potter's apprentice."

The mayor nodded. When Ibolya mentioned the potter, he remembered hearing the gossip.

"Ah! The potter. How is he these days, Ibolya? I hear you have competition."

Ibolya shot him a glance that wiped the smile from his face.

"Nothing I can't figure out."

"Really? Because I hear Valeria's quite the hellion," he giggled.

Ibolya thew her dish towel down in front him.

"She is just bored," Ibolya snapped. "That's all. Her chimney had cobwebs in it is all. Anyway, it seems the chimney sweep has put an end to that. I understand he cleaned her out in no time. She'll forget all about the potter now. Everything will be fine. I have work to do."

And Ibolya walked away.

Seventeen

The potter was still conflicted. Insofar as his present situation was concerned, he found himself immobilized by doubt. He simply didn't know what to do. He didn't know which woman he wanted. Furthermore, he didn't know how to make that kind of decision. Surely, if the heart of the matter rested in the fact that his present situation was a matter of the heart, then his own heart must have been dodgy, because it told him nothing and would not give him a clear answer. Not the slightest clue. All he knew was that he was fond of Valeria and Ibolya, and had they come into his life independently, he could have built a relationship with either. So, unlike the chimney sweep, who could act with selfish intent, in this case the potter felt that he was a man with good intentions who couldn't act at all.

Like most men in uncomfortable personal situations, he buried himself in work.

But he did for a moment remember his dead wife and he felt a sudden appreciation for her, if for no other reason than simply because there had been no romantic crisis in their time together. His life was much simpler. He was married and that was all there was to it. In their years together, even when her melancholy had made her physically ill, he had never tarried and was committed to her. But now! The potter shuddered at the thought of his situation. He had barricaded himself inside his workshop and he was thankful for it. When he had enough of that, he went to the yurt and worked there. He was thankful that he had tangible tasks, because by focusing on those alone, he didn't have to focus on anything else.

But there was something else, and maybe it was selfish. Whereas the construction of the ewer was the moment at which the potter understood that his craft could be an art, since then, his new focus in life was in being able to create that art at will. The heart of the matter lay in the fact that he discovered for the first time in his career that he could enjoy the act of creating something. Add this to his dilemma and neither woman stood a chance. In his time away from both women the potter learned that he enjoyed the challenge of finding the right technique and of molding globs of clay into just the right shape. And if what he made wasn't exactly what he wanted, he destroyed it and started again. When he considered his situation, he realized that he enjoyed the clay as much, if not more, than he enjoyed being with Valeria or Ibolya. So, yes, he had shut himself in for weeks. He was living like a hermit and didn't care. His work was the perfect respite from an uncomfortable situation. He was in the perfect state of being to keep from having to make a choice.

He was also wholly unaware of the village's troubles. He was unaware of any strangers making advances and winning advantages. When those women came to see him after being in front of Valeria's cottage, he shooed them away before they could speak. He knew nothing of Valeria and the chimney sweep, or Ibolya and the chimney sweep, and it is impossible to know what he would have thought if he did. How much personal crisis does the artist need?

Pacing in his workshop, the potter felt dust settling between the balls of his feet and his slippers. The workshop was a shambles. His phone was still off the hook. Mail had piled up in front of the mailbox. For three weeks not even his apprentice had been allowed to enter. Turnip vases and a fountain. These were his concern.

He had not slept enough. He was losing weight, not having eaten enough. His face was craggy and rough from not having shaved. First, he was intent on finishing the vases—his and hers, side by side, complementing one another, orbiting one another. They were like a pair of spinning tops, or dervishes with their skirts blown wide.

The potter had made a larger turnip vase first. Its shape was like a V. Under the rim of it he had painted a series of flowers —pansies—purple and white ones. He did the same around the base—purple and white pansies. The vase was easy to hold. It felt snug in the hand. It was smooth. It was slick. It even captured the potter's warmth and radiated it back to him. When he picked up the second turnip and held both of them in front of him, carried both of them, he felt as if he were holding a pair of misshapen breasts. Strangely, they reminded him of Valeria's breasts. Perhaps that was his heart reminding him of something, he thought. The promise of her breasts? He remembered the night he had held her. She seemed so hard and cold and big in the daylight, but she wasn't at all. She was small, like a bird. She was small and soft and bony, exactly like a fat pigeon. He remembered holding her. He looked again at the vases. She had inspired this.

At the fountain, he experienced a similar type of feeling. He had constructed a cast model by hand, out of beeswax and paraffin. It was a new medium for him, but when the potter finished it was as rich in detail as the original clay figurine. The statue stood and looked past him. An invisible wind blew its skirt and tugged at its blouse. Its kerchief seemed ready to flutter off. A container was resting on its shoulder and a bicycle was at its feet. It stood a head taller than he was. The potter nodded at it. He had to admit, then, that it really was Valeria. He took it all in. He was done. The men from the foundry took over. They began to cover it with clay.

"Do you have the original plans?" they asked.

"Yes, why?" the potter said.

"We have to destroy it. The model."

"How do you mean?" the potter asked. "Why?"

"Well, this clay we're covering it with now is the mold. Before we pour the bronze, we have to melt the wax. See how we're leaving those spaces at the bottom? We'll let the wax drain out there. If anything happens to the cast after the wax has melted you'll have to start over from the beginning."

The potter felt his stomach turn, but he nodded. Yes, maybe this was the answer. While his heart couldn't consciously decide, it had led him to this. He could allow them to do this because the original model was sitting at home, and she was probably furious at him.

"Do it. Melt it," he said, and then he left. Back to the workshop.

He intended to take the vases to Valeria right away. He was sidetracked, however, because he found himself suddenly inspired again. Without any prodding, he had decided to sculpt Valeria her own wedding platter. He would make something fantastic that he would surprise her with.

The potter was energized, and he finished a very basic wedding platter quickly. He had been making them for years, after all. Then he thought to look at his mail. He found that most of it was stationery of some kind from Ibolya or Valeria. Love letters, as best as those two formidable women were capable of writing.

He sorted them in two piles. Ibolya had sent him the greater number. He couldn't help but feel regret then, at how he had treated her since meeting Valeria. It was true that she had reawakened him to his desires. It was true that she reminded him of his virility. Had Valeria not come along, it was true that by now the pair might have been in a full-blown relationship, but the argument was in the might. They might have been. He couldn't say for sure. Anyway, relations with Valeria were similar, and then there was this added bonus of his work. The potter realized that the main difference between the two women was that he was inspired to create with one while he was merely content and comfortable with the other.

The potter understood himself better then. He understood a lot of things better then. He telephoned his apprentice and asked him to return to the shop. The young man arrived within an hour of the call. He looked gaunt as well and seemed to be struggling for air.

"What is the matter with you?" the potter asked. "You look horrible."

"You don't look so great yourself," the young man said. "I gave the teapot to Zsofi, along with the cake platter. No thanks to you, I might add. I've been crazy ever since."

"I am sorry. I had forgotten. How did they turn out?"

"They were wonderful. Zsofi loved them."

"Stupendous," the potter said. "I knew you were more than ready to work on your own. But tell me, what seems to be your trouble? You really look terrible."

The apprentice scoffed. "When I was leaving her home, Zsofi walked me out the door and before I turned to leave, she threw her arms around my neck, kissed me, and told me that we should be together."

"Ah!" the potter said. "I see. Well, what did you do?"

"I left as quickly as I was able. She has a nice figure and it was hard to break away, but no way. She's a crazy girl. She has nothing but marriage on the mind."

"So, what happened next?"

"She called me a couple of times after that. I never spoke with her though. She spoke to my brothers and those imbeciles told her I was a homosexual."

"What?"

"They don't like the thought of me getting a girl like Zsofi. She's much better looking than their wives."

"So, what happened?"

"I don't think she believed them. When we bumped into one another at the market, she was all smiles. She even brushed against me. I just ignored her, though, and kept walking."

"That was a foolish thing to do."

"Was it?"

"It might be. Are you playing hard to get?"

The apprentice thought about the question. There was nothing really wrong with Zsofi. He just didn't understand the need to settle down. Had Zsofi ever said that she was interested in a casual relationship, a stress-free fling, the potter's apprentice felt like he would have been more than happy to partake in that.

"She's nice enough, I guess," he said.

"So what's the problem?"

"Ibolya has hired her at the pub."

"What?"

"Ibolya has hired her to be her assistant. After what happened with Valeria and that damned chimney sweep, business is booming over there. The whole village is in the bar drinking. Even the mayor has practically moved in. He's been making eyes at Zsofi. The mayor! Now Zsofi works every day from six in the morning until two in the afternoon. She looks ridiculous. She's wearing too much makeup and she wears the exact same outfits as Ibolya. Only she looks much better than that old lady, and so now men are going just to drink and ogle her. I even heard men saying that they've petted her legs and pinched her bottom. Since she started working there I've been in five scrapes. I could just kill them. I can't stand seeing her there. I haven't been there in a week. What do you think she's thinking? What is she thinking? That's not a place for her at all."

The potter had stopped listening.

"What did you say about Valeria and a chimney sweep? You mean the one that stuck his head in here?"

The apprentice looked at the potter.

"What?"

"What did you just say about Valeria?" the potter answered. "You just said something."

The apprentice looked frightened. He fidgeted.

"You don't know? I thought you knew. Everyone knows. They spent ten days in her cottage. They say Valeria was moaning like a bear the whole time."

The potter sat down.

"I don't believe you."

The apprentice grimaced.

"I'm sorry. How could you not know this? This town has been an asylum for the last ten days. The guy only just left her cottage a few days ago. Have you really not heard anything about it?"

"No, damn you. I haven't heard anything. Who is he? What is he doing here?"

"I don't know. He's some chimney sweep. Just passing through. All the women are crazy over him, but he's a nasty little fellow. The men in this town are ready to burn him at the stake. The town has been falling apart since he rode in. Apparently, he and Valeria hit it off immediately. Ibolya also. He and Ibolya are like old friends. He's been here for three weeks almost. How can you not know any of this? Some women came by to tell you."

The potter put his head into his hands.

"I've been making turnips," he said to himself, and laughed. "And a statue. I've been making these damned turnips."

The apprentice looked over to the vases on the workbench. He walked over to them and picked them up, one in each hand. He held them in front of him.

"These are marvelous," he said. "We could get a lot of money out of these."

The potter was looking at his feet.

"These are truly beautiful."

The potter looked up.

"Really?"

"They even feel like . . . breasts," the apprentice remarked.

The potter smiled.

"They're even warm. How did you do this?"

The potter shrugged.

Then the apprentice saw the clay model of Valeria.

"What is that? What are you doing there? Is that what's going on at the rail station? Is that what you're working on under the yurt? It's a big mystery, you know."

The potter was embarrassed. "Yes, I'm trying to build a fountain."

"Of Valeria?" The apprentice looked confused.

"Yes. It will be a statue of Valeria."

"I don't understand. What's happening here? You're a potter. You're supposed to be a potter. You're supposed to be teaching me to be a potter."

The potter stood up suddenly and shook his head. The apprentice took a step back.

"No. No more. Not anymore. I'm not a potter anymore. Something has happened to me. I don't know what, but you listen to me now. You listen carefully. I want to give you the shop. The shop is yours. I'm giving it to you. Right now. This moment. That quickly. Will you take it? I will not tell you how to run it. You run it how you see fit. I won't bother you about it. I don't want to hear anything about it. I don't care about it. I will stay in my flat and use the workshop, but from now on you're the potter. You're more than ready for it. Once that damned fool of a mayor has finished his train station, you might even have a customer or two. Tourists maybe. Who knows? I know I can't prepare for that. I'm an old man. That's not my future. That's your future. And your wife's. You and your wife's, because you won't be able to do it by yourself. So, if you are a smart man, you will go to that pub and grab Miss Zsofi Toth this instant. You will take her to the mayor and make him marry you. If he gives her a look or gives you any lip, then I expect you to punch him in the nose. If Zsofi takes you after the way you've behaved, then consider yourself lucky. The workshop and the business are my wedding present to both of you. You're both young and strong and can do everything you want. I'm finished. I will stay here until I die, but I will never make anything I don't want to make again. I want to create art. That's all. That's all I intend to do. Make art and love the woman who makes me want to. Do you understand that? Valeria is the woman who makes me want to do that. I can see that. It's in the clay. It's everywhere. Do you understand what I'm telling you?"

The apprentice was dumbfounded. He nodded.

"Then what are you standing here like a donkey for? Go and find Zsofi. Grab her. Propose to her. Make love to her. Have babies with her. Go!"

The apprentice was worked up. He nodded and stormed out of the workshop. The potter looked around and smiled. He felt like a weight had been lifted and that for the first time since childhood, he was allowed to live. He went into his flat, pulled his suit out, and prepared himself for another visit to Valeria's cottage. He hoped it wasn't too late.

Valeria had a lot of cleaning to do. It seemed to never end. Ten days indoors with the chimney sweep, and not a bit of work had been done around the house. Cupboards had been left unlocked and opened. Food and sherry bottles were left on countertops and tables. Outside, her plants were just beginning to wilt, while the animals had to fend for themselves. They dug for roots and ate grass. Someone had come by and milked the cow. They had even tossed it some fresh hay. And somehow, Valeria didn't care about any of it. She thought she would, but she didn't. It was okay. The world hadn't imploded.

She thought it would be best to start by doing laundry. She put her bedsheets in her old washing machine and then drew herself a warm bath. The bath was a luxury, something she would not have indulged in before the chimney sweep's visit, but she had also indulged his vigor and that act had made her tired. She was still tired, and it had been three days since he'd left. A long bath, she felt, would ease the fever that was deep in her muscles.

She sat in the bathtub and sighed. She smiled to herself as she thought about the chimney sweep on top of her. At one point she even giggled. What a silly little man. Poetry recitals on the front steps. In front of the villagers. Idiot. She rested her head back and put a washrag over her forehead. The soap stung the love bites on her shoulders. She shuddered. Then she thought about the potter. She shrugged to herself.

"We're not getting any younger," she said aloud. "He knew where I lived. He could have come to see me. He could have sent a word, at least. Nearly a month with no word."

Valeria rested in the bath for a long while. She felt like she had earned it. She fell asleep.

The knocking on her door woke her up. She tried to ignore it, but it became a pounding—an insistent pounding. She stirred from her bath. She wrapped a towel around her body and put on a robe. She grabbed her key ring hanging from the doorknob and walked barefoot to the front door.

"Who's there?" she asked.

"Valeria, it's me," the potter said. "Please let me in."

Valeria swallowed hard. She was too relaxed to shout at him, though she wanted to. She cracked the door open and stuck her head out. He stood in front of her, wearing the same suit he had worn a month before. His white hair was pomaded. His moustache was brushed. He was holding presents in his hand.

"What are you doing here?" she asked.

"I've made these for you." He offered the gifts.

"What are they?"

The potter looked up at her. "Your vases. You said you wanted vases. I've been working on them for a month. It wasn't easy. It took a lot of tries, but I finally got it right. I have more presents. I want to give them all to you. Right now. But first you have to accept the vases and my apologies."

Valeria looked at the wrapped gifts. Then she looked at him. He seemed content.

"You mean I haven't heard a peep from you all month because you've been making me vases?" Valeria asked. "What about that stunt you pulled at the market?"

The potter nodded. "Don't you remember? You asked for turnips."

Valeria shook her head. "Can a man really be this stupid?" she said. "That was a month ago. I thought you ran away."

"I did the best I could," the potter said testily. "It takes time. I could never run away. . . . If you don't want them, I can always sell them. But there's more. There's much more."

Valeria took the vases and opened the door wider for the potter to pass.

"You may come in."

The potter entered and followed Valeria to her kitchen table. He looked around.

"Valeria, are you all right?"

"What? Oh, the mess. I was entertaining."

"Entertaining," the potter said. "Who? Soldiers?"

"Don't be silly. I was entertaining a visitor."

The potter feigned ignorance. "What's that? A man?"

"Yes. I thought you had deserted me. I had a gentleman caller," she said matter-of-factly. "He wooed me with poetry right on the front step there. In front of the whole village. We're not getting any younger, you know."

The potter cleared his throat. Valeria tore the wrapping paper from the vases.

"Oh, my!"

"Do you like them? I hope you like them."

Valeria examined them.

"They are beautiful. The most beautiful vases I've ever seen."

"I shaped them like turnips, just like you asked. I painted them purple and then painted pansies over them. What do you think?"

"Marvelous. These are marvelous. Thank you so much. I am speechless."

Valeria held the vases in her hand and smiled at them. Not normally a sentimental woman, Valeria couldn't hold the vases and not think of her grandfather. Of her childhood. Looking at the vases, even the moments of her childhood that were sad seemed joyful in a way she couldn't relate to anymore. The vases were beautiful to her because they reminded her of childhood joy. It was the subtlest piece of art that the potter had created. It worked on Valeria in a wholly emotional way. Like she could laugh and weep at the same time. Like she had stumbled upon a music box from her youth, the sound of which released a life that once pleasurably was, but is no more, but would very much be welcome.

"I've made you an even more special present," the potter said, "and I've given my shop to my apprentice as a wedding gift. So, you know, I have nothing but time now."

Valeria smiled at him and held the turnips in front of her.

"I don't see how it could be any better than this." Valeria said. "This is perfect."

"I have time for you and my art," he said.

She looked at him. "What do you want from me?" she asked.

The potter slid his hand into her robe and pulled her towel away. Her skin was damp. He pulled her close.

"What are you doing?" Valeria whispered.

"I've missed you, Valeria." He stepped toward her.

Valeria wrapped her arms around his neck. She was still holding her vases. They kissed for a long time. Her towel fell completely away. He caressed her body. She whispered in his ear. They hurried to her bedroom.

She pulled away from him suddenly. "I'm washing the sheets," she said. "Let me get fresh ones."

"We're not getting any younger," he said, nuzzling her throat. "To hell with bedsheets. Let's consummate this thing right now.

He pressed himself against her and cupped her bottom.

"I'm going to end up in a hospital," Valeria remarked.

"Then I want to marry you as quickly as possible," the potter said.

Valeria began unbuttoning his shirt. "How's that?"

The potter was kissing her throat; he didn't answer her right away.

"You will marry me," he finally said.

She didn't speak, only nodded her head. Her skin was flushed in all the places he had touched and kissed. *At last*, she thought to herself.

Eighteen

It was Ibolya who finally got the mayor back on his feet. He might have gone on sitting at the bar making scenes without a care in the world. Especially when he decided he was making progress with Zsofi. She was afraid the girl might forget the potter's apprentice, that she might consider the older man's advances. Ibolya could not be a party to that. She didn't consider herself intentionally cruel. She took to cheering the mayor on about his train station until the man was reminded of what it was he wanted to accomplish. She pressed him with questions. She gasped appreciatively when he told her how big it was. It worked. She saw the pilot light flickering in his eyes. The mayor finally stood up, slammed his hand on the table, and declared that she was right.

"I've got a job to finish," he said. "I've got a future to make."

The mayor left the tavern and drove to the train station. The alcohol hadn't left his system yet, but he made himself presentable. He combed his hair with his fingers and tucked his shirt in. Save for the potter's project, the rest of the site was empty. It was dark out. He could see men working in the yurt, their movement showcased in silhouette. He stepped inside to check the progress. The men from the foundry were at the last stage of constructing the statue. They were pouring bronze. It was hot inside the tent. Two of the men wore heavy aprons and long gloves. Only two men at a time had room to pour the metal. The other two men were in short sleeves. They waited for their turn at pouring. The potter, who couldn't help this part of the process, had unbuttoned his shirt to his sternum and stood silently taking it all in.

The mayor tried to engage him in a friendly repartee. The potter was not responding. He stared intently at the men doing their work. He looked like an expectant father, the mayor thought. These were the potter's final moments. His statue was nearly complete. All of the work had been done—and successfully, thought the mayor—and now the potter couldn't do anything but watch the final push and hope for the best. The mayor understood what the older man must have been feeling. He was suddenly impatient to feel the same way. To feel that same sense of victory over his train station. He patted the potter on the shoulder and went to the door of the yurt, to let the old man be.

The men poured the molten bronze. They called out to one another as the liquid sputtered.

"Careful. Careful. Don't spill. This stuff's expensive."

One of the workers who wasn't pouring held up some bottles for the potter to take a look at. They were deciding on patinas. The potter was nodding.

"Yes, yes," he said. "In a minute. In a minute."

The potter broke away from this man and turned toward the mayor. He approached him.

"This is too much. Too much. I can't take much more of this. They'll be pouring for the next thirty minutes. Would you join me for a smoke outside?"

The mayor followed the potter outside. They walked a good hundred meters away from the yurt. The potter lit a cigarette and passed it to the mayor. He lit a second and inhaled it. He looked around the construction site.

"You've got to get those last cross ties in," he sighed.

"I know it." The mayor nodded.

"The inside of the station needs another coat of paint," he said. "And the chandelier needs a more secure fastening."

The mayor nodded again. The potter was prickly.

"What's the problem, mayor? You're making my fountain look bad. The pump just arrived from Vienna. We're almost ready to go."

The mayor laughed. "Your fountain! Well, aren't you a funny old man. This is my station."

The potter harrumphed. "Well, it's my fountain. I made it. I'm paying for the bulk of it."

The mayor agreed. He looked around the station and sighed.

"I can't seem to get out of this funk," he said. "I thought I could, but now that I'm here, I'm lost again. What's the point?"

The potter took a drag off of his cigarette.

"You've come too far to back off now," the potter said. "It's really almost done. Just those last cross ties, some paint, a few more shingles. This could be finished within a week or two."

"What's going on with you and Valeria, anyway?" the mayor asked, changing the subject.

The potter finished his cigarette and lit a second.

"I'll marry her just as soon as I'm done here. This is her wedding present."

The mayor looked at the yurt. The silhouettes were pouring bronze. The steam rose from the bucket. Out of earshot the workers looked like shadow puppets. They looked like they were dancing around the sculpture. The mayor felt comforted.

"Maybe the train station could be a present for my wife? I could name it after her instead of myself."

"I suppose you could."

"Like a Taj Mahal."

"In the middle of the prairie. Why not?"

"Would she accept it, you think? She threw me out, you know. Do you think she could forgive me?"

"I don't know. What's the hairdresser's part in all this?"

The mayor considered this. He hadn't before. He decided there was no part. She was just a hairdresser. Julietta was her name. She had hazel eyes with green specks and a bum that extended out into the world the way the continental shelf extended out into the abyss. The mayor remembered slipping into that abyss. It was an incomparable pleasure, but that's all it was: an affliction of the senses. A slippery, woozy, euphoric narcosis of the ass.

"Look, she was available," he said. "That's all it was. Surely *you* of all people understand that sort of thing."

The potter harrumphed.

"It won't happen again," the mayor said hopefully. "Her hairdresser is off-limits. Just bad form."

"Fix your train station," the potter said, leaving the mayor and making his way back to the yurt. "You're making my fountain look bad. I won't be able to convince Valeria to visit if she hears this place is a mess. And tell your wife whatever you want, but don't make promises you're not going to keep. And don't knock yourself out over it; you didn't invent infidelity."

The mayor raised his hand. It was a wave or a salute. He couldn't tell.

For the record, the mayor's young wife was named Klara. After throwing him out, she packed all of his belongings into a suitcase and had them waiting in the front closet. She had telephoned her relatives and through them was arranging for an attorney to handle her divorce. She wasn't interested in hearing anything about Taj Mahals or narcosis for that matter.

When the mayor arrived home from the train station, hopeful that he could convince her that he was sorry and that he would do whatever it took to make her love him again, she was on the phone reserving a microbus.

The mayor entered the house and found her sitting on their sofa. She was looking at him while she spoke, and this made him feel more hopeful. When he caught on that she was arranging for transportation his stomach fell. She hung up. Her whole demeanor had changed. She was cool.

"I came to apologize," he said.

She was standing already. She made her way to their kitchen.

"A bus is coming to collect me. I've contacted an attorney. We're divorcing."

"But I'm here to apologize. I wanted to let you know that I'm naming the train station after you. It'll be your train station. You're like a ray of sunlight in this town. You must forgive me."

Klara scoffed at him and opened the closet door.

"Keep your train station. You made a fool out of me. Those peasants will look at me and always remember how you preferred a cow. You've shamed me. Absolutely shamed me. I won't forgive you. My bus arrives tomorrow. I'll be gone after that. You can sleep with anyone you want to. I'll be doing the same, only it'll be a minister of some kind."

The mayor shook his head.

"That's it? You can walk away from it all that quickly?"

She screamed and attacked him. The mayor backed away, all the way to the door. She opened it for him and pushed him out.

"That's right. That's it," she said. "It's the best decision for both of us."

She turned off the light.

*   *   *

Disasters were one thing. Certainly disaster sold drinks and helped Ibolya make a profit; she wouldn't argue that. Long legs sold just as many, though. Zsofi had long legs. Of all the smart investments Ibolya had made in her life, hiring young Zsofi Toth to work in the pub was among the best. Zsofi was smart. She had loose waves of bright yellow hair that fell across her shoulders and framed her angular face. Once Ibolya bought her some new clothes—the same outfits she wore—the men of the village never stood a chance. At Ibolya's Nonstop Tavern there was now a woman for every generation. The younger woman was bringing in a lot of new business. Young men were actually spending time at the bar, rather than coming in for a drink or two and then leaving. Ibolya knew what the score was. She wasn't offended that they weren't interested in her. She didn't mind if those barrel-chested, strapping boys ignored her as though she were their friendly aunt. She didn't care about any of it as long as those young men sat, drank, and then drank some more. In fact, she stopped serving them altogether and happily insisted to Zsofi that she serve them instead. She even allowed the girl to keep all the tips for herself.

"I'm making enough on sales, dearie. You have a whole life ahead of you. Just promise me you won't spend it on more dresses and makeup than you can use. Put it away someplace safe. That's what I do."

Zsofi thanked her and put the money in her apron. She smiled. She was always smiling. She was neutrally pleasant. Smiled just enough to get the job done, was able to be friendly without being flirty. She was like everyone's attractive kid sister, and except for the mayor, most of the other men were respectful while she served them. It was only when she was out of earshot that they talked.

Ibolya's instincts told her there was something more to the young girl, though. She knew that there was something else behind the younger woman's smiles and head tosses. It was mostly in her eyes. At first Ibolya thought it was nerves at having the new job and having to wear the revealing outfits. Later, Ibolya realized that the only problem with the girl was that she was forlorn. Every time a young man walked in through the gaping hole in the wall, Zsofi looked up like she was expecting somebody. She would light up for the briefest of moments in a mixture of love and defiance; then, when she saw that the person who had entered was not the one she was expecting, her face fell in on itself. She was still beautiful, but a subtle shadow crossed her features. None of the men noticed, but Ibolya did.

Ibolya knew the young woman fancied the potter's apprentice. She shook her head. *Those damned potters*, she thought to herself. What was it about them? Their hands? The fact that they weren't bashful about using their fingers?

"It's the potter's apprentice you're hoping will walk in that door, isn't it?" Ibolya asked the young girl finally. She had decided to become an indulgent aunt—no, big sister—to this younger woman. "Is that why you're always making moon eyes at the entrance? Is that who you're waiting on to walk through the door?"

Zsofi nodded and looked over at the hole in the wall.

"I love him, but he's not very bright," she remarked. "Not at all."

"None of them are, dearie. I'm waiting for a potter too," Ibolya laughed. "He sent me over the moon, my little goat. He was a magnificent lover. The gentlest. Oh, the way he caressed me. Did his apprentice do the same thing? I swear, if I were a younger woman and a man did that to me, I'd be making eyes at that entrance myself. Consider yourself lucky to have found one so early in life. My husband was a horrible lover. An ape would have done a better job of it. A couple of grunts and off to bed.

I never should have married him. He was a horrible man. Horrible. Come to think of it, he didn't have a single redeeming quality. He owned a pub. That was it. That's all he had. I was a poor girl, you see. It seemed like a good way to make a living. But do you know I had to take lovers very early on? A girl's got to take her pleasure when she can. There's nothing shameful about it."

Zsofi shifted and looked about the room. "I'm sorry," she said. She hoped that nobody had heard the older woman. "What are you talking about?"

"You know. Down there," Ibolya said louder. A few men looked up. She stared them down before pulling Zsofi behind the bar. She lowered her voice to a whisper. "You know. When you made love," she continued. "It's okay. You can tell me. You don't have to be shy about it. The old potter? He's a randy goat. Really. I know it's hard to believe. He seems so distinguished with that gorgeous hair and moustache. You would never know it by looking at him, but he did things with his fingers that just about drove me mad. Did his apprentice make love like that?"

The girl shook her head. "I don't know what you're talking about."

"We even did it once leaning up against that wheel in his workshop." Ibolya laughed remembering it. "What a kook!"

The young girl blushed and walked away. Ibolya figured it was because she was too embarrassed to talk about it. *Youth today*, Ibolya thought. What was there to be embarrassed about?

"I understand, dearie," Ibolya called after her. "Really, though, it's okay to talk about it. I promise it'll make you feel better."

Zsofi occupied herself by cleaning a table. It was her luck that the chimney sweep walked in, a smile plastered to his face. He couldn't help but smile. He saw Zsofi and sidled up beside her while she was still leaning over and wiping the table. From his leather blazer's chest pocket he pulled out three one-thousand-forint notes. He wrapped his arm around her waist and kissed her on the cheek. He put the money in her hand.

"For the prettiest maiden in the whole village," he said, and even doffed his cap at her. Zsofi thanked him and put the money in her apron. She went on cleaning.

Ibolya noticed the chill that traveled among the men when the chimney sweep entered the room. She couldn't read what his reaction was toward them. He seemed generally disinterested. He had over two hundred thousand forints on his person. He'd shown it to her the night before.

"More money then I've ever had at one time," he said.

He'd actually started to believe in the possibility that he was lucky. Ibolya also noticed that he had almost started to take his job seriously. She advised him to stay around the bar, though. Just for a short while.

"But I can feel it now," he'd said in response. "The luck coursing through my veins. Do you feel it too? Anybody could touch me now and it'd be good for them."

The change in his demeanor was profound. He was friendly and jokey. He was trying to make friends. He was even petting the strays.

"Contempt," she reminded him. "They won't love you if you love them back. Don't get complacent. There are quite a few men in this village who want your head."

"Bah," he'd said. "I'm not afraid of peasants."

"Hello, old girl," he said to Ibolya as he sat at the bar. "Your finest wine, please. And pour one for yourself."

Ibolya shrugged and poured two glasses of wine.

"Look at you," Ibolya said. "You have such a faraway look in your eyes. I swear, I couldn't have planned any of this better than how it has all turned out. Between you and that girl there, I might become a rich woman after all."

"My dear," the chimney sweep said, "I feel like I've gotten a new lease on life. Like I said before, everything is going my way. For the first time in my life, I'm on top. And it's mostly thanks to you."

The pair clinked glasses. Ibolya was surprised that she still had not pried from him the story of what he had done in Valeria's cottage for so long. Every time she'd ask him, the chimney sweep would just shake his head and mutter, "What a woman!" She noticed that he also looked pained if she criticized Valeria too harshly. But Ibolya was dying to know the details. She tried to bring it up again.

"Now, I insist that you tell me what happened over there," she said. "You spent ten days in that woman's cottage. Ten days! You have excellent stamina for such a small man. It must be from all that bicycling. We should sign you up for the Tour de France. Tell me what happened there, dearie. Is she a screamer? Were you a brute? Did you smack her once for me?"

The chimney sweep—who had been smiling—suddenly frowned. Then he scowled. He swallowed the rest of his drink quickly.

"Give me a beer," he ordered.

She pulled a bottle from a cooler. She popped off the top and tossed it in the trash. She handed him the drink and watched as he threw his head back, polishing it off in a few seconds.

"Well, what's eating you?" she said. "You look as lovesick as that young girl of mine. I just paid you a compliment. Didn't you hear?"

"Yeah, I heard. It wasn't very funny."

Ibolya reached across the bar and squeezed his arm.

"Hey! Who would have thought you could be such a brooding animal? It's almost exciting."

The chimney sweep pulled away.

"Give it a rest," he said. "Your tricks don't work on me, and I'm not interested in your jokes."

"Take it easy, why don't you?" Ibolya couldn't understand this man. He was too changeable, too fickle. He came into her life a nihilist, became a cynic, and was now, unexpectedly, in love.

"You know, she's not what you make her out to be," the chimney sweep said sharply. "If anyone deserves a little bit of roughhousing, I'd say it's you."

When she attacked Valeria, he found his ire rising. He wanted to defend her.

"Look at what you did to that poor sap of a mayor. I just spotted him wandering around his hotel and station. And really, what did his wife ever do to you? Telling on him like that was plain mean. Meanness without provocation."

The men in the bar looked up. Zsofi looked up. Ibolya felt their stares. She was stunned. What was happening here? She shook her head and smiled. She rolled her eyes. She would put an end to this, this instant.

"Please. You're not about to tell me all this is about you falling in love with Valeria? I could care less. That would just be too ridiculous. Everybody in this village is lovesick and abandoned. You're the one who came in here whining three weeks ago and looking to bilk a woman. You're the one running over children and pawing men's wives. You're the one pocketing heaven knows how many hundreds of thousands of forints from cleaning chimneys. If anyone has been mean without provocation, I'd say it's you. I've had my reasons for keeping the mayor in check. Heaven knows. Any of these men in the bar can tell you. If I gave him even a centimeter, this tavern would be closed down in an instant. I have a real reason for the things I do. And while, true, I might also benefit, so do the men who need a place to come and drink. I'm the patroness in this town. Who are you? What have you done for this village, except infect it with your bad luck?"

The men nodded. The chimney sweep glared at them all. He snorted.

"You're the one who told me to show them contempt. So what if I found something that makes me want to change my mind? Why can't I change the way I live in this world? I have a chance. It's a last chance."

Ibolya shook her head. "I can't believe it! You really do think you're in love. And I thought you were a smarter man than that. I really gave you too much credit. I should have known. You know, everybody heard that little speech you made on her front step. Craziness. Stupidity, really. Yes, I said offer them contempt, and instead you go off and spew nonsense. What's the matter with you? Wake up. A marathon lay doesn't make her your wife. You must realize this by now. She would never marry you after that show of yours. She might be a quarrelsome old bitch, but she's not dumb." The hair on Ibolya's head was beginning to quiver to life. Out of the corner of her eye she spotted Zsofi, and that made her think of the potter. Unfortunately for the girl, this made Ibolya angrier. She turned to her. "And just because he used his fingers or mouth or whatever on you, young lady, doesn't mean he's going to propose."

The men in the bar snickered; Zsofi turned red.

"It's not that," she stammered. "It's not that at all."

"Well then, what is it?" Ibolya asked. "Why won't you kiss and tell?"

Zsofi looked around. There were tears in her eyes now. She shook her head.

"Spit it out," Ibolya said.

"Tell us, little Zsofi. Tell us what that scoundrel did to you." The tears in her eyes had raised the men's hackles.

"Nothing!" Zsofi cried. "He won't do anything. That's the trouble. I swear, I really am starting to think he is a homosexual!"

Zsofi gasped and covered her mouth after she said it. She ran into the bathroom. They heard her sobbing through the closed door.

The men looked at one another. They all looked back at Ibolya. Ibolya shrugged.

"What is he?" a man asked.

"He's a what?" said another.

"I don't know," Ibolya said.

"God, you're all bumpkins!" the chimney sweep shouted. "He's a fairy. He likes men."

Ibolya gasped. The men shifted uncomfortably in their chairs.

"Valeria is a good woman," the chimney sweep said after an uncomfortable moment of silence. "You just don't understand."

Ibolya moaned loudly enough for the other patrons to stop listening to Zsofi crying in the restroom and focus their attention back on the bar.

"At last, you are absolutely correct," she said. "I do not understand a hair on that old hag's muff, or what it is that is making you men so silly over her."

The chimney sweep didn't answer. He almost looked wistful. Ibolya could tell he was thinking of Valeria.

"Well, can you tell me?" she asked. "Can you explain it to me?"

"Nothing to explain," the chimney sweep said. "She's just like you said. Hera incarnate."

Ibolya shrugged and poured the chimney sweep a drink. She poured one for herself as well.

"Can you explain what that means?"

The chimney sweep drank and considered.

"A man could settle down and still be inspired," he said. "That's all it is. She's a woman who inspires."

"That means nothing to me."

"I know," the chimney sweep said. "Valeria's inspiring. I would like to marry her."

"You little twerp. I've been married." Ibolya's ire was slowly rising again. "I understand it all too well. I'm not interested in wiping a man's ass and cooking what he likes for dinner. No thank you."

She was trying not to react, but she couldn't help but feel angered. She couldn't stomach the thought that another man she had found first would throw himself into Valeria's arms at the first opportunity. Standing there, talking to the chimney sweep, she decided she would confront the potter. If a cretin like the chimney sweep could feel these things—subtleties, she understood—then maybe her position with the potter was in more trouble than she had anticipated.

The chimney sweep began to mutter. Through bits and pieces that Ibolya was able to make out, she began to glean that he was, in fact, attempting to explain his feelings for Valeria and how they were different from his feelings toward her. He was attempting to explain the changes that had come over him.

"Oh, spare me!" Ibolya cut him off. "Christ, what does she keep down there, cotton candy? She's at least six years older than you are. She's practically got one foot in the grave."

"Valeria is unlike any woman I have paid money to, gotten drunk, or begged to be with," the chimney sweep said simply.

He sat in a reflective state and stared at the dregs in his beer bottle. Ibolya was now beyond containing herself. Her nostrils flared; she began taking deeper breaths. The chimney sweep was unaware of her temper. However, other men in the pub noticed that her hair—freshly dyed, permed, and swept onto the top of her head—was growing like an angry flame. It was the sort of flame that launches out of a fire pit unexpectedly, that bursts out and catches hold of a stray twig during a drought. They backed away from the bar.

"Tell me all about it, why don't you!" she shouted while throwing a heavy brown beer bottle at his head. Maybe she shouldn't have done it, she thought afterward. Later she would remember that this was the act that set him into motion. The bottle only glanced off his forehead, but he fell to the ground and the men around him snickered. She leaned over the bar to shout at him. "While you were busy tickling her bottom did her lover stop by for a visit?"

The chimney sweep snapped to attention. The other men, who had been snickering, stopped and pursed their lips. Even young Zsofi Toth stuck her head out of the bathroom but was otherwise still as a doe.

"What are you talking about?" the chimney sweep said in a growl. He stood up and leaned his face into hers. "What are you talking about?" The growl in his voice was the only sound in the pub. The question hung in the air like a noose. Men sensed the violence behind it. Zsofi put her hand to her throat. "What are you talking about?" The chimney sweep asked it a third time and grabbed her chin with his hand.

"Ha!" Ibolya laughed. She felt the violence as well but took it as a challenge. She batted his hand away and glared at him. "She certainly pulled the wool over your eyes. Why, she and the potter are lovers as well. I suspect if you were to pay her a visit, you'd find her sitting on his lap right now. He had not been gone from her bed a few days before she brought you in. I wonder if she even had time to change the sheets."

"We never used sheets," the chimney sweep shot back. "Too bourgeois for me. If you must know, we rutted like pigs right in her kitchen. Which potter is this?"

Young Zsofi moaned and shook her head, but Ibolya ignored her.

"The potter who is madly in love with her," Ibolya said, surprising herself. "The potter she thinks she is madly in love with. The potter who made her that ridiculous pitcher. The potter who is down at the train station doing only God knows what, who won't come to see me, who won't spend time with me, and who won't even call me, all because his precious Valeria has asked him to make her some foolish gift to put on her windowsill."

The chimney sweep shook his head. He looked winded. Ibolya smiled.

"Oh? Don't you know anything about it? How awful for you. It seems, you filthy little man, that the potter must have awakened some kind of fire in her, and you just happened to be the first piece of meat her famished body came across. It's funny really. A switch, actually. You were convenient. She used you for your sooty little pecker. How much luck does that warrant, I wonder?"

Ibolya laughed—a head-back, openmouthed laugh. She pointed at him.

"Change your life?" she giggled at him. "Last chance? You really thought these things? You never had a chance at all. You're the same miserable wretch you always were. You're going to die that way."

She couldn't have hurt him more than this. She knew it. The color left his face. He shook his head and turned to leave. She laughed at him as he left.

"Where is he? In that shop up the hill? I've seen him."

"Yes, his studio. Ask him about her. You'll see."

The chimney sweep was shaking. He left the pub and walked up the hill. A torrent of emotion swept through him. He felt his heart quicken. His skin felt tight around his bones. He remembered his life. It had been a trap from the beginning. He was trapped with who he was. Valeria was not the hope he sought. There was no hope at all. No hope, no hope, no hope. By the time he reached the potter's door he was a changed man again. He was a man scorned. He was an envious man. A beaten man. He banged the

211

door with his fist. There was no answer. He looked in through a window and then threw a stone through a glass pane and waited. There was still no answer. Unable to think of anything else, he urinated on the doormat. Then he returned to the pub. He walked in just behind the potter's apprentice.

"He's not there," the chimney sweep announced. "He's not in his workshop."

Ibolya pointed her chin at the apprentice. "Ask him where the potter is. That's his apprentice. Another shiftless Casanova. Shame on you," she said to the apprentice. "Stringing innocent young Zsofi along. You're a pervert."

The apprentice had gone home after speaking with the potter and informed his family about the potter's offer. They argued, but the apprentice announced that he would be moving out and that he would propose to Zsofi Toth. He was carrying flowers from his mother's garden. He was wearing a smart new shirt that a cousin in London had sent him. He was, at this moment, so single-minded that he did not notice Ibolya's anger, the chimney sweep behind him, or the other patrons at the bar as they stared mockingly at him. He looked at Ibolya and then turned his head toward Zsofi.

"Zsofi Toth!"

Zsofi was serving a table of young men. They had been laughing together. She noticed the flowers and stepped toward him. "Yes?"

He extended his hand.

"I've treated you horribly."

The chimney sweep grabbed the apprentice's shoulder from behind. "Hey, fairy, I want to talk to you."

The apprentice was staring into Zsofi's face. He pulled his shoulder away.

"Zsofi, I want you to quit working here and marry me. Marry me."

"Now wait just a minute!" Ibolya shouted. "Zsofi, hold on."

"Is he wearing a blouse?" one of Ibolya's patrons whispered; the others shrugged.

"I said I wanted to talk to you, fairy," the chimney sweep said.

"Marry me, Zsofi. Will you marry me?" the apprentice asked again.

"You're an idiot," Zsofi Toth answered. "But of course I'll marry you." She looked at Ibolya. "Ibolya, I'll have to quit. My fiancé doesn't like me working here."

"That's right," the potter's apprentice said.

The men in the pub groaned.

Ibolya shook her head. "Now wait just a minute."

The apprentice smiled and tried to embrace his bride to be, but Zsofi's face suddenly contorted. She wasn't smiling. She wasn't even looking at him. She was looking past him. She looked shocked. Frightened. The apprentice was about to ask her what the matter was when something landed against the back of his head.

The chimney sweep had picked up the brown beer bottle and clobbered him with it. The dregs spilled down the apprentice's back and soiled his shirt.

The chimney sweep remembered that before he arrived in this village, he had never been wrong about human nature. It was a large part of what depressed him. People never grew and they died as stupidly as they lived. Somehow he had forgotten it. These weeks in the village, he had forgotten it, but Ibolya had reminded him. He saw it all too clearly now. Of course he hadn't changed. He couldn't change. Life was a hopeless affair.

He stood over the apprentice and eyed the younger man viciously. He didn't feel any pity. He didn't feel any hope. He was lost to himself. The fact that the apprentice's shirt looked like a woman's blouse didn't help. The chimney sweep felt superior to him. To all of them, really. What kind of man dresses like a woman and proposes? What kind of man plays with clay for a living? The gangly apprentice was grasping the back of his head. He looked so soft. Like he'd never earned a hard day's living. The chimney sweep scoffed and kicked him. Apprentice indeed.

Zsofi screamed and lunged at him. Ibolya was frozen, her mouth agape. The men rose from their chairs.

"I said I wanted to talk to you, fairy!" the chimney sweep shouted into the apprentice's face, and pushed Zsofi aside. "Where's your boss?"

The apprentice clutched his head, more stunned than hurt, more embarrassed than injured. "You hit me with a bottle! You stupid little shit. You kicked me. Are you crazy?"

The apprentice propped himself up on his elbows and then sat up. The chimney sweep was directly over him, so he was unable to rest on his haunches and spring at the man. His body was tense and quivering, though, as though it was ready and straining to attack.

Zsofi had retreated behind him and was hovering by his head, holding him up by his shoulders.

"You're a maniac," he said to the chimney sweep, and then somehow was back on his feet. He pushed him. "I should kick your ass. This shirt cost a lot of money."

"Brute!" Ibolya shouted, coming to her senses. "Leave that boy alone. The potter is probably with Valeria right now, or down at the station."

The chimney sweep turned to scurry off through the hole in the wall. The apprentice reached out and grabbed his shoulder. As if on a mechanical swivel, the chimney sweep pirouetted and landed a solid punch in the younger man's stomach. A straight shot to the solar plexus. The apprentice doubled over.

"Sit down, princess," the chimney sweep growled. "You'll get yourself hurt before your wedding day. I'm not fucking about."

The apprentice fell into a chair, his face colorless. The chimney sweep was gone.

Ibolya couldn't help herself from getting one last dig at him. "If you're off to visit Valeria, be sure to knock!"

"Call the inspector!" Zsofi shouted right after.

Nineteen

The chimney sweep was shouting curses when he jumped through the hole in the wall and tore off on his bicycle toward Valeria's. A few pedestrians he saw along the way heard him coming long before they saw him, and when they saw him they didn't know whether to laugh or run for cover. The truth was, they were perplexed, because he was screaming, bellowing like an elephant. And he was such a small man! He decided he would bellow. It was a warning: he would lash at them with his teeth, or tusks, as the case might be.

When he reached Valeria's home he loosened a brick from her stairs. He was wholly conscious of everything he did. In fact, there was even a moment when a small voice warned him against carrying things too far.

"Ah well," he muttered, and he let loose the brick. It set out hard and fast and crashed against Valeria's door with a loud bang. The noise made him feel better. Valeria's curtains rustled as she hurried past.

"Of all the nerve!" she shouted. "If it's you brats, I'll fix all of you."

She opened the door with a broom held at the ready in her hands. She was prepared to sweep children off her portico. When she saw the chimney sweep, she put her broomstick down. She was still wearing her robe. The potter had left, gone back to the train station to oversee the pouring of the bronze.

"Hello," Valeria said to the chimney sweep.

He was in a fit. A scornful rage. His eyes were menacing and bright. While the satchel full of money he carried eased him somewhat, he was angry with resentment. When he thought of how foolish he had been to think he could change anything about his life, he wanted to share that disappointment as much as he could. If he could have he would have smothered the village with it. Most of all, he would have suffocated Valeria. He decided that the fault was hers. He stepped toward her and questioned her straightaway.

"Is it true? You have a lover? Are you in love with a potter?"

Valeria looked taken aback. She glanced up and down her street. She raised her eyebrows at him.

"My dear, a week in bed is very nice, but it does not make you my husband," she said. "Would you like to come in? We can talk about it."

The chimney sweep's eyelids twitched. He stammered for a moment.

"What? How can you say something like that? I expect that kind of talk from Ibolya. I don't understand."

Valeria sighed at him. A long, breathy sigh—like she had run out of patience.

"Stop thinking like a peasant," she said. "You don't own me."

It was oil to fire. The chimney sweep couldn't stop shaking his head. He had never been in this position before. Normally, he was the one trying to break himself free of a tearful woman. He stepped closer.

"Why does this matter to you anyway? You're a traveling chimney sweep. You're passing through. I figured you did this sort of thing all the time."

The chimney sweep saw a chance. Was she giving him a chance? Did she want to be pursued? Hope raised his eyebrow.

"I've been thinking of sticking around. I thought I might stay here." Valeria laughed and killed his hope again.

"No, no. I'm afraid that won't do." Valeria shook her head. She was still laughing. "That wouldn't do at all."

Damned right this wouldn't do. He took a threatening step closer. He took off his hat and twisted it.

"Don't laugh at me," he growled. Valeria silenced herself.

"Who is he, eh? That oaf in the workshop. The old man with the moustache and the little assistant. You would choose him over me? We had something."

"I don't like your tone," she said. "Let's go inside and have some tea. It really is better than shouting in the street."

She turned to enter her home. The chimney sweep followed.

When the door closed, the chimney sweep grabbed her and pulled her close. He kissed her throat.

"Stop slobbering on me," she said.

The chimney sweep put his hands inside her robe and groped her breasts.

"Please, Valeria. Please."

Valeria couldn't help but laugh. "What a day!" she giggled. "No, stop this immediately."

The chimney sweep's hands fell. He followed her to the kitchen. She pulled out a pair of teacups.

"I don't want any damned tea. I detest tea."

"Well, I need some."

"Who is this man? Who is this potter?"

"We are to be married."

"What? What do you mean? Why didn't you tell me?"

"I just discovered it myself. He came to propose. Listen, you're not quite the man I have in mind for myself," she said. She tried to make it sound gentle, but the look on his face told her she had failed. He looked hurt, like she had stepped on his toe.

The chimney sweep spied the vases on the table. He reached over and picked them up. He held them in front of him. They felt like breasts. He looked closer at them. It dawned on him that they were Valeria's breasts. He became sickened. His intestines heaved. He threw the vases to the ground and they shattered.

"Worthless trash," he said.

Valeria was stunned. She picked up the hot kettle and held it in front of her threateningly.

"Get out!" she shouted.

The chimney sweep turned and ran out. She threw a mug at him, but he had already slammed the door.

Valeria swept up the broken pieces. She felt sorry for the vases and also for the potter, who would be disappointed when he returned. What a silly mistake to have made, she thought to herself. Being with the chimney sweep certainly wasn't worth this. Valeria sighed. She understood that she should have had more faith.

"But how does one ever know until they know?" she said to herself.

She tossed the shards of pottery into the trash and sat down at her kitchen table. She looked up at the black plates hanging on her kitchen wall. She looked at the patched-up ewer. She smiled.

"He can make me new ones," she said, "and I'll have faith that everything can work."

She was unsure for a moment about whether she believed that or not, but she decided that she would believe it, and in the decision to do so, she found the strength to finish dressing and wait for the potter to return.

However, the chimney sweep had not left. He was sitting outside her door. He sat there for a good ten minutes plotting his next move. He stood up and knocked again.

"Who is it?" Valeria asked.

She opened it.

"What about us?" the chimney sweep argued one last time. "It meant something."

Valeria's stare withered him.

"We had a nice time," she corrected him firmly and coldly. "That's all. You're making it mean more than it did. Now you're behaving crazily."

The chimney sweep's mind went blank. He slapped her. He didn't think about it. His hand simply shot out and pressed against her cheek. He stunned them both. He was immediately sorry. A red welt grew across her cheek.

Valeria screamed, pulled away, and her face darkened in an instant. Then he tried to step back, to step away from her. She picked up the broom and swung it in his face. He tripped over his heels and landed on his bottom, at the bottom of the stairs.

He was looking up at her now. She ran down after him swinging the broom and shouting at the top of her voice. He only had a second to break away. He scurried backward, then got to his feet. He ran to the other side of the gate.

"I'll kill him," he spat at her. "I'll kill him."

A few of Valeria's neighbors heard the shouting. At first they tittered.

"It's like a cathouse," they giggled. They saw the chimney sweep running past. Valeria was standing at her gate swinging her broom and shouting after him.

"What's the matter, Valeria? Men troubles?"

"He hit me," she gasped. She was shocked and embarrassed that it had happened. She went and sat on her steps. She shook her head.

The neighbors looked at one another. They stopped smiling. A few of them went to visit her. She looked meek and tired. They grew concerned.

"Did he hurt you?"

"That bastard."

"He smacked a woman."

The others went to spread the news: something disgusting had happened at Valeria's house. The potter and the chimney sweep had been there on the same day! The bed hadn't cooled down between them. The chimney sweep got angry and belted her. She had a black eye. He'd broken her leg.

The number of visitors at her side grew quickly from a handful to twenty. Then it grew from twenty to fifty. It seemed that within a few minutes her yard was full of people who let themselves in. They didn't even ask. The gate was open and they walked in. *Serves me right for not locking it*, Valeria thought.

Her neighbors brought food. They brought wet cloths and hot water bottles.

"Are you okay?" a woman asked.

"We heard he beat you," a second said.

"I'm fine," Valeria answered. "Really. I'm fine. It's not that serious. I've called the police station."

Valeria tried to rise to go inside, but she was pinned in from all sides. She couldn't get away. It seemed that the harder she tried, the harder her neighbors kept their eyes on her.

"Don't let her leave until the police come."

"She might be suicidal."

Valeria resigned herself to her fate and hoped the inspector would arrive soon.

Twenty

At Ibolya's tavern, a group of hard-drinking men, men who'd seen or carried out all manner of violence, were partially sobered up and helping to make sure the potter's apprentice was all right. He was fine, only wounded pride. Many of them patted him on the shoulder and then left. They walked home in silence and spent the night with their wives.

"There's blood in the air," they muttered when their wives asked them why they were home so early.

Then their wives nodded and told them about the stories coming from across the village from Valeria's street.

"He broke her arm and gave her a fat lip," they repeated. "The whole affair is just too revolting."

"Hrmph," said the men. "That's not the way to do things."

They closed their curtains and turned on their televisions.

Zsofi Toth and the potter's apprentice embraced outside Ibolya's tavern. She rubbed his head and kissed his cheek. Ibolya had apologized and given him a red kerchief and ice. His brothers had all been called and came quickly to pick him up. They wanted to wait for the chimney sweep to return, or go out looking for him— "We'll fix him," they said. "Maybe lock him in one of those oversized cellar safes"—but the potter's apprentice shook his head and convinced the lot of them to leave.

"Let's go visit Zsofi's mother," he said. "She baked some pies."

They didn't say good-bye to Ibolya or even acknowledge her. They drove off as she came out to offer them refreshments—free of charge. She spied the backs of their heads in the car. The apprentice had his arm around Zsofi's shoulder and Zsofi's head rested against him. They were laughing in that car. Ibolya saw the way their heads tilted back and their mouths opened wide and carefree. She felt a kick in her stomach. She shivered. They looked so good. They looked so young and happy. The car's wheels spun a cloud of dust at her, and then they were gone. She couldn't help but feel hopeful for the young couple. *I bet they'll last*, she thought.

Feeling hopeful herself, Ibolya was emboldened to chase down her own desires. Why not? Everyone else was doing it. Why not go to the potter and declare her feelings once and for all? Yes, she would do exactly that. Ibolya went to the restroom and washed her face. She let her hair down and shook it out. She changed blouses and dabbed a bit of White Musk behind her ears.

"Watch the bar," she called out as she left, and marched up the hill to the potter's workshop. It was now good and dark out. The sky was clear. The air was cool. The moon was full and bright. She even had a bounce in her step.

As she climbed the small hill, the potter pulled up on his bicycle alongside her. He was just returning from the train station. She straightened her back and smiled at him. Two rows of perfect teeth. Teeth anyone would be proud of. Her own teeth.

"Hello, stranger," she said pleasantly. "Coming from the station? I was just coming to visit you."

The potter nodded and smiled. He got off his bicycle and walked beside her.

"Were you?" he said. "I was coming to visit you."

Ibolya's heart quickened. They reached his workshop, and the potter spotted the broken window. He looked through the hole in the glass.

"Let's go in," she said, and motioned to the latch on the door. "It's chilly out."

The potter shifted. The time had come. He would have to let her know his intentions. He couldn't carry on like this. He nodded, unfastened the latch, and opened the door. Ibolya bustled in noisily. She took off her shawl. She made large movements, hoping her perfume would waft over to him. It was the perfume she wore when she knew they would be intimate. She had been training him. Like Pavlov.

"Well," she huffed, "I figured if you would not come to me, I would come to you. How do you like that, eh? Aren't you flattered? You have me behaving like an eager schoolgirl."

The potter put his hands into his pockets and rocked on his heels. Ibolya looked him up and down. He looked wretched. Wasted away. His skin was yellowed. His cheekbones pressed through his flesh. She tried not to register her disappointment on her face. She was afraid that he might see her expression and take offense.

"Somebody threw a brick at my window," he said. "Who would do that? Why would someone do that?"

"What's that?" Ibolya asked. She would ignore the question and steer it in a different direction. "I come to visit and you ask about a window? Don't you even appreciate my coming? Don't you realize what the graceless women in the village will be saying about me tomorrow? You've got quite the reputation now, you know. Oh, yes! A real Casanova. They'll think I'm shameless, visiting you so late at night. I would expect a smile from you at least."

"I'm sorry, Ibolya!" the potter exclaimed.

That was more like it! He was apologizing. It was a good sign. Ibolya shook her head and waved him off. She let down her guard and looked around his workshop. It was as unkempt as the potter was. Bread crusts were thrown into a corner. A paint bucket was filled with coffee grounds and orange peels.

"You look horrible," she said. "What on earth is the matter with you? Why is this place so filthy? What are you doing in here?"

"I've been busy. I've been working."

"So the mayor tells me, not to mention your apprentice." Ibolya spotted the botched turnips and figurines that were strewn about the room. She peeked around, trying to get her bearings, trying to get a footing. "In fact, he's been telling us quite a bit. He had a scrape at the bar."

The potter looked concerned.

"What? Is he all right?"

Ibolya put her hand on his shoulder. "He's fine. He proposed; she accepted. It was very romantic. I think they'll be okay together. They're good kids."

The potter nodded.

"He also mentioned to me that you're retiring," Ibolya continued. "I think that's fabulous."

"It is," the potter said.

Ibolya went to a table and looked at the turnip models.

"He also said that you're making our old lady friend a bushel of . . . terra-cotta apples?"

"They're not apples." The potter sighed.

"Tomatoes then?"

"No."

His reticence was pestering her. He didn't seem happy to see her. She was embarrassing herself like some dumb woman who couldn't let go, who couldn't realize that the man she was hounding just wasn't interested.

"Well, I don't really care what they are!" Ibolya suddenly shouted and moved at him. She couldn't stop herself. It made her feel better. "I just want you to stop making them. I want you to forget about her. Can't you do that for me?"

She rubbed her body against him. She caressed his face. Her palms rubbed his cheekbones. The potter tilted his head back as if to avoid her mouth, as if to get a better look at her.

"Why?" he asked.

Ibolya remembered what the chimney sweep had told her he felt about Valeria. Her hands felt like stones. She kept them on the potter's face, though. She would not lose. This was a test of wills. Nothing more.

"Were you this stupid with your wife?" she asked. "I can take care of you, you know. We can make a home together. We're good for each other in so many ways. I think our relationship should be more exclusive after all."

The potter nodded.

"Silly man, I really miss you."

The potter knitted his eyebrows together.

"Yes, but why?" he said.

Ibolya threw her arms around his neck and embraced him. She buried her head into his chest. He returned the embrace, but it wasn't the embrace of a lover. He was indulging her. Like a friend. A kind old friend.

He kissed her on the forehead. She could have killed him for that.

"Why are you wasting your time on her?"

"I have to. I am inspired by her. I love her."

And there it was. As easy as that. Moonlight or broad daylight, there was no arguing facts. The potter felt a load lifted from him the moment he uttered the words, that instant. He could breathe again. Life was easy after all.

Ibolya frowned. Valeria had nothing to seduce a man with, no charms to give. Yet somehow, the old woman, a woman nobody in their right mind would have thought of as anything but an old hen, a hag, was really a weasel, and while Ibolya wasn't watching, the crafty weasel had stolen her lover away and left her the clucking hen.

Ibolya hated mewling, but she had to understand. She kept asking him to explain himself. She kept trying to negotiate. The potter answered as best he could, but after a few moments he realized there would be no end to the conversation. He shook his head.

"Ibolya, you have been kind. I am very fond of you. But the truth is that you do not inspire me. You have never inspired me. You have never made me feel like I could be a bigger man. You have never made me feel like I could have a larger life."

"Ibolya motioned to the pieces of pottery around them. "They're only plates. You're only making saucers."

The potter stepped away from her and walked to his workbench.

"And that is the reason," he said. "That is the reason why I don't love you. Plates are all they could ever be to you. But Valeria loves them. Loves that I do them. Believes that there is value in them. And it was the same with my Magda. She cherished them also. I felt cherished. Even though she was ill. That is the reason why Valeria inspires me."

Ibolya reddened. A quiver of anger was dancing in a lock of her hair. She was tired, though, and so it fell limply against her cheek. Defeated. She brushed it aside and tucked the stray tendrils behind her ear.

"What does a woman get, I wonder?" Ibolya asked. "What was in it for Magda? What's in it for Valeria? What's in it for me? For any woman? She gets a man? That's all? That's the prize? That's not much of a prize, mister." She pointed at one of the botched turnips. "That is only a piece of clay. I am real. I am a person. I have a heart. What about you, bastard? Do you have a heart?"

"Of course I do," the potter answered. "You are a person I am very fond of."

Ibolya shook her head and laughed. She pointed at the turnips. "They look like breasts! Why are you in here squeezing breasts out of clay when I would be happy and willing to let you squeeze mine?" A sound came out of her. Not a shout or moan. It was frustration. "I positively hate this."

She snatched a turnip from his workbench and smashed it to the ground.

"I won't allow you to ignore me over this! I won't." She swept the table with her arm and everything on it fell. She felt better. She even laughed.

"There. Does that inspire you?" she asked. She was daring him.

The potter's face trembled. He looked at the shattered pottery on the floor. His hand shot out and pointed at the shattered pieces.

The two were silent a moment.

"Ibolya," he said finally, talking himself down, trying to keep from hoisting her up and throwing her out on her ear. "I would choose those chips over you. Every sliver, every shard means more to me than you ever could. You don't understand that, you couldn't, but Valeria does. She understands that exactly. That is why I will be devoted. Neither of us has to explain anything to the other. Now please just take this as a fact and leave me alone."

Ibolya fell back. Her mouth opened. Her hand rose to her cheek. It felt hot, like she had just been smacked. She teared up. This made her hotter. She turned and left without saying another word. She hoped her trembling legs would carry her. She walked out of his workshop and back toward her pub with her hand on her face.

"That bastard," she whispered to herself, over and over again. "I can't believe it."

She repeated those words as she made her way down the hill and back to her tavern. When she reached the tavern and walked

228

inside, she was still saying them. Even when she stepped behind her bar, she was repeating them. When her customers looked at her and saw her mumbling to herself, though they couldn't make out what she was saying, they understood the look on her face and kept quiet.

The chimney sweep returned only a moment later. He looked angrier than she. He saw her holding her hand against her cheek and mumbling to herself, and he also understood. He immediately understood. She didn't need to explain. Indeed, he understood so well that he grabbed the bottle of beer that was still on the ground where he had attacked the potter's apprentice, and he hammered it until the bottle neck broke off in his hands. Jagged ends of glass stuck out and the other men sitting in the bar grew quiet.

"Is he home?" he asked in that same low growl.

Ibolya nodded.

"You can watch him get a thrashing if you like," he said.

And Ibolya turned around, right around, without hesitation. She even smiled. *Here's a man,* she thought. She didn't require any further explanation. She just walked from behind her bar, took the chimney sweep's hand, and leaned up against him.

"I'm going to hurt him," the chimney sweep whispered. "You watch."

"Good," she said. "Hurt him."

They left. They were like a pair of Furies of olden times, each consumed and pulling the other to greater depths. They headed back up the hill, back toward the potter's workshop. It was abysmally silent when they left.

Twenty-one

There was silence in the tavern until the pair were out of earshot. The men looked from one to another hoping that someone else would speak first. That a murder in their small village was about to take place seemed certain. At least the intent had a stench, thick and overbearing. It stunk all around them. They felt dirty just being there. Whose murder, though? Valeria's or the potter's? Perhaps both? Of this they were not so certain, but the simple fact, the intent, why, it was as clear as the bottom of their beer glasses. The chimney sweep seemed a dangerous enough character on his own. But now, with Ibolya at his side, there was no telling what the two were capable of. The men in the pub shuffled and hesitated, knowing that every second in silence was a step closer to the potter's workshop. Finally, the soberest of them all, the redhaired man named Ferenc, spoke. He had long ago decided that he would always protect Ibolya, even from herself. He pointed to a pair of men.

"The two of you hunt down the mayor and the chief inspector. The rest of us will stop Ibolya and the twerp."

The two men nodded and set off. The rest of the pub—ten men in all—followed Ferenc as he followed Ibolya and the chimney sweep toward the potter's.

"The poor potter," said one of the men, suddenly figuring things out.

"Why's that?" asked another.

"Are you blind? It's the potter they're going after. I can't believe it. He never hurt anybody."

"Bah. It's all poppycock to me. Disgusting. The lot of them. Disgusting. Especially that Valeria. She's so old. She's a lot older than the chimney sweep, older than Ibolya too."

"She's older than me," announced one of the men.

They began to argue. They were drunk, after all.

"I thought chimney sweeps were supposed to be lucky?"

"Don't you remember those caterpillars? He was here when the caterpillars hatched."

"He destroyed my sugar beets," Ferenc said. "Remember when he first came in and asked me about my fields? Why, I bet that little twerp was mucking about on my land. That bastard!"

"That wasn't the chimney sweep's fault."

"Wasn't it? Then my wife gave him ten thousand forints and practically lifted her skirt for him right in front of me. Right in front of me she's panting and rubbing up against him like a cat. Frankly, he can have her. It was the money that made me angry. That money was two weeks' work. I swear I could have boxed her ears in when he left. Show her who's boss. And has my life changed? Have your lives changed? Since he arrived, I'd say things have gotten worse. My asshole brings me more luck and relief than that midget ever did."

"Well, let's go and get him!"

The men began running, as quickly as the drunk are able. They overtook Ibolya and the chimney sweep fifty meters from the potter's home.

"Go back and sit down," Ibolya ordered as the group of men surrounded them. "This isn't any of your concern."

"We can't let you hurt the potter," Ferenc said to her. "Run away with me instead, Ibolya."

"Why don't you get your ugly mugs out of here," the chimney sweep said. He brandished his beer bottle.

"I wouldn't be giving any orders just now, midget. You'll be lucky to get out of this with all your teeth."

"Ah! I'm not scared of you. I've been in worse scrapes than this. You're just a bunch of dirty hick farmers."

The men pushed him from all sides. The chimney sweep slashed with his bottle.

Ferenc punched first. He punched the chimney sweep in the nose.

"Get back to the bar right now," Ibolya commanded.

But they weren't listening to her anymore. They were focusing their attention on the little man standing beside her. Once Ferenc threw the punch, the others moved in and pummeled him.

The half of the men who couldn't get through to get their own crack at him didn't hesitate. They snatched Ibolya, hoisted her into the air above them, and carried her back to the pub. She screamed and thrashed, but they were gentle with her. They set her down behind her bar.

"This is where you belong," they tried to convince her good-naturedly. "Why do you want to hurt the potter? He's nice man. He made all of us those wonderful plates and steins. Forget about him. You can have any of us instead. Take Ferenc, for instance. Ferenc really loves you, you know. He has for years. You've made him suffer so much. We've all had to hear about it, you know. You can have Ferenc. Just say the word and he'd be yours. He's a nice guy. Think about it."

All the men nodded and straightened up.

"You stupid, filthy farmers!" she shouted. "I'd become a nun before marrying another one of you!"

They booed her. Then they slapped their hands against the bar. They ordered drinks.

"We're going to spend a lot of money tonight, old girl," one of them said.

"Whatever it takes to make you happy. That's how much we love you."

Ibolya wasn't listening. She had begun to cry. Her head fell to the bar and she really wept. Cried right into the dish towel. The men were taken aback. They looked at one another and shrugged. One man motioned to another and they went behind the bar beside her. They served themselves. They paid double what they normally would. It was the only generous thing they could think to do.

On the road to the potter's, the rest of the men were beating the chimney sweep soundly. They had tried to wrench his arm to make him let go of the bottle, but the chimney sweep wasn't as easy to roughhouse as they had thought. He fought back viciously. His fists seemed to come at them from five different directions. They didn't have much weight to them, but drunk as the men were, the chimney sweep's fists stung their brows and noses and dizzied them into vertigo. One of the attackers even fell. His vertigo, his heavy supper—he could not help himself. He hunched over and lost his stomach.

"Phew," the others said, and tried not to step near him.

The chimney sweep kicked. He hadn't let up fighting a single moment. When the others tried to break away to look to their comrade, the chimney sweep was all over them.

Finally, several of the largest men jostled him into the gully alongside the road.

"Whoa. He's scrappy, this chimney sweep. It's like fighting a cat."

The chimney sweep, furious, stood up and tried to charge up the embankment.

"I'm going to kill you all!" he shouted.

The men saw him coming and laughed.

"What a dwarf!"

They threw stones at him and one caught the chimney sweep in the forehead. He stumbled and slipped back down the embankment. The men laughed. They taunted him from their position.

The chimney sweep looked up. He couldn't see their faces through his bruised eyes, but he made out their figures. Someone was peeing. He heard it hitting the grass.

"Your mothers are all bitches," he answered.

"You cut our mechanic's hand pretty bad," Ferenc said. "He's pretty angry with you right now. As for me, I'm ready to bash your skull in. My wife paid you ten thousand forints and lifted her skirt for you. Isn't that true?"

"Well? Chimney sweep? Is it true? Did she lift her skirt?"

"I'm not sure," the chimney sweep called out. He had been looking for a way to escape. The gully seemed to run beside the road all the way to the centrum. If he could make it there, he might make it back to Valeria's cottage. "Is your wife the fat one with the hairy ass?"

The men above laughed.

"Ferenc!" one man shouted. "The dwarf knows your wife!"

Ferenc ripped his shirt off and tried to jump down into the gully, but the other men held him back. The chimney sweep could hear them arguing.

"You see? I'll kill him!" Ferenc shouted. "I'll kill you, you dickhead!"

Ferenc spat into the gully. He kicked dirt.

"Hey, chimney sweep!" one of the men shouted. "Play nice. You're in a world of trouble right now. If Ferenc's wife really did show you her whiskers, what color were they?"

"Rat brown. Same as yours."

The men laughed again.

The chimney sweep couldn't help but snicker.

"You know, you're very stupid people," he said.

"That may be," Ferenc answered, "but we're up here and you're down there."

"True enough. I'm coming up. I give up."

The chimney sweep pulled himself up the side of the embankment. He was too tired to run. He could barely claw his way back up. His face pressed against mud and scraped against stone. His fingers pulled out clumps of grass. When he reached the top, a hand pulled him to his feet.

"You tell good jokes."

"Thanks. Fuck you," the chimney sweep said.

A fist landed against his jaw. A fresh barrage of punches pummeled him.

The chimney sweep spat his broken teeth at them and made a lot of noise trying to get away from them. The more he did and the louder he cursed, the more violent the men became. They beat him mercilessly now. Fists hammered across his breast and on his back. Kicks pummeled his belly and groin. The chimney sweep was hunched over, on his knees, unable to defend himself.

"You're not much of a chimney sweep anyway!" a voice cried out. "You're not very lucky!"

The others agreed and punched him some more.

"You're not very friendly!"

The chimney sweep felt hands searching through his pockets and grabbing his satchel. He thrashed about trying to keep them away.

"Look at this! He's loaded! Would you take a look at this?"

Money was spilling out of the chimney sweep's satchel. The men looked at one another and grabbed what they could. They turned his pockets out and tore through his bag until his stash was gone. All of it. Two hundred thousand forints gone in an instant.

"You had better get out of our village," they said nervously. "While you're still breathing. You've brought nothing but trouble here."

"Thieves!" the chimney sweep shouted and grabbed at the bills. "Give me my money. I earned it. I suffered for it. Give it back."

The broken bottle neck was at their feet. One of them men picked it up and tossed it over the embankment with a sneer of disgust.

Twenty-two

Violence has its sounds. A repertoire of them. The sounds of grunts and screams, of breaking bones and popping joints, of bloodletting and cracked vertebrae. Recognizing the sounds is no large feat. Surely the noises reside in an atavistic memory stored in DNA carried over from the era of the earliest tribes. After all, it was the sounds of distant violence that informed a tribe that they had to fight or flee.

And even in a more modern, civilized era, violence holds the same sway. Over meters, through walls, and into a muffled work-shop, the whisper of violence seeps in. In this particular case, the shouting and cursing, the bludgeoning of fists against teeth, against muscle—this din could not help but reach the potter inside his workshop. When he first thought he heard it, he stopped what he was doing—which was lamenting and cleaning up his shattered turnips—and opened his door. He was hit with more of the noise and he looked around in the darkness. In the moonlight, he spotted a band of shadows beating someone, just down the road from his doorstep and close enough to the ravine that he winced for all their safety, frightened that the man they were beating, and all of them as well, might accidentally fall over and into the gully. Though it was not a deep gully, they could easily hurt themselves if they landed the wrong way, he thought. Break an arm, perhaps, especially if they tried to break their fall and failed. He cursed and stepped outside. He walked down the hill.

He approached the men lost in a reverie. He was thinking of his future. He was thinking of Valeria's fountain. He was content. His insides stirred, however, at the sound of that last blow. A knuckle had cracked and a man had cried out.

"Hey!" He was surprised at the harshness in his own voice. It was barely checked. Fight or flee. It was a moment of self-awareness for the potter. He recognized which way he'd like to run, but it was too late to change his mind. The men stopped what they were doing and watched him approach. He kicked gravel over the side of the precipice. He was still in his suit.

"What's going on here? What are you doing? Ferenc, is that you? You had better stop this nonsense before I call the inspector. What kind of night is this? That moon has made us all loonies."

The potter looked down at the chimney sweep. It was their first time seeing one another since the chimney sweep had arrived. The potter, now fully aware of what had gone on between Valeria and the chimney sweep, didn't feel immediately sorry for the other man, but the chimney sweep looked a miserable figure. The men beating him were bleary eyed. They had an unfair advantage over him. What they were doing was wrong, he thought. They looked like a band of apes mauling a banana. They were breathing hard and rubbing their hands.

"You would do well to shut up, potter," Ferenc said. "If anything, you should be thanking us and buying us drinks. We're doing this for you, you know. So that you can make your plates in peace."

"Thieves," the chimney sweep spat. "Thieves! Help! Police!"

Someone punched him.

The potter stepped closer to the drunken men.

"What are you talking about? I'm right here. Nothing's happened to me. Ibolya came over and started throwing some of my plates around is all. I told her to leave." He began pulling them away from the chimney sweep. "There, there. Enough of this. What are you doing out here? Stop it and go home. Go home, all of you. Go home or go back to the pub. Leave this man alone. He could fall over and really hurt himself."

"Thieves! Help! Police!"

"What are you talking about?" the potter asked the chimney sweep. "Did they take something from you? Did you all take something from him? You had better give it back."

The men tried to push the potter out of the way, but the potter was far tougher than they imagined, and his feet were planted firmly on the ground. He would not be pushed aside too easily. The men were too winded to entertain the idea of another skirmish. The potter continued pulling them away from the chimney sweep —who by this time looked like a tattered scarecrow at their feet.

"You daft idiot!" One of the men had finally had enough. He boxed the potter against his ear. "What did you want with Valeria anyway? Wasn't one old woman enough for you?"

The men laughed. They had spent a lot of energy fighting with the chimney sweep. In their stupor they thought the potter coming out and defending him the way he had was insulting. A slap in their faces. They pointed at him and the chimney sweep.

"You two should fight it out yourselves."

The potter felt a foot kick his knee out from behind him. Then a pair of hands pushed him and he tipped over and tumbled headfirst down the embankment. The men cheered. Even the chimney sweep looked up and smiled when the potter sailed past.

"Good show! Good show!" he wheezed at the men's feet.

"Shut up, you bastard. Nobody asked you," said one of the men.

"Yeah, but since you like it so much, maybe you should join him," said a second.

"Yeah, screw this. Let them fight it out. I'm thirsty."

The men hoisted the chimney sweep over their heads as easily as if he had been a pillow. They tossed him over the side of the gully. He landed feet away from the potter with a thud and a grunt. He landed next to his broken bottle. The men above shouted insults and kicked pebbles. The potter was sitting and rubbing his ear and back. He crawled over to the chimney sweep's side and shook him on his shoulder.

"Hey, fella, are you all right? These men are crazy tonight. Let's lie low and you can spend the night at my workshop. You can set off tomorrow morning."

"They took my money," the chimney sweep whined. He opened an eye but it couldn't focus; it rolled about in its socket. The potter shuddered. The small man looked mad.

"Are you all right?" the potter shook him and asked again.

"They took my money!" His eye danced around and finally came to rest on the potter. It seemed to focus all of a sudden and the eyebrow that was able knitted furiously.

"You!"

"Let's not worry about money now. We'll get it back. When they leave, I'll get you out of here."

"No," the chimney sweep protested, and pushed away. "I don't need your help."

The potter wasn't sure he understood him correctly. He leaned in closer.

"Don't be silly," the potter said. "I'll take you to the inspector in the morning."

"I don't need your help." The chimney sweep pushed the potter again. He patted the ground around them.

"Be still," the potter said. "Calm down. I'll get you fixed up, but be still."

The chimney sweep found the broken beer bottle. He was smiling and sputtering, laughing and hacking.

"What's that you've got there?" the potter asked.

The chimney sweep lunged at him. He swiped and slashed wildly. It was frightening how quickly he moved. The potter was only just able to get his body away and his hands out in front of him. The chimney sweep slashed. The potter shouted to the men above, who were walking away.

"Help! Help! He's cut me! Ferenc, he's cut me! I'm bleeding. My God, I'm bleeding badly. My hands. Help me."

The men above stopped and turned around. They began to curse and yell at each other. The chimney sweep looked frantically about. His eyeball started dancing in its socket again. He tried to attack the potter a second time, but this time the potter kicked and caught him in the jaw. Then the chimney sweep turned over. He began to crawl away. The potter reached for his leg and tried to grab him, but a bolt of electricity shot up his arm. His hand slid off the chimney sweep's heel. He shouted out in pain.

The men stumbled their way down the embankment. A pair of them easily caught up with the chimney sweep, who had mustered enough strength to scurry. The others surrounded the potter and scratched their heads. The potter was holding his hands together. Ferenc used his torn shirt as a tourniquet and tied it around the potter's right arm. They lifted him to his feet and carried him up the hill. They apologized all the while. He was cursing back at them. He looked pale and shriveled. The other pair lifted the chimney sweep and brought him back up the hill as well. They marched down to Ibolya's tavern and dropped both men off. The bloodlust left them. The men were good and sober now. They asked if the inspector had arrived and when they discovered he hadn't, they called the police station.

Twenty-three

The police station in Zivatar was a forgotten, decrepit building around the corner from the mayor's office. In the nineteenth century it had been a stable. It was a simple structure with solid walls and shingles, and the arched doorways were tall enough for a man to ride a horse through. The police force was generally as forgotten by the populace as the building and only consisted of an officer and his deputy. The officer liked to be addressed as chief inspector. His deputy was referred to as deputy. The village had no real need for a police force. There wasn't any violence to speak of. Theft wasn't normally a problem. Generally, the chief inspector and his deputy served as the mayor's lackeys when foreign dignitaries arrived. They did the driving and fetched fresh drinks. They were both armed but felt uneasy about it. As a result, they over-compensated and were quick to brandish their weapons at the slightest provocation, the deputy especially. The inspector was the smarter of the two. He had a wife, a daughter, and a small weekend garden where he grew pear trees.

When the phone rang, the chief inspector was not sitting in his plush chair. His deputy wasn't either. Thirty minutes before the call was placed, the pair of men Ferenc had sent had arrived from Ibolya's tavern. They were sweating and out of breath. They looked around the police station uncomfortably and spotted the chief inspector and his deputy playing cards in one of the cells. Both men were former classmates of the chief inspector, but they knew that didn't help their situation. They understood that the chief inspector had long ago decided he need not associate with the lower classes. He liked to keep his personal relations as seemly as possible, in order, he thought, to help the mayor succeed in all his endeavors.

So before the two men from the pub could say a word about the goings-on at Ibolya's tavern, the chief inspector told them he wasn't interested in anything they had to say. He told them he was unavailable, as he needed to be near the phone should the mayor call for any kind of assistance with his foreign guests.

"In fact, you should leave this instant," he said.

His former classmates looked at the wall clock and saw how much time had passed since they left the pub. They wouldn't budge. They didn't dare. They implored the inspector to follow them.

"There really is trouble tonight," they said.

Then they pleaded until the inspector gave in with a sigh and a shrug.

"At least let us finish this round of gin," the chief said. "I've almost got him."

The two men nodded, understanding the importance of a card game. They tried to hurry the game along by assisting the unfortunate deputy—especially when it became all too obvious that the young man had no talent for playing cards and that the game was bound to last another hour without their help.

"That's sweet," one of them said to the deputy, pointing at the card he should drop. "You must come from a nice home."

"Deputy, what kind of a sissy are you? Does your pistol even have bullets?" the second man asked, picking cards up from the deck and handing them to the young man.

The deputy shrugged. He was a good-natured lad. Everyone knew he was only made deputy because the mayor's wife liked to look at him in his uniform.

After they had suffered through the final round of play and the chief inspector had sufficiently castigated his young deputy, he stood and announced that they were departing.

"First, though, we must stop by Valeria's cottage. There was an incident there earlier. Then we must check in with my good friend the mayor at the new hotel."

The two men groused. "We have no time. There's murder in the air over at Ibolya's."

The chief inspector scoffed.

"Did you witness a murder?"

"No, sir," the men responded.

"Has anything actually transpired?

"No, sir." The men looked sheepish. "But it will. We're sure of it. That little chimney sweep."

"Gentlemen. There's a reason why I'm the chief inspector and you're not. This is a peaceful village. We shall drive to Valeria's, and then on to the mayor's, and then on to Ibolya's tavern. Don't worry about a thing. Please, now, put your faith in me and my six years of experience."

The men agreed and followed the chief inspector to his automobile.

The chief inspector was not a stupid man. In reality he knew that, either way, the mayor would be angry about being disturbed. If there really was a murder, it made sense to the inspector that they visit before finding out anything for certain. The chief inspector hated to be the bearer of bad news. In the event of any trouble, he could send the deputy to the mayor's and he could stay at the scene . . . keeping everything under control. Yes, that is exactly what he would do.

The two men were uneasy sitting in back of the police car, and they looked to one another for support in the chief inspector's presence. The inspector had attained a level of sophistication neither of them possessed. They were simple farmers. The first man owned an orchard of plums. The second owned an orchard of pears. They were the best of friends and indistinguishable from one another. Both men were of medium height and build. They had married sisters from a different village and lived next door to one another. Mr. Plum owned a truck. Mr. Pear owned a tractor. They worked each other's orchards and supplied Ibolya's tavern with strong homemade brandy. Though not too bright, they were an amiable pair.

"Is the mayor entertaining American investors?" Mr. Plum asked from the backseat of the police cruiser.

The chief inspector laughed. "Don't be ridiculous. Those same Asians—from Korea or some such place." Then he began to curse. "The whole fucking country gets Americans. Army bases everywhere. We get Koreans. Why are we so unlucky?"

"The chimney sweep?" the deputy volunteered. "Maybe Valeria sucked it all out of him. Maybe he's not lucky at all."

The two men in back laughed and shrugged. It was all the same to them.

They arrived at Valeria's cottage. She was sitting on her steps and was surrounded by her neighbors. They were consoling her, and by the look of boredom on her face it was obvious she was tired of being consoled. She certainly wasn't feeling sorry for herself. She was more angry than anything else.

"Get away already," she complained.

Her neighbors shook their heads.

"You poor woman."

"What a miserable wretch that chimney sweep is."

When the police car pulled up and the inspector pulled his

window down, Valeria burst through the crowd, rushed to the car, and pointed down the street.

"You certainly took your time," she said. "The chimney sweep hit me and ran that way. I think he'll do something terrible," she said.

Mr. Plum and Mr. Pear nodded in the backseat.

"We've told them that," they said. "We're on our way to the tavern now."

Valeria's neighbors followed her. They tried to pull her back to her steps. She could see they were prepared to console her all night. The thought of that actually made her shiver. She opened the back door to the police car.

"Move over," she said. "Let me in. I think I'd rather come with you." She didn't wait for the two men to move. She nearly sat on top of Mr. Plum in her attempt to escape her cloying neighbors.

"Now wait just a minute," the inspector said. He turned to protest.

She raised an eyebrow.

"Be careful," was all he muttered. "Don't stick your hands or head out the window."

The car pulled off. The crowd waved at her.

"Be strong," a woman offered.

When they arrived at the hotel, the chief inspector parked and exited. He was gone for what seemed a long while. Valeria and the two men began to grow impatient. They harassed the deputy.

"Listen, we really have to go. We don't have time for this," Mr. Pear said.

"Hold your horses. The chief inspector will be with you shortly."

"I'm going in to get him," said Valeria.

"Now hold on there. You can't do that," the deputy said, and got out of the car first. He blocked her door with his hand resting on the butt of his pistol. "That's to be a three-star hotel, and I'm sorry, but you're not dressed properly. There's a private meeting going on in there. You can't just walk in on that. I'd have to shoot you."

The men were ready to open the other car door when the hotel's sliding doors opened and the chief inspector and the mayor stepped out. The mayor did not look happy. The deputy hurried back to his seat. None of them could hear what the mayor and the chief inspector were talking about, but they could see the spittle flying from the mayor's mouth into the chief inspector's eye. They wondered if he would wipe it away, but he never did. He stood there and listened, nodding his head and smiling. He was the perfect subordinate. The mayor stopped talking and turned toward their window. He looked into the car at Valeria and the two men but did not say hello or acknowledge them in any way. Mr. Plum and Mr. Pear shrank back at the sight of him. The mayor had fully recovered his senses and confidence. His hair was coiffed and his teeth were a brilliant white. His time at the pub was a memory past, an anomaly in his otherwise triumphant life. He motioned for Valeria to open their window and she obliged.

"Good evening, Miss Valeria."

"Good evening, mayor."

"Good evening, mayor," the two men beside her said. "Nice to see you again. You're looking well. How's the missus?"

"Fucking hell!" the mayor shouted at them, and then he looked at Valeria and apologized. He returned his gaze to the men. "Tell Ibolya that she has until morning to fix all this or I will have the chief inspector close that pub down for good. Enough is enough. That place is more trouble than it's worth. I'm holding you two personally responsible for any trouble that goes on down there."

Mr. Plum and Mr. Pear looked at one another and shook their heads.

"We didn't have anything to do with it, mayor," they protested. "We had just arrived there ourselves looking to play a game of cards, get away from the wives. The place looked a mess. People shouting. You couldn't play cards there. Not tonight, anyway."

"To hell with it!" the mayor shouted at them, and excused himself to Valeria. "I hope the place burns down. I'm serious. I don't have time to worry about this now. Consider yourselves deputized. All of you. Do whatever is necessary. Just help the chief inspector straighten it out."

Mr. Plum and Mr. Pear smiled and nodded at him. Despite herself, Valeria smiled as well. She was to be in law enforcement then! How wonderful. She tugged her key ring. She snuck a glance at the mayor. She decided if he did not make her angry in the coming weeks, she might reconsider her opinion of him.

"And get that filthy chimney sweep and lock him up," the mayor said to the chief inspector. "I heard all about how he mistreated you, Miss Valeria."

"Yes," Valeria said. "I fully intend to press charges."

"What if he's run away?" the chief inspector asked.

"Then find him!" the mayor shouted, spittle landing on the man's cheeks. "We're going to get luck out of the bastard if we have to squeeze it out."

The other men laughed at this and congratulated the mayor on his improved demeanor and professionalism. Valeria shook her head at them. No need to gloat. They quieted down. The chief inspector hurried back to the driver's seat. The mayor turned around and marched back toward the hotel.

"Um, good night, mayor," the two men in the backseat called, and waved after him. "We'll take care of it. Just you wait. And you're right to be angry with Ibolya. Telling your wife about the hairdresser was bad form. Absolutely. We just want you to know that her doing that didn't sit right with us at all."

The mayor stopped and turned around.

"What?"

The two men flinched. Neither could think of a reason for having blurted this out. Perhaps it had been the excitement of their new job.

The mayor approached them. His eyes were squinted, but he stared straight ahead.

"What did you just say?"

The two men hesitated but didn't want to risk running afoul of him, especially as they had just been deputized and were hoping to get pistols of their own.

"It's true, mayor," Mr. Plum said.

"She sent a message with the chimney sweep. He announced it tonight at the pub," said Mr. Pear. "We felt bad that she did it to you, we did. Now that we're deputies, I guess we have to tell you these things."

It was all clear to the mayor. He imagined every conversation Ibolya and the chimney sweep had had. He imagined conversations they hadn't had. He looked to the chief inspector.

"Arrest her."

The chief inspector nodded. "What charge?"

"I don't know; make something up," the mayor said.

"Public nuisance," Valeria volunteered. "Health violations. Safety violations. Indecency."

"Yeah," agreed the mayor. "All that. I want her to rot as long as the chimney sweep."

Then the mayor cursed and went back inside the hotel.

"Of all the fucking troubles," the chief inspector said when he got to the front seat. "Deputy, do we have gasoline in the trunk?"

The two men in back began coughing.

"You're not really going to burn it down, are you?" Mr. Pear asked.

"That's what the mayor said to do," Valeria chirped.

The two men shook their heads.

"I'm not sure I like that idea," Mr. Plum said.

"Yeah. You know. I don't really think I'm cut out for police work," Mr. Pear said.

The inspector looked back at them and shook his head.

"Fuck that," he said, and then apologized to Valeria. "We were playing cards, minding our own business, when you two walked in. Now, if I have to go swing my dick in a field of nettles, you two deputies are coming with me and going in first. In fact, I'll let you clear the place out and make the arrests yourselves. I'm sure your drinking buddies will love you for that."

The original deputy laughed. The two men in back didn't respond. They sat quietly. They were all quiet for a moment before Mr. Plum finally piped up.

"You think I could be mayor one day?"

"Heaven forbid," Valeria muttered.

The police car arrived at Ibolya's tavern. A crowd had gathered in a circle outside. Valeria could make out a body sitting on the ground and her heart began to beat quickly. She began to breathe heavily. They heard Ibolya shouting orders before they opened the door. A few men were scurrying like ants, some bringing vodka, others bringing towels.

"We're too late," the men said. "The poor potter must have gotten it by now."

Valeria pushed the car door open and rushed to the potter's side.

"My dear," she said. "My poor darling."

The potter was moaning. Someone had cut his sleeves away. Both of his hands and forearms were badly slashed. Skin had been torn.

The deputy followed close behind her. He was shining his flashlight in men's faces while he kept his hand on his pistol. He elbowed people who didn't move quickly enough.

250

"Make way! Make way! Give the potter some room."

"For fuck's sake, calm down!" the chief inspector shouted at him. "They've already got their blood up. You'll get our asses kicked if you don't stop."

The deputy sighed and put his flashlight down. Ibolya looked up at the chief inspector.

"The chimney sweep cut him with a beer bottle."

The inspector laughed. "Well then, I'd say if he survives he's going to be a pretty lucky man for the rest of his life."

Ibolya glared at him. She clearly had no time for jokes. When they had carried the potter in and she saw the blood that had soaked into his shirt and heard him moaning, she felt sick. She was immediately sorry for what she'd done, for what she'd led the chimney sweep to do. She knew the end was near. It had to be. She was disappointed in herself.

"He's hurt badly," she said. "His hands are all gashed up. We stopped the bleeding, but I think he's cut a tendon."

The chief inspector whistled. The deputy raised his flashlight again, this time on the wound. "Look it, it's just a cord. Is that your nerve then, potter?"

Beside the visible cord in his forearm, his palms were slashed and even the tip of his right index finger was dangling. Ibolya was nursing him the best she could. Over the years, she had become adept at nursing the injuries that came with running a pub. Broken noses and swollen eyes were common enough. Nobody had ever been stabbed at her bar, though. She cleaned the potter's wounds and wrapped them with wet towels. Her hands trembled and she had to keep rubbing the tears out of her eyes. She felt miserable. Ferenc stood behind her. He looked harried.

"My poor little potter," she said. "My little billy goat. I'm so sorry. Please, please forgive me." She threw her arms around him and kissed his cheek. "I egged him on, I did. I'm so sorry. I was angry at you and at her. I'm so sorry."

Valeria was holding the potter's neck. For the briefest of moments both women were draped over him. Some of the men in the crowd tittered.

"Well, Ibolya, you're in the shithouse for certain," the chief inspector announced. "The mayor wants you on a stick."

The potter was moaning.

Ibolya sobbed into her hands. Valeria wasn't sobbing, but she was scared and she trembled a little. She reminded herself that the world was a frightening place.

Ferenc tugged at Ibolya's shoulder.

"I'm afraid you're under arrest," the chief inspector said.

"Oh, leave her alone," the potter muttered. "It's not all her fault. I'm to blame for what's happened to me as much as anyone."

Valeria stroked his white hair.

"Well, I honestly wouldn't mind running the lot of you in," the chief inspector said, "but you look like you've been punished enough, and as far as we can tell, Ibolya's at the center of it all. You overplayed your hand, darling."

"Ibolya, go with Ferenc," the potter said, ignoring the inspector. "Get out of here."

"Now hold on there. I'll look after her," the chief inspector argued. "She'll get all the breaks."

"Aw, Zoli, she didn't really do anything. Just leave her alone," the potter said. "I'm not pressing any charges."

"Mayor's orders. It's not just this, potter. He knows everything, Ibolya. Everything. We're here to burn it down."

Ibolya's hands fell from her face. She looked at the inspector. It was really over then. She'd lost. She'd lost everything. She looked around. She was trapped. She shook her head. There had to be some way. There had to be some escape. She grabbed on to Ferenc's arm.

"To hell with the mayor," Ferenc said, springing to her rescue. "And you can tell him I said so. That irrigation system he got me was shit. Killed all my beets. Ibolya's leaving with me. We're leaving the village tonight. You have a problem with that?"

Ferenc stood several heads over the chief inspector. The two men eyeballed one another. The deputy put his hand on his gun. The crowd began making wagers.

"Let her go," the potter said. "Just let her go and call me a doctor."

The chief inspector put his hand on his young deputy's arm to still him. He nodded his head like he had heard the potter and understood. Or maybe he nodded at Ferenc. Or maybe it was for his own benefit, to remind himself that he cared less than they all could have possibly imagined. The chief inspector decided he wasn't getting into an actual scrape on the mayor's behalf. Regardless of who the nod was meant for, Ferenc nodded back and pulled Ibolya close to him. He swaddled her in his arms.

"Thank you, potter," Ferenc said.

The potter smiled at them.

"You behave yourself, Ibolya," he said. "I think you found a real man there."

Ibolya looked warily at Ferenc and then at the potter. She looked at the chief inspector. She looked at Valeria.

"I guess you win this one, you old bag."

Valeria nodded.

"I told you I would."

Ibolya relented. "I guess you did. Good luck to you."

The chief inspector turned around. He tapped his deputy on the shoulder and the young man turned around as well.

"Has anyone called the doctor yet?" he asked the crowd.

The men in the crowd shook their heads and shrugged.

The chief inspector looked at his deputy.

"Why don't you go and pick up the doctor," he said.

The young man nodded and ran off to the car. He sped away. Ibolya touched the inspector's shoulder. He didn't turn around.

"Thank you," she said.

He nodded. He walked a few paces away.

She looked up at her customers standing all around them. She smiled at them.

"Well, fellas, I guess that's it. They've won. It'll be drinks at overpriced hotel bars from now on."

The men moaned and cursed. Ibolya looked back at her bar. She was sad, but licked was licked. She put a wide smile on her face. She forced it there, but they wouldn't get any more tears out of her.

"Go ahead and drink what your stomachs will hold," she announced. "Drink it all and then watch it burn."

More moans, a few cheers.

She quieted them down. "You're my darling little piglets. Every last one of you. Remember me at the next election. Maybe you can write me in. I think you're allowed to do that. I think I would make a fine mayor."

Valeria sighed.

"Hear, hear!" they shouted.

And that was the end of it: Ibolya's Nonstop Tavern was officially closed. It was as if their world had lost a little bit of color. They could all feel it. Even Valeria could feel it. Things were different already. And what was odd about the difference was that one couldn't tell if it was better or worse. One couldn't tell much of anything except that the world had changed and they would have to change with it.

Ibolya turned to Ferenc and smiled.

"And as for you, Rusty, you're the last man standing, as they say. I've been a fool, I guess. I hope you will forgive me. Let's get started on a life. Yes, I'll run away with you. Absolutely. Wherever you want."

The redhaired man named Ferenc, Rusty forevermore, exploded with pride. The men cheered for him and patted him on the back as he finally grabbed his woman and carried her to her quarters to collect her things.

Inside they kissed, and it was like the first time for both of them. Ibolya's knees quivered.

"Rusty!" she giggled. "Who knew?"

She laughed and pulled back a carpet. She pried away the floorboards. A safe was under them. She opened it and pulled out two satchels of money. Hundreds of thousands of notes. A lifetime of savings.

"My dowry," she quipped, and then blushed. "We can open a proper pub somewhere. With a satellite television and music. Let's get out of here, Rusty. Let's never come back."

Twenty-four

"Last call!" the chief inspector shouted as he doused the walls of the pub with gasoline. "Get it while it's hot! Last call! Your last chance until the opening of the hotel's pub next month. That'll be twice as expensive, but worth every penny. New booths, a billiard table, and three satellite televisions. Last call!"

The walls were wet. Mr. Plum and Mr. Pear poured their home-made brandy onto the bar. They doused every piece of wood. Every stool. Every table was soaked. They opened the wash closet door to get in there and they found the chimney sweep sitting on the commode. The men had gagged and tied him. He was writhing about, trying to escape.

When the crowd of men in the pub spotted him, they booed and threw whatever was in their hands—bottles mostly. They didn't even wait for Mr. Plum or Mr. Pear to get out of their way. The two men ducked to avoid the attack. The bottles that didn't hit them exploded against the walls and floor.

"You stop that this instant!" Valeria shouted at them. She was on her feet and had gone inside the pub. "This instant!"

The room grew quiet.

Valeria was the only one who felt hopeful about the changes.

She'd turned a lot of fresh pages recently. She decided this latest change for all of them could be good. It really could be.

"There will be none of that," she said. "No more of that. Never again. You have all been behaving disgracefully these last few weeks. Leave that man alone. He's suffered enough tonight and he has more suffering in store."

The rabble protested, but Valeria acknowledged that rabble would always protest. It's not easy to change. She would be resolute. She would even be obstinate. She could only lead by example.

"Look at what he did to the potter," they argued. "He hit you! The village has been falling apart since he got here."

"Oh, don't be ridiculous," she said. "He's no more guilty than any of us. You're making a scapegoat out of him is what you're doing. Look at you. It might as well be a riot."

The men muttered under their breaths.

"Have your drinks and go home. Let the chief inspector do his job. He knows what needs doing. The chimney sweep will pay for his actions."

The men grew somber, genuinely somber, for six seconds. That was the number of seconds it took for the first of them to get behind the bar and a set a mug under the tap. After that, it was a free-for-all. They helped themselves to the last of the liquor. They did what Ibolya had said and drank as much as their stomachs could hold. They ran home and returned with their wives and girl-friends, who got drunk as well. They danced. They sang. They threw each other up in the air. It was the biggest party the town had ever seen. The noise from the revelers carried through the village and even reached the mayor and his visitors in the hotel. They were surveying the town from the roof. A glow started up that lit up the centrum like a spotlight. The Koreans oohed and aahed. They promised another factory. The mayor felt a tear roll down his cheek. Progress.

Ibolya and Ferenc saw the glow in their rearview mirror as well. They stopped and looked back. Then they smiled at one another and never looked back again.

Dogs came. Children awoke from their slumbers. The entire village, every man, woman, cow, and mouse, saw the glow of light. The future had arrived.

For many years afterward, people present that night would remember it as the most exciting night of their lives. Everyone alive that day would talk about where they were the night Ibolya's tavern burned down.

The potter sat quietly and watched the events unfold. He already felt a pang of nostalgia for the way the village used to be when he was younger, when they were all younger. He couldn't help but feel a tug of sympathy for the lot of them. If it wasn't clear before, it was clear now that tomorrow they would wake up in a new world and have to navigate their way through it. Only this time, they would be older and feebler. Hopefully they were wiser as well. They would have to be or they would be lost. They would have to adapt or be left behind. He looked at Valeria. At least they didn't have to do it alone.

"Doctor's here," the chief inspector announced. "Don't worry, old man. You should be all right. Nothing a few stitches and some gauze won't fix. Though I imagine it will be plenty hard to make a plate from here on out. See what two-timing gets you? Stick to big-city prostitutes. That's my motto. Excuse me, Miss Valeria."

The potter moaned. Valeria shook her head.

The chief inspector stood up and looked around for his deputies. He spotted them singing in front of the fire, the chimney sweep pinned between them.

"Hey! What are you shitheads doing?" he called out. "Get him to a cell. Then come back and we can all get drunk."

The doctor approached and examined the potter's wounds. He looked at the potter's hands, especially the right one, for a few minutes. He pursed his lips.

"Not good," he said. "We'll need to get you to the clinic. I'm afraid you're going to miss the festivities. You need a thorough cleaning and lots of stitches. You'll need a lot of pain medication. A tendon in your right wrist is severed. We can stitch the tip of your finger back. The left hand isn't so bad. It's just a gash. Considering your age, though, you won't be able to use the right one for a long time, maybe never. You'll need looking after until you get enough strength back to really grip something. Do you want us to call your apprentice?"

The potter shook his head.

"I'm here," Valeria said. "He's with me."

The doctor nodded and led them back to his car. "We really need to get you to the clinic as quickly as we can," he said.

"Can we drive by the train station?" the potter asked. "Only for a minute. It can't wait anymore. There's something we need to see."

He turned to Valeria.

"I've made you a present," he said, smiling. "This one won't ever break."

Valeria smiled back. She looked out the window at the rising whorls of smoke, at the men beginning to stumble home, at the strays that were watching warily from the shadows. She rested her hand on the potter's leg. She had done it. She had yielded. She had allowed herself to open up. For the first time in fifty years she felt hopeful about something, and that feeling—it was love—filled her up. It filled her up so much she felt like she could cry. She didn't. Instead she began to whistle. It seemed appropriate. She whistled and looked forward to the rest of her life.

ACKNOWLEDGMENTS

There are always so many family and friends to thank. Too many. Here's my list; Zita and Benji. Mom and Dad. Karinda, Jason, Eli, and Ezra. Thank you Karoly and Margit, Roland, Robi, and Emily. The Lawleys—every last one of them. My readers: Christine Lawley, David Goldsmith, Sarah Pennington, Veronika Gunter, Anthony Grooms, Rita Olah, and Brenda Mills. My really smart friends and mentors: Jo Ann Adkins, Lawrence Hetrick, Alisan Atvur, Brigid Hughes, Judit Sollosy, CLMP, Laurel Snyder, Rick Campbell, John Lawley, Andrew Jozak, Rob Jenkins, Jack Riggs, Steve Wallace, and Roland Weekley. I want to thank Agnes Krup for helping work through the earliest drafts and talking the book up. More important, I want to thank her for seeing the possibilities and encouraging me before anybody else did. Thank you, Agnes. And of course, I might not have gotten anywhere without the literary magazine *Prairie Schooner* and the excellent instincts of one Mr. Bill Clegg at the William Morris Agency. He cold-called me from London and made suggestions that made the book better overnight. Thank you for your tireless help, Bill.

Reading Group Guide

These discussion questions are designed to enhance your group's conversation about *Valeria's Last Stand*, a wry folktale about life, love, and capitalism in a tiny village off the map of Hungary.

About this book

Valeria has a long list of things she disapproves of. Whistling, tropical fruit, free-market capitalism, and the mayor of her Hungarian village top that list. And Valeria especially doesn't believe in love past a certain age. Until she bumps into the potter, a widower with white hair and a thick moustache. Suddenly Valeria, the village's least popular senior citizen, finds herself awash in an unfamiliar feeling: desire.

The potter is equally surprised to respond to Valeria's overtures; he was enjoying a casual affair with Ibolya, the proprietress of the village's only tavern. But Valeria inspires the potter to reinvent himself as an artist: he makes her the most beautiful pottery the village has ever seen, then moves on to bigger, less fragile projects. Ibolya tries to break up this unlikely love affair by enlisting an itinerant chimney sweep to distract Valeria. But Ibolya doesn't count on the chimney sweep's violent tendencies. The villagers will never be the same after the powerful forces of modern capitalism and old-fashioned sexual desire sweep through town.

For discussion

1. *Valeria's Last Stand* opens with an epigraph by Milan Kundera: "The great matters of nations cannot make us forget the modest matters of the heart." How does this quotation comment on the story that follows?

2. "Valeria never whistled," the opening line of the first chapter declares (3). Why does Valeria disapprove of whistling? What does she associate with this small musical act? When does she finally begin to whistle herself, and why?

3. Zivatar, the name of Valeria's village, means "thunderstorm" in Hungarian. How does this name suit the village? What "storms" have bypassed Zivatar in the past? What kinds of turbulence are taking place now?

4. Many of the novel's characters are named by their jobs, such as the mayor, the potter, and the chimney sweep. Why do these characters remain unnamed? Near the end of the novel, after the mayor's infidelity, we learn, "For the record, the mayor's young wife was named Klara" (199). Why does the mayor's wife gain a first name at this point of the novel?

5. Discuss Valeria's social standing. Why do the women of the village despise her? Why do the old men of the town call her a "firework" (16)? How do the villagers' attitudes toward Valeria change over the course of the novel?

6. Describe the initial attraction between Valeria and the potter. Which of the potter's qualities does Valeria find attractive? Which

traits eventually bother her? Why is the potter drawn to such an unlikely lover?

7. The mayor is characterized as a "driven opportunist" (43). Why is he the "most dangerous of individuals" (43)? Does he prove dangerous by the end of the novel? Why or why not?

8. The chimney sweep is first introduced through the history of his bicycle. What does the bicycle reveal about the chimney sweep's personality and history?

9. The potter says of Ibolya and Valeria, "One's a volcano, the other is an ocean. It's a difficult choice to make" (99). What are Ibolya's volcanic qualities? How is Valeria oceanic? Why is it Valeria who inspires the potter artistically, and not Ibolya?

10. Imagine if Valeria, the potter, Ibolya, and the chimney sweep were in their twenties instead of their fifties and sixties. How would their affairs be different if they were forty years younger?

11. *Valeria's Last Stand* features a colorful array of secondary characters, from the scheming mayor to the potter's clueless apprentice to the lovelorn Ferenc. Which smaller character is the most interesting and vibrant?

12. Consider the potter's evolution from craftsman to artist. What are the stages of his transition? What leads him to declare, "I'm not a potter anymore" (189)? Why is he still called the potter to the last page of the novel if this is so? What might the potter's future be like, after the grave injuries to his hands?

13. *Valeria's Last Stand* is a novel of great changes, individual and collective. Which character evolves the most over the course of the novel? Who changes the least? At the end of the story, "Valeria was the only one who felt hopeful about the changes" (256). What accounts for Valeria's optimism and the villagers' dark view of the future?

14. The mayor senses a kindred spirit in the potter; he believes they are both "Men who know what they want and how to go after it—whether it's train stations, hotels, fountains, or women" (147). Why does the potter object to this comparison? How are the potter and the mayor alike? How are they different?

15. Discuss the differences between the older generation and the younger generation of the village. Why has the older generation stayed in Zivatar, while the youngsters "embraced the anonymity of globalism" (137)? What does the future hold for this tiny village?

Suggested reading

Gary Shteyngart, *Absurdistan* and *The Russian Debutante's Handbook*; Joanne Harris, *Chocolat*; Rivka Galchen, *Atmospheric Disturbances*; Muriel Barbery, *The Elegance of the Hedgehog*; Alessandro Baricco, *Silk*; Kate Maloy, *Every Last Cuckoo*; Milan Kundera, *The Unbearable Lightness of Being*; Gabriel García Márquez, *Love in the Time of Cholera*.

Marc Fitten lives in Atlanta, where he edits the *Chattahoochee Review*. He has written for newspapers and literary journals, including the *New York Times*, the *International Herald Tribune*, the *Atlanta Journal-Constitution*, and *Prairie Schooner*. *Valeria's Last Stand*, his first novel, was published in ten countries.